The Gentle Care
for
Broken Things

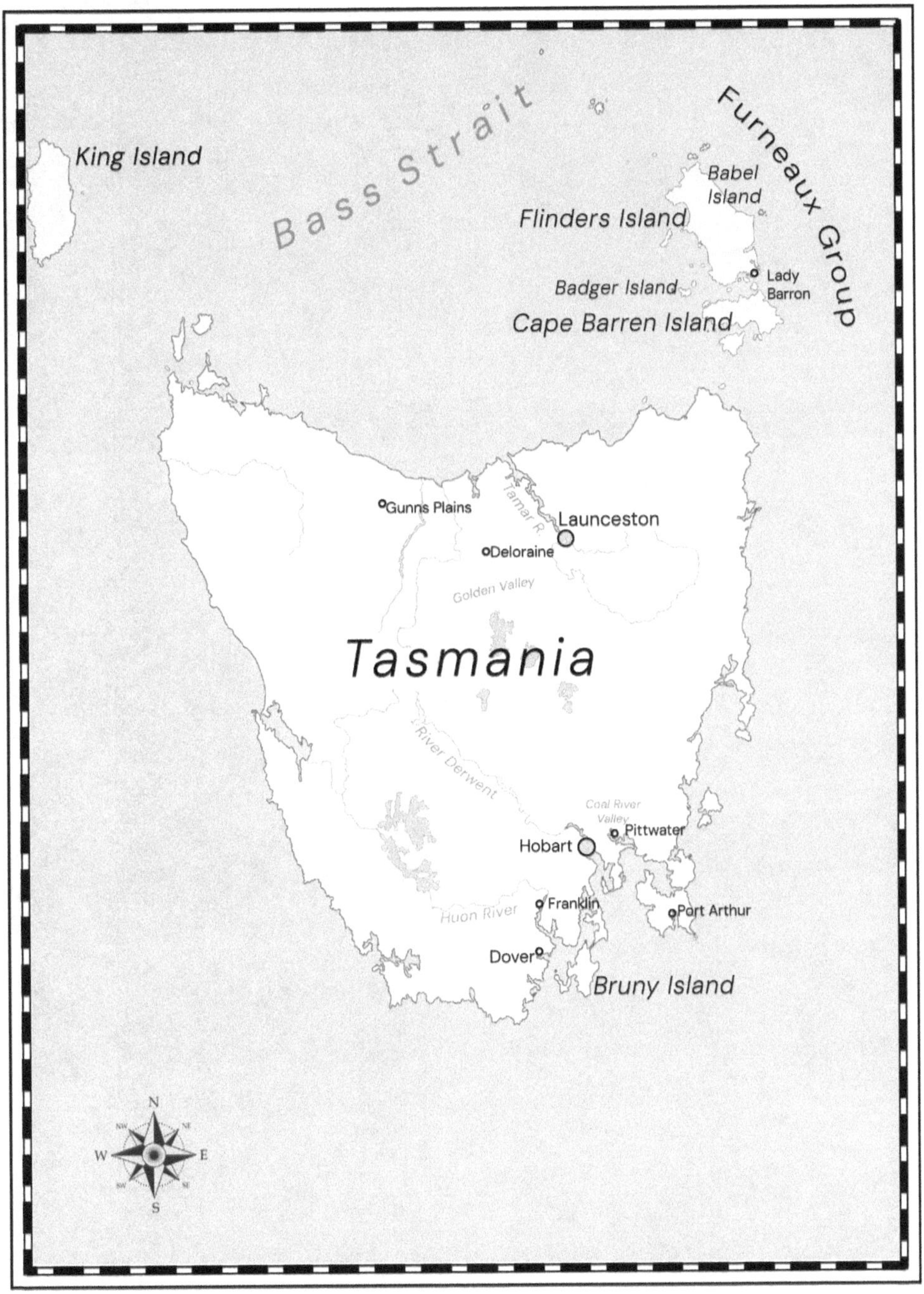

King Island

Bass Strait

Furneaux Group

Babel Island

Flinders Island

Badger Island

Lady Barron

Cape Barren Island

Tamar R.

Gunns Plains

Launceston

Deloraine

Golden Valley

Tasmania

River Derwent

Coal River Valley

Pittwater

Hobart

Huon River

Franklin

Port Arthur

Dover

Bruny Island

N
NW NE
W E
SW SE
S

The Gentle Care

for

Broken Things

Steven Gadd

ASHWOOD
PUBLISHING

ISBN–print: 978-0-6452045-9-9
ISBN–epub: 978-0-6459137-0-5

Ashwood Publishing
Cradoc, Tasmania
ashwoodpublishing.com.au

Set in Adriane Text 11/16

Cover design: Susan Young
Violin image: Iotas/Depositphotos
Dover image: Kristie Knight @krillknight

A catalogue record for this work is available from the National Library of Australia

Steve Gadd lives in the village of Franklin, in Tasmania's Huon Valley.

He has worked as a mine labourer, supervisor at a shelter for the homeless, a lecturer in political philosophy, and as a festival curator. Prior to retirement in 2021 Steve worked for 23 years as a musician and teacher of instrumental music and as a collector and promoter of folkloric music.

With his wife Marjorie, he has published collections of the traditional country dance music of rural Tasmania, including the influential *Tasmanian Heritage Apple Shed Tune Book*.

With historian Peter MacFie, Steve and Marjorie published *On the Fiddle*, the life and music of the colonial fiddler Alexander Laing.

Steve has also published *Contemporary Tasmanian Fiddle Tunes* and *Tasmanian Airs and Tone Poems*, plus two books of poetry and stories, *Tales from the Three-Layered Island*, Volume I in 2021 and Volume II in 2022.

Together Steve and Marjorie Gadd founded the Tasmanian Heritage Fiddle Ensemble and the Huon Heritage Ensemble.

The Journey of the Beast

Timeline of the Testore violin and its custodians

Italy

Milan	1700	Paulo Testore
Milan	1700	Francesco Geminiani
Lucca, Tuscany	1704	Francesco Geminiani
Naples	1711	Francesco Geminiani

United Kingdom

London	1714	Francesco Geminiani
Dublin County	1733	Francesco Geminiani, Turlough O'Carolan
Belfast	1734–1810	Michael, Ryan and Arthur McBride
Scotland, Banff, Paisley	1811–1812	Alexander Laing
Perthshire, Scotland	1813	Alexander Laing

New South Wales

Sydney Cove	1813	Alexander Laing

Van Diemen's Land

Pittwater	1815–1817	Alexander Laing
Sorell	1820	Alexander Laing
Richmond	1840	Alexander Laing
Port Arthur	1847	William Champ
Port Arthur	1849–1867	Neil Gow Foggo

Tasmania

Golden Valley/ Deloraine	1867-1925	Liam Donohue, Fergus Donohue, Lenny Donohue
Badger Island, Furneaux Group	1925	Affie Saltmarsh
Flinders Island and Cape Barren Island, Furneaux Group	1925	Affie Saltmarsh, Anthony Wheeler
Launceston	1926–1929	Launceston Emporium of Fine Musical Instruments
Gunns Plains	1929	Eileen McCoy
Devonport	1932–1968	Eileen McCoy
Coal River Valley near One Tree Hill	1968	Tommy McGuire
Franklin	1968–1976	Marek Wozniak
Franklin	1976–1979	Mick and Helen Flanagan
Braeside Road, Franklin	1979–2023	Pop Joe Flakemore
The Glen and Hobart	March– May 2023	Haley McGribben and Aaron Larsen
Dover Beach	29 May 2023	Jesse Doolan

Prologue

Dover, Tasmania, January 2022

She had loved the late summer light, the play of silver-white on the wide blue palette of the bay. She loved, too, the warmth of the mornings before the cool of the sea breeze touched all of Dover at the cusp of noon.

Now things were different. The light seemed stark, unforgiving, and brought with it a particular nausea. Jesse moved abruptly, pulling the bedroom curtains closed until not a hint of day entered her room.

She choked back a scream of frustration before it became audible to her mother at the other end of the house. She had been trying to tighten the strapping that she had used to bind and flatten her breasts for the last year or more, but they had kept growing and now the discomfort of the procedure was too much.

She sought to deny womanhood one last time. She had avoided eating whenever possible. Sometimes she would arise early, before her mother, and leave toast crumbs on the table along with jars of peanut butter or vegemite left open, so that her mother would surmise that she had eaten. However, she did not break her fast. She refused lunch and ate only nibbles at dinner. Sitting on the bed she tried not to think about what it was like to know that her father would not be around, never come back, never hug her, never take her out in his boat.

She had been different then. Someone else, full of curiosity and music. She could make things happen then. Bit by bit she had lost that person and lost control.

Sometimes she imagined that thing under the bed, locked in its case, calling out for her, begging to be loved again. But she could no longer love it. It was a cruel reminder, that is all. It must go!

The vocabulary for such feelings is stilted and incomplete. Jesse was not sure if she was angry, sad or both. She knew that she couldn't keep binding her breasts and thus needed to assert some other form of control. The pain was terrible but when she made fine slices on her arm with the razor she knew that this was a pain that for a time would overshadow the others. It was a pain that she alone could will.

Beyond the house, across the road and some way down the coastal strand, a lone sea eagle lay in a stony hollow, crippled by a broken wing.

Chapter 1

Dover, Tasmania, 2023

*N*o, *it's not here! Am I blind or just stupid?* Haley could not believe that yet again she had failed to find it.

She had driven down that pitted gravel road slowly and carefully, past old houses, young forest plantations, neat orchards, and rambling blackberry thickets, scanning both directions.

She was looking, for the third time, for the turn-off to the road that her father had described; one that led to the old dairy and the humble family home that she had seen in old photographs.

Trying to shake off the inevitable burden of small disappointments, she asked herself, *Why is this even important? Why am I so pissed off?* She was being disingenuous and knew it. Haley smiled, remembering the gentle timbre of her dad's voice. He had told her a thousand stories of his childhood in these hills. She wanted to see for herself, grasping for a more tangible connection to this strange land. *Where is it, Dad?* She knew she would never receive an answer. She still missed him so much.

Arthur MacGribben, McGribben's Dairy, Claytons Drive, Dover, Tasmania. That was the address inscribed upon the inner sleeve in each one of her dad's musty old textbooks, forever on the shelf at their home in Hove, Adelaide. Why had he kept them? Pride, she supposed: Artie was the first of the Dover McGribbens to go beyond high school, the first of his family to attend teacher's college, the first to leave the milking and the herding and other chores at the dairy behind, moving to South Australia to teach and eventually securing a coveted tenured position in a private school in genteel Adelaide.

Now, forty-eight years since he had left Tasmania and crossed the Strait to teach, there seemed to be no discernible trace of the dirt track that had once stretched west into the forested land off Dales Rd and up to the McGribben dairy on its hilly clearing. Haley had looked for Claytons Drive on the tourist maps, and had consulted Google Earth on her phone, but there was never a mention or sign of it. It was almost as if fire, or regrowth, or time itself, had simply erased any remnant of her family's Tasmanian past.

'Oh shit!' The corrugations of the dirt road were worse after the recent dry spell, jolting the suspension and causing the two marimbas in the boot to thump together in an unholy discord. Haley, though, was more concerned about her violin on the back seat, loose in its case, even though it was wrapped in a satin scarf for padding.

Better pull over and check. She found a safe place to park and, having assured herself that the instruments were still intact, decided to take a breather.

Perhaps she should write to her mum and tell her she just couldn't find her dad's old home, or even the road that led there. Her mother did not do emails – the digital age, it seemed, had simply passed her by.

And so, pulling a sheet from her notebook, she penned a letter to her mother, who had relocated from Adelaide to beachside Port Elliot when she had remarried, several years after Artie had passed on.

Dear Liza

Hope all is well for you and Jack there in sunny Elliot, Mum.

After a few classes at Dover District today, I tried, yet again, to find Claytons Drive to no avail. Maybe it has been renamed?

I know you only visited Dad's folks a few times, but I was wondering if you remember any landmarks that might help me get my bearings?

Maybe I am destined to live in the same valley where my father grew up, but to never know exactly where that place was. My incompetence as a navigator is getting obvious, but the fact that the modern maps don't have the road or turn-off marked doesn't help.

PS, did you and Jack get my last card?

Your loving, fiddling daughter,

Haley

Driving home to the Glen, Haley had the impression that autumn was late this year. Summer had not relinquished its grip on the land and there was no sign yet of the leaves in the apple orchards turning, despite April being only a few weeks away. Coming from a place of broad flat plains, she never stopped feeling a little awed by the grandeur of the mountains and the steep sweeping of the forested foothills down to hamlets, towns and villages nestled close to the river.

The descent down the winding highway once again brought her father to mind. Sometimes when he had been homesick for Tasmania, he would drive the family to a part of the Adelaide Hills where the curving roads, orchards and cooler climate were almost reminiscent of home. There, far from the bustle of the city, they would stroll together beneath pink-gums and cup-gums and wattles.

On such days, he had taught her to recognise the various raptors that flew through those hills. He would place a finger to his mouth with an almost inaudible 'Shhhh', put an arm around her, and direct her attention to this bough or that where some rare bird of prey was perching, almost hidden. Now living in Tasmania, she continued the family tradition. She had bought *The Illustrated Book of Tasmanian Birds* as an aid to spotting and naming kestrels, harriers, eagles, goshawks and peregrines and other birds of prey. This routine kept her alert as she drove through Waterloo, Port Huon, and Castle Forbes Bay, to South Franklin where sea eagles nested in a tree near the point. Today, however, she saw no eagles.

Remembering to buy an envelope and stamp, she pulled her car up outside the Franklin Post Office, then walked in, past the hairdressers and the florist's street stall.

Sandra, who ran the post office, was a transplant from Oregon, friendly, helpful, and always ready for a chat. This day there was a bit of a queue as each person collected their mail, sent off parcels, paid bills and exchanged stories.

Haley, realising she would have to wait until the current backlog of customers had cleared, opted to have a coffee and a sweet treat in the café located towards the rear of the post office.

She noticed the tall glass case towards the end of the cake bar. It was full of books for sale. Opening the cabinet to peruse the contents, she was surprised to find that all the books were written by local authors.

'So, there be novelists and poets in the Huon Valley. Who would have guessed?' she said sardonically, half mumbled but audible.

Jake at the cake bar heard, and laughed at her comment, looking directly at her with one eyebrow partly raised. 'So you're new to the valley? If you're interested in getting a better feel for this place, maybe read one of these tomes and soak up some yarns and local folklore.'

Haley, for some reason she could not quite understand, half-blushed.

'Yeah, I'm a blow-in from South Oz, but my father grew up down here, a bit further south, near Dover. His stories put me to sleep at night, and I loved them. Even though I've always had a suspicion that folklore is simply another term for bold-faced lies, I might take up your suggestion.'

They shared a quick glance at each other, and both smiled.

Jake had always had a thing for pretty women with curly red hair and glasses, and was honest enough to admit to himself that he was flirting, something he usually steered clear of with customers.

Haley, in turn, considered it prudent to go about her business despite admitting to herself, reluctantly, that she was enjoying the attention. She selected four books to take home to adorn her bookshelf. First, a book of poems by someone called David Hume, then a murder mystery titled *On Shipstern Bluff* by John Tully. In addition, she chose a longish novel, *Golden Valley*, with a cover picture of a mountainscape reminiscent of the view from her backyard in the Glen; and finally, another book of poetry and short stories titled, enigmatically, *Tales from the Three-Layered Island*.

When the genial hordes at the post office counter had left, she purchased the envelope and stamp and posted the letter to her mother before buying the books.

At the counter, she exchanged some friendly small talk with Sandra, who had noticed the name and return address on the back of the letter envelope.

'Haley McGribben! Your name sounds familiar. Aren't you that new fiddle teacher in the valley?'

Surprised that word of her private teaching had got around so quickly, Haley smiled and nodded, in an eruption of ginger curls.

'Yes, that's me. I've always taught mostly classical violin, but down here there seems to be a lot of interest in folk fiddling, so I have been schooling myself in all that is involved: the tunes, the bowing, the different rhythms. I've even been frequenting the Irish sessions at the New Sydney on Saturdays and occasionally the gypsy-jazz sessions at the Cascade, if ever I can get there on a weeknight. So, I guess I am a fiddle teacher now!'

Sandra, smiling, replied that it had been lovely to meet her and dropped a hint that she might know of some violin students in the area who were looking for a new teacher.

'That would be great. Here's my number for anyone that wants to get in touch.'

Haley slipped Sandra a little handout that she had printed off. Lime coloured, with a magenta violin drawn in the centre, it provided Haley's contact details, qualifications and places of work, and included a request for any second-hand violins that might be for sale in the valley and suitable for students.

'If you have another of those little posters handy, please feel free to pin it up on the notice board. Good luck with everything.'

❦

Haley, an Adelaide girl through and through, was raised in a world of long suburban beaches, cafés, high jetties, and those enduring hot summer days relieved only by slightly milder nights.

She had attended Brighton High, both because of its proximity to home and because of its special emphasis on musical education. Artie had recognised that his daughter had a passion, and maybe even a vocation, and so supplemented her school music with private lessons on piano and violin.

Later, Haley attended the Elder Conservatorium and gained an honours degree, 2nd class, having studied under Dr Elizabeth Layton and been tutored by Keith Crelin, for a while, during a brief flirtation with that outlier among the strings, the viola.

At first her heart was set on being an orchestral player or even a soloist. She worked hard at her craft and was always a better-than-average violin student. Yet she bore no delusions. This was a field in which, as her teacher often reminded her, 'Many are called but few are chosen.'

Eventually, realising that she was never going to be an orchestral player, Haley downsized her dreams, shelved her disappointment and added a teaching diploma to her CV. Thus, like her father, she had become a teacher, albeit in the specialised field of music, a field for which, in budget-tight times, there seemed to be decreasing funding and few secure positions. Consequently, Haley spent some months scouring vacancy notifications interstate, while living on the meagre income received from a few private students and some fairly demeaning retail work.

When an apparently good teaching position did arise, it came from where she least expected it. So it happened that, in an inversion of her father Artie's trajectory, Haley McGribben secured her first teaching position, south, across the Strait, in Tasmania. The island state was a place that, for her, had always seemed story-filled, time-frozen and remote, as if it was not quite part of the wide, dry Australia she knew.

Arriving in Hobart, she took up a position in the Catholic education system. For just a while her future seemed stable. It was a picturesque old school of sandstone and red bricks overgrown with ivy. She enjoyed the students, and the music room had good enough acoustics. The demons of small disappointments had not yet finished with her, however. She was there for not quite two years before she was told that the music stream was being slashed.

The school's managerial team had called her in for a meeting. Rather than the principal it was the treasurer, an officious little man in an expensive suit, who addressed her.

'Dear Miss McGribben, or may I call you Haley? Due to a looming funding issue we are being forced to do... more with less. We have decided to cut the music program down to bare bones and reallocate resources where they are most necessary.'

Haley took a quick guess at what was coming next, and choking down the rising despair, decided to hold her ground. 'I'd like to remind you that I relocated here, from interstate, to teach music. I have a binding contract that guarantees me four years of fulltime teaching at this school.'

This time it was the board's secretary, a pallid and expressionless woman who looked old for her years, who spoke.

'Haley, we can still promise you employment for the rest of your contract, but it just won't all be in music. We desperately need a year eight maths and science teacher and want to ask you if you are willing to do half your load in those areas?'

Not knowing whether to laugh or cry, Haley tried to imagine teaching in subjects in which she had neither qualifications nor any interest. 'Sorry to waste your time. I am a well-trained musician and music teacher. I have not one iota of desire to compromise on this issue. Music education is not some added extra to me. It is, when done well, fundamental to helping the young soul soar. Also, I am sure that you are well aware of the research regarding the effects of musical training on the brain and on its cross-over benefits to mathematical performance, pattern recognition and to literacy!' A cowl of silence fell over the room as she paused. Haley ground her teeth with inevitable frustration before concluding, 'Please, let me save us all further embarrassment by resigning outright now.'

Haley's decision to quit the job that she had so long sought brought her more than a little heartbreak, and a few nights of tears. More than before, she now realised that she was missing South Australia and all she had left there.

Making the decision to leave her position, however, she was not quite jumping blind into the void. By that time, Haley had already taken on an affordable mortgage on a little riverside cabin in a place called the Glen, in the Huon Valley, a drivable distance just south of the capital.

Having first gathered into itself the water from a dozen smaller rivers and countless creeks, the Huon opens to the

D'Entrecasteaux Channel and the Southern Ocean. There the river valley with its mountains and hills gives way to wild beaches and rocky coastlines. To Haley, the valley seemed its own little world, hemmed in by craggy blue peaks; a place where tall forests, quaint towns, and emerald pastures snuggled into the gullies and hollows of graduated foothills.

So it came to be that she made her new home not too far from where her ancestors had apparently lived, in that mountain-rimmed, tree-clad place of sleepy villages, farms and orchards.

There, already, she had begun to accumulate, via word of mouth, a growing bevy of private violin students. Meanwhile, one area school and two regional schools had given her enough hours a week, as a casual music teacher, to make ends meet by rote-drilling country kids in marimba compositions and screeching recorder tunes.

Fortune had it that not long before she had made the Huon Valley her home, a popular local violin teacher, Marjorie Gadd, had retired, leaving a pool of eager young fiddlers looking for a new teacher. This was serendipitous, and Haley was most happy to take up the slack.

From these fragments of employment, she found that she could patch together a living and thus ensure that she could pay the bills.

That night, back in the little cottage in the Glen, Haley did her lesson preparations for the next day, all the while ruminating over the day that had been. The chaos of marimba group, the after-school drive to try and find the road to her dad's old family home, the natural village friendliness and bonhomie of the good folk from the Franklin Post Office, all blending together, were laid out in her mind like an unfinished tapestry.

She then dragged out her recent purchases, placing three upon the shelf, but leaving out *Tales from the Three-Layered Island*, a collection of miniatures, because at this time of night her concentration was unlikely to permit much more than a short story or two.

She opened the book, randomly settling on a page. The story, titled 'The Blue Violin', was in sprung prose, not quite a poem and not too long. She wiped her glasses and immersed herself in the tale.

The Blue Violin

She had gone through the book with her teacher,
Moved swiftly from the beginner's tunes
To real songs, songs that people knew,
Had the dots removed from the fingerboard,
Found her own way.

She played for herself in her room,
Because she loved the pieces,
Loved how they came to life,
Danced for her, sang along
With the sweet voice in her head.

When she played through her homework
For her mother and grandmother,
And they smiled and clapped,
She felt proud
And stood taller.

With her friends there was
That healthy competition,
That engendered camaraderie,
Rather than spite.

She pulled and pushed her bow,
Through one melody and the next,
Letting them know,
That she could do more,
Than just keep up.

Soon she was out-growing the half-sized violin
And dreamed of owning a full-sized instrument,
One that would be distinct,
Unlike all of the others.
To reward her progress the wish was granted.

Choosing her new instrument she passed by
All of the violins in the store,
Shunning the grained timber and the French-polish,
And picked one of bright blue,
Her favourite colour,
The colour of the water at the Dover beach
In summer.

On that first night she slept with her new fiddle,
And woke up playing her first tune,
Before rising from the bed,
Playing it for the dawn,
For the birds and the clouds,
Playing it loud so that it would ring on
Down the corridor and tell the whole family,
'That she loved her new violin, her blue violin'.

She took it to school and to ensemble.
She showed it to the other girls,
Who gasped at the brilliant colour,
And who noticed that she was playing
With new-found authority and flair.

The greater the acknowledgement
And the kudos,

The more she practised,
Until the true musician arose in her.

More and more her playing,
Surpassed that of her peers,
In that country school,
And in the valley ensemble.

She started playing the harder lines
The ones that the older kids played.
And each night, before sleep,
She kissed the blue fiddle,
Wrapped it in a satin scarf,
And placed it, carefully, in its case.

Noticing her progress her teacher recommended
To her parents that she go to the summer string camp,
At the other end of the island,
Where students, from all over the state,
Would go to learn, play together,
Polish repertoire and practise ensemble skills.

When they agreed
She was beside herself with anticipation.
She knew that she would be the only one
From her town there,
But vowed not to be afraid,
But to play like a demon,
To show everyone what her blue violin could do.

When she arrived there the others seemed friendly,
Lots of kids from the city, from private schools,
Who seemed to know each other,
From Youth Orchestra, or previous camps.

On first orchestra day she smiled,
And smiles were returned.
When it seemed to be the right time,

The players took their instruments from their cases,
Tightened their bows
And rubbed them with rosin.

There was a short moment there
Where being part of something this grand
Filled her with a joy and a light.

Everywhere girls and boys were warming up,
Playing sparkling cadenzas,
Or melancholy lines,
With weeping vibrato.
She looked around and saw,
Their old instruments,
Grained wood, French-polished.
German instruments,
Italian instruments,
Instruments like those she had walked past
In the store.

In turn they looked at hers and fell silent,
Turned away as if embarrassed for her,
As if trying not to be seen to sneer,
For they were brought up to value manners.

And then for the first time she understood
That her blue violin was somehow wrong,
A folly, a toy, a childish mistake,
Garish, loud and without the complexity of voice,
These other instruments seemed to speak.

She fell out of love with her violin that day,
Endured the camp, bit her lip,
Refused tears,
Hardened her heart.

When she returned to the valley
She packed her instrument away,
And before her twelfth birthday,
Said farewell to music,
As if her ears had closed,
And her fingers had frozen,
And as if she refused even to recall
The joy that it had brought,
And refused to remember the lonely blue violin,
Packed forever under the bed,
In its case,
Gathering dust.

Haley felt a lump choking in her throat and became aware of a tear running down her cheek.

This was not her story, but she understood it acutely. She remembered when country girls auditioned for Youth Orchestra back in Adelaide. They were often naively unaware of the unsaid protocols, the deeper layers of competitiveness, and the tacit snobbery that oft times oozed to the surface.

She also felt that she knew this girl, though clearly she did not and could not. Was this story based on a real person or a composite of students whose love of music had been crushed, or was it just a fiction conjured by the poet to serve some malign muse?

That evening, lying in bed, the weight of responsibility that was ever a teacher's to bear asserted itself, even into her dreams. She stretched out her arm, reaching for the warm assurance of a once constant presence. There was nothing there; only a vacuity that she thought she had banished.

Chapter 2

Milan, 1700

To Maestro Giuliano Geminiani
Care of the Palatine Orchestra of Lucca
Lucca, Tuscany

Dearest Father,

I hope and trust that this letter finds you well and in good spirits. Please pass on my love to Mother and to all my sisters and brothers. Tell them that I am well, but that I miss their good cheer and their conversation.

Maestro Lonati also says to send his regards. He is certainly a competent teacher, if a little harsh and quick to judgement at times. He encouraged me to take up the guitar, an instrument that I have previously held in low regard, as a way for me to attain a more profound understanding of accompaniment, harmony, and polyphony. I must say that after four hours of scales and études on the violin, playing the guitar offers some relief for my neck and shoulders.

Sometimes I get the suspicion that Maestro Lonati only requires that I play guitar so that he can have an accompanist at hand to help him test out his latest compositional ideas.

I have made some friends here, mostly young men a few years older than I, with whom I occasionally perform.

However, I have some unfortunate tidings to convey. These months have made evident that my apprenticeship stipend is barely enough for me to live on in this expensive city. Saying as much, let me be clear that I understand that neither you, nor Lonati, are in the position to increase my allowance. So, taking things into my own hands, I have, along with my new friends, started playing in the local tavernas. Though I am only 13, I am allowed into these places with the older musicians provided we play for the patrons, and play specifically what they wish to hear or dance to. They don't seem to appreciate serious music, so we end up having to learn and play the cruder village and tavern dances that are popular here.

Four or more nights a week I spend some hours sawing away stridently at the Saltarello Romagna, (a dance nothing like the elegant Salterellos that you taught me), French and English set dances such as La Contradanza, Quadriglia and Il Codiglione, and most of all a southern peasant dance which is becoming obscenely popular called the Tarantella.

These are rowdy affairs and don't inspire musical finesse, but I have gained great stamina for bowing continuo in semi-quavers, something you always felt was lacking in my playing. Last week a patron came over to tip me after requesting a Tarantella, unfortunately after the frenetic dance his balance was askew. He knocked my violin onto the floor before stumbling on top of it. It was smashed and ruined beyond repair. I was inconsolable, knowing that he would not offer to pay for an adequate replacement.

Maestro Lonati was furious at me. He lectured me about how every true violinist considers their violin to be part of their very being and something they must protect with their life. Nevertheless, he has given me the loan of his *secondi*, albeit temporarily, and he refuses me permission to take it outside the studio and the concert room.

So it is, dear Father, that I find myself without a violin of my own and unable to supplement my income as required. I know too well, that with ten other children and a wife to feed and clothe, you would be hard stretched to help financially. But I wondered perhaps if you might consider asking the patron of the Palatine Orchestra to help. If he is so forthcoming, I promise that in two years, when my apprenticeship here is over, I will return to Lucca and take a seat in the orchestra while foregoing any remuneration for 12 months.

Dear Father, I must convey that appealing to you in such a way brings me no little shame, but such is the force of necessity.

Your faithful son and servant, Fra
    Francesco Xaverio Geminiani
     July 7*th*, The Year of Our Lord 1700

Chapter 3

Tasmania, 2023

That Saturday, Haley began her morning with every intention of driving the fifty-six kilometres into Hobart to participate in the Irish tune session at the New Sydney, a great old hotel that struck her, ironically, as being far from new and totally devoid of any associations with Sydney.

Haley had not expected that the notice she pinned on the board at the Franklin Post Office on Thursday would have drawn anyone's attention so soon. Consequently, the two phone calls, one on Friday evening, the next early that morning, had taken her by surprise. Both callers had rung to inform her that they had full-sized violins that might suit students upgrading from smaller instruments. One was offered for free, and the other at a very reasonable price.

The second caller, a Diane Doolan from Dover, had seemed to want to converse about something else, but had pulled back from elaborating over the phone, saying, 'Maybe when you come down here to get the violin we can chat more, about music and kids and stuff.' She left it at that.

Haley replied politely, 'Sure thing, and thanks again for the call. I can always find a home for a fiddle with some eager youngster. Look forward to meeting you this arvo, Di. Cheers!'

The other call was from a woman called Kerry Flakemore. Kerry conveyed that while organising an estate sale after the recent passing of her grandfather, she had come across an old damaged fiddle in the shed. She said to Haley, 'Don't think it's worth anything, but if it is a goodun, I would like to see it find a good home.'

Haley figured that after doing the rounds in the valley to pick up the two student violins, she could still get to Hobart around 5 p.m. Still hoping to catch up, she group-messaged her session mates, Rose Murphy, Charlie Dempsey, and Michelle Pearson.

> Stuff has come up, looks like I won't make the session today, but I would like to pop into the New Syd after, for a counter meal, if any of you want to stick around and join me?

Each replied with a yes or a thumbs up. And so, it was.

Haley found Kerry Flakemore's place at the end of a gravel track running off Braeside, a steep road leading to a cluster of hillside farms in South Franklin. She paused for a while to take in the view. The Huon River was laid out like a blue mirror, kissed by the slightest remnant fog, with tiny wind-ripples catching the midday sun making sprinkles of silver on the water, flaws in the glass.

She recognised, in the distance, the brown and gold of a solitary swamp harrier winging over the delta inlets of South Egg Island, while closer, near the driveway gate, a cluster of currawongs were scouring the ground for lunch.

'You must be Miss McGribben then! Nice to meet ya,' Kerry called out in husky tones from the steps up to the front door. 'D'ya find the place alright? Seems ya did!'

'Hello, Kerry. Please call me Haley! Yes, your directions were clear as day and easy to follow.'

'That's all good then. Yous is not from Dover then? The old Dad used to know some McGribbens from down that way. Used to get fresh cream from their dairy, for making the butter when our cows weren't lactating, y'know.'

'No, I'm a drift-in from the mainland, nowadays I live at the Glen, but my father was born down there. You don't happen to know where the old McGribben dairy was located do you?' asked Haley hopefully.

'No bleeding idea, love. Never went there myself and Dad is long gone. Tractor accident in his early forties. The orchards, you see, the rows went right up the hill, too steep and angled for safe driving, but work had to be done! Was a blow to all of us, but his father took it worst of all. It's a curse outliving your children. The old bloke lived more than twenty years after Dad had gone. Hardly saw him smile again in all that time, unless he was on the turps, which he often was, right up until the end, just around a month back.'

Haley was taking an immediate liking to Kerry, though she felt disappointed that Kerry could not cast any light on the location of the McGribben dairy and homestead. Kerry saw that Haley looked a little disappointed and chipped in, 'My daughter Liz is a cop. I'll ask her if she knows where you could find any records of the dairy and the track up to it.

You'll have to be patient though, her boss, Jack Martin, keeps her busy helping him solve murder cases, so she tells me.'

They entered a weathered grey timber shed next to the house. There Kerry showed Haley the fiddle, taking it down from the wall where it seemed to have hung for some forty years, covered in decades of straw, dust, birds' droppings and spider webs. By way of explaining its provenance, Kerry offered, 'My grandfather, Pop Joe we used to call him, won this violin in a pub raffle at the Franklin Tavern, you know, Kon's pub. It was one of those raffles they used to have to raise money for the volunteer fire brigade. A bloke called Mick Flanagan, what used to organise the folk music club down there, donated that fiddle. Apparently neither he nor his missus played fiddle, though they played squeeze-boxes and other sorts of instruments. He wasn't sure if it was worth much. He told Pop he found it in one of the cupboards in his house up Teetotallers Lane when he first moved in there around 1977. I can see now that it looks a bit cracked, and it's covered in filth, but if you want it then it's yours.'

Haley was going to say that she had seen worse, but in truth she realised that saying so would have probably been to lie.

She took the instrument over to her car and opened the boot. From within she drew out a bag of utilities and knick-knacks, the like of which any violin teacher worth their salt would carry. There was a dusting cloth, polish, a buffing cloth, old cakes of rosin, half serviceable chin rests, some spare tuning pegs, a few spare tail pieces from defunct instruments and most importantly, neat coils of her used violin strings, each arranged in tidy paper envelopes.

She dusted off the worst of the detritus from the fiddle, then used a knitting needle to get inside the f-holes. There she removed cobwebs, straw, and part of what appeared to be an abandoned wasp nursery, after which she gave it a quick clean with a rag.

While Haley began to restring it, Kerry returned indoors to fetch a cup of tea, saying, 'I'll leave you to it, dear.'

By the time Kerry had returned with two cups of tea and some Anzac biscuits, Haley had restrung the old beast and was ready to tickle its strings, with her spare bow already rosined and ready to go.

For both player and listener, the first reaction was a kind of shock. The violin had an unusually loud voice, with a strident chorus of overtones helping shout the notes out. Haley played some scales before launching into a sprightly little jig that she had recently committed to memory. Immediately she found herself thinking out loud, 'This beast would blow them away at the sessions.' Despite wanting to blend in, Haley sometimes fantasised about what it would be like to have an instrument loud enough to cut through the wall of sound made by assembled fiddles, whistles, pipes, the piano accordions, the melodeons, the bodhrans, bouzoukis and the rest. *Oh, to actually be able to hear one's own playing.*

Next, she tried a partita by J.S. Bach, and soon stumbled, realising that further up the neck the action was too high. To make things worse, the intonation in the higher register was terrible. It was clear to her that the accurate and flowing position work required for Baroque, Classical, and Romantic performance pieces would be impossible on a recalcitrant instrument such as this.

'Would do very well as a student's first violin,' she said audibly. Kerry was not attuned enough to nuance to detect that Haley was damning by faint praise. Instead, she was most happy to offer it to anyone who might get some use from it.

⁓

'It's been lovely to meet you, dear. All the best luck with your teaching business. Things can be fickle down here in the valley. Ooroo! I must get back to sorting Pop's things.'

After she had thanked Kerry and exchanged farewells, Haley headed towards Dover, further south, for her second appointment. While she was driving, some peculiarity of the Flakemore violin came to mind. She pulled over near the river towards the far end of Castle Forbes Bay, grabbed the instrument from the back seat and proceeded to have a closer look.

The top of the violin had more than one hairline crack. Leaving aside the cracks, stains, some obvious attempts to revarnish the wood, and a host of other crimes, she thought that she recognised something in the wide grain pattern of what appeared to be some unidentifiable European pine.

She looked inside, and while there was no label, there seemed to be a remnant insignia that had been deliberately, though carelessly, scratched out. The purfling, chipped in several places, resembled the pear wood she had seen on one or two antique instruments. The ribs seemed to be of a timber related to that used for the belly but of a fainter, broader curl. What would have been a golden varnish at the side was covered in places with a carpentry glue of a kind that would never have been used by a violin maker or luthier worth their salt, but instead, probably indicated later amateur attempts to re-join the panels.

Haley was not sure what to make of all this, but she had begun to think that the old beast might have a story to tell; one that stretched back way before Pop Flakemore had won it in a pub raffle, before leaving it on his shed wall for four decades. These observations alone were enough to pique her interest and to see it as being more than a throwaway student violin.

The layout of Dover proper was becoming more familiar to Haley, hardly surprising considering that two days a week she worked at the school, and usually lunched in the town. She found Diane Doolan's place easily enough, just half a kilometre around the corner on the beachside road. When she had time to spare, she sometimes drove home this way after work, following the longer coastal route past salmon pens, idyllic hobby farms and the stony beaches of Police Point. She never tired of the view from just out of the town. Looking south one could see that magnificent bay with its little islands, and in a southwesterly direction, the view stretched back towards the dock, the town, and the picture postcard vista of Adamson's Peak, looking like an Antipodean Mt Fuji.

Haley checked the address and street numbers, and determined that it was the square timber place, lodged on a tidy block, between a large A-frame and an ostentatious white brick mansion of the kind that absentee owners kept as a summer folly. She had been told to park in the drive and to knock on the side door, under the carport canopy.

The door was already open. Before Haley had a chance to get her hand to the knocker a voice came from inside the room. 'Hi there, you must be Haley. I'm Di. And thanks so much for coming round so soon after I rang. Just come through please. I hope I haven't interrupted your plans for the weekend!'

'Not at all, I had another violin to pick up back near

Franklin, so I decided to drive down here afterwards and make a morning of it. I have a growing number of school-aged students who are on the cusp of graduating from three-quarter-sized violins to full size, so your call has come at just the right time.'

At her host's beckoning, Haley took a seat at the sunroom table, lodged amid a leafy canopy of indoor plants of various sizes and kinds. The first thing that caught her eye was, of course, the seemingly new violin case, dark against the gold oval of the pine table. Haley scanned the room before turning her attention to Diane. A mixture of freshly cut flowers filled a simple vase sitting atop an ornately welded iron stand replete with bird and ivy motifs cut from steel plate. The room was tidy, recently cleaned and arrayed, here and there, with just a few touches of colour, ornaments, hangings, and the like. Guests would, at first glance, get an impression both of order and taste.

Diane herself seemed at first sight to be around Haley's age, but on reflection, Haley surmised that she might be a little older, perhaps anywhere between her late thirties and mid-forties. She wore her blonde hair in a long bob that she had only just managed to tie back into a short ponytail. She was clearly an attractive woman, but it seemed she wore a cowl of sadness that gave the impression of someone who had aged suddenly and prematurely.

'The violin is a Valencia, it's in as-new condition, we paid $210 for it but I'll take $100 for it if you think that it's worth it.'

'Did you play at some stage?'

'Ha, no not me. It belongs to my daughter, Jesse. It was a present for her twelfth birthday. She used to love it so much, played all the time and we thought she was playing beautifully. She got so far, even did string camp, then she just stopped. She said that violin was stupid. No matter how many people asked her to play she just refused. She became an angry teenager, I guess. Some of her classmates, ones that she started with, have kept at it. A few are in your string ensemble at Dover District High. That's how I got your name; one of the kids, Anthea, well her mum, Sherry, is a dear mate. That friendship has been a great comfort to me since Alf, Jesse's dad, died a year and a bit back. Life has felt so empty ever since. And if anything, it's been even harder on Jesse who had been a real Daddy's girl.'

Haley had questions, but she refrained from interrupting Diane Doolan's outpouring.

'You see Alf got killed by a widow-maker when he was setting the chains and wedges for a logging operation. He never even saw the big dead branch that struck him from above. We found out an hour later that we had lost him. I was paralysed with the grief and the shock of it. Luckily Sherry had heard what had happened and she got Jesse out of school and brought her home for me.'

Diane had begun choking up at the recollection. As she paused, Haley, knowing what it was like to lose a father if not a husband, broke the silence. 'Oh, how terrible, so sorry that you and your daughter had to suffer such a loss, I am lost for words.'

'Thanks,' Di replied. 'Sometimes I still feel so certain that he'll come back through the door any minute. But realistically I know that it's just the grief that conjures up such thoughts. You know, Jess had already become an angry, closed-up girl when she hit puberty at twelve. Then after Alf died, she became depressive as well. Wouldn't eat for days, stopped communicating, and for a month she wouldn't leave her room. She became desperately thin and then her periods even stopped. Nothing I could do or say helped. The education department psychologist was a little help to the extent that Jesse started seeing her friends and going to school again.

'The string teacher before you knew what Jesse was going through and tried to coax her back into the ensemble. But Jesse insisted that her violin was stupid. She used to love it. I tried to console her and promised to find her a new violin for her fifteenth birthday, which is coming up in a few months, a genuine professional one, not a cheap brand, or student violin. After that she showed a glimmer of interest for a day or two, until she found out that her old violin teacher, Marjorie, had retired from teaching. She seemed to lose interest again straight away. Then, when I told her that you were taking on private students, she let on that maybe she would give music another go, seeing that some of her friends said you were nice.'

Haley gave a coy smile. 'She'll certainly be welcome in the string ensemble if she does start up again!'

'Thanks Haley,' Diane replied, 'but the truth is though, I don't have the money now to get her a really classy instrument. I was holding out for the possibility that you might be able to source a good enough second-hand one for us. Even so, I have my doubts that Jesse will agree to play again.'

Haley wanted to reply with *Never say never, let's wait and see!* but it was as if her mouth and tongue would not oblige and the words would not come. Something about this situation seemed oddly familiar to Haley, something unsettling. Following an intuition, she reached over the table and opened the violin case. Slowly, she unfolded the covering cloth and there it was, almost in shop condition, the bright blue, Chinese-made, Valencia student violin.

Haley went pale and gasped for air, struggling to hold back tears and shock in equal measure. Just at that moment, a pallid teenaged girl with sandy hair and a severe fringe came through the door. She wore a sombre expression on her thin face as she turned to address Haley.

'Hello, Miss McGribben, I've seen you around the school, what are you doing here at our place?' Then she snapped out, in a narky turn of phrase, 'Mum's not talking about trying to get me to play violin again, is she?'

Haley could hardly get her words out. 'You are her, her, the Girl with the Blue Violin.'

Jesse didn't grasp the reference but replied abrasively, 'No! I am not. Take the bloody violin and give it to someone who might want it because I certainly don't.' She stormed out of the room to a banging of doors. All the time Diane was shouting to Jesse to apologise to Miss McGribben.

Haley, who was visibly shaken, quietly requested that Di let Jesse be. 'It's fine, I'm not offended at all. I deal with teenagers every week and I've seen and heard things that would make a wharfie blush. I best go now though, but I'll keep in touch. Here is $100 in twenties, that's all I have in cash. I'll soon find the violin a new owner. Here's hoping it finds a new home and everything works out next time.'

'Sorry about all the drama, dear. It's been nice talking to you. Thanks again for listening to our story. You know I'm still holding out hope that a new violin might turn my daughter's state of mind. She needs something to focus on. So, if you come across one that's not too expensive, tell me. We can only try.'

The coast road home was, as ever, picturesque enough that it distracted Haley from her fractured mood. *That bloody poem, turns out to be about a real person. How the fuck could the writer have known all of that, right down to the details? It has to just be a coincidence! Ah well, I need to go to Hobart and share food and drink with friends, now, more than ever.*

Before heading into Hobart and the New Sydney, she stopped in at the Glen and dropped the blue Valencia home. On a hunch, she kept the old wrecked Flakemore offering in the car. There was still a mystery or two to be figured out about that thing.

Chapter 4

Contrada larga di Milano al segno dell'Aquilla, Milan, 1700

(The Sign of the Eagle Workshop on the Contrada Larga, Milan, 1700)

Returning from a trip back to Novara for the funeral of an ancient aunt, whom he had only vaguely remembered from his childhood, here he was, tired, hot and flustered. The workshop floor clearly had not been swept for a week. At least *i ragazzi* had been busy keeping up with orders. He went across the room and began inspecting the instruments on the drying rack.

Four completed violins, newly crafted by the hands of his sons, were there drying. The shellac and spirits had been rubbed in, time and again, over a number of days, and only the finishing layer remained to make French polishing complete.

One after the other, Carlo Giuseppe Testore picked them up to inspect the work. He nodded to himself, until he came to the last one, picking it up then examining the joints, the contour of the back and belly, the position of the f-holes, the scroll work. He tapped the instrument here and there and was pleased to hear the resonance of the timber, loud and sonorous. It was when he sighted the angle of the neck and the small but definite twist in the carved lines that his blood boiled.

'*Spazzatura totale!*' Carlo Giuseppe screamed, before calling to his youngest son, Paolo Antonio, who cringed being only too familiar with the berating to come.

'Who are you named after?' Carlo Giuseppe roared.

His son answered meekly, 'Your teacher Paolo Grancino, Padre, as you have oft times told me.'

'Yes!' announced Carlo. 'Grancino, may his soul rest with the angels. My teacher who learnt the craft directly from Nicolo Amati and alongside Antonio Stradivari, the other great light of the Amati stable. And tell me, Paolo, what is this place? Tell me now, loudly, boy!'

Paolo knew he had to follow the usual routine. 'It is the Sign of the Eagle Workshop, Padre. Named after our insignia, *lo stemma della Famiglia*, here in the same workshop once graced by Maestro Paolo Grancino.'

'Then how and why, in the name of Lucifer's Great Balls,' begged Carlo, 'do you insist on presenting me with such rubbish? Look at your brother's violins over here! Even those made from the scraps of indifferent timbers he hoards end up being excellent, better than most of the over-rated crap coming out of Roma.'

Paolo could never bring himself to hate, nor even envy, his older brother, Carlo Antonio. He adored him, but he lived perpetually in his shadow. He granted that Carlo Antonio crafted with more care and attention to detail, but Paolo knew that his own violins were serviceable, attractive to the eye, and made in less than half the time it took his obsessive brother. Further, he could not bring himself to tell his father that two of the three violins on the drying rack, that he seemed to so admire, were his creations, not Carlo Antonio's. He vowed to himself that one day he would shake off the shackles of family and open his own workshop somewhere over town.

In a day or so, things had settled back to normal at the studio on the Contrada Larga. The polishing was done and each instrument was strung with new strings. Two of the four new pieces had been commissioned and were already paid for. Carlo Giuseppe played each in turn and found that the first three more than met the standard discerning customers usually demanded. He insisted that Paolo play the fourth instrument, believing that it was beneath himself to touch it. When Paolo began to saw on the strings the sheer volume of the violin silenced the workshop, as apprentices and journeymen alike gasped at the sound.

As soon as he tried a passage in third position, however, the sound became truncated by the awkward action in the higher register. Then, when Paolo tested the harmonics, it became clear that the instrument did not hold true temperament along the length of the neck.

While his father mumbled dismissively, in his familiar *I told you so* manner, all that Paolo could think about was that he had crafted a perfect instrument for the raucous dance music of the tavernas and villages, places where the more subtle concert instruments often struggled to be heard.

Paolo had just convinced himself that he had made something of value, after all, when his father came and, grabbing it from him, inserted a fine chisel into one f-hole and did what he could to scratch the eagle insignia from the interior. 'Let some gypsy buy this, but I won't have our name on it,' he announced, for the benefit of the other apprentices as much as Paolo.

Chapter 5

Tasmania, 2023

The late afternoon sun dappled the stony tops of the mountains as Haley made her way up the highway to Vinces Saddle, before descending towards Kingston, where the road turned off to the city of Hobart. On the descent, she could see into the distance across the wide river mouth to South Arm and there was Betsy Island, already arrayed in its first autumn green. The majesty of the scene helped quell the disquiet that she still felt after the visit to the Doolan home.

There were dark gold-rimmed clouds, heavy over Storm Bay, and a beam of light from the mountain, kunanyi, fell upon a pair of yachts sailing past the Iron Pot Lighthouse, and in towards the Derwent River.

I will never get sick of this view, she thought. She could not help but compare the richness of this scene with the dusty golden plains and low dry hills of South Australia. In her current estimation these dolerite mountains, forested hills, wild seas and coastal islands won hands down. Her thoughts turned for a moment to the battered old Flakemore violin on the back seat and its scratched-out insignia inside. She wondered again what that mark had represented. With that question still on her mind, she drove towards the round-about. Just before she took the turn towards the city, the shadow of a great wedge-tailed eagle fell across the road, as the bird swept low to grab a roadkill wallaby from the verge.

When she first moved to Tasmania, Haley had lived in Hobart for around eighteen months. Looking for musical outlets she had subbed for a while with the Van Diemen's Band, a wonderful Baroque ensemble that also delved into folk and ethnic genres from time to time. She had played in two of their themed shows but, given that their roll call of non-core players was extensive, and being a newcomer, she rarely received the phone call for work.

One time, outside a café in Hobart, she had run into Rachel, a regular player with the Van Diemen's Band. Rachel's dark eyes scanned Haley's face, and before Haley could raise the matter Rachel had anticipated what Haley was feeling.

'Hi, Haley, hope all is well. It has been a while. Sorry there's not much work available with the ensemble at present. Julia really appreciated your playing, but our latest shows have just required a smaller core group. Do you have any other musical projects to float your bow?'

'Thanks Rach! I was beginning to wonder if it was me. To tell the truth I do feel a bit musically frustrated. I can feel a little culturally deprived down in the valley. I was thinking of joining the Derwent Symphony, but I can't fit the trips up to Hobart for rehearsals around my teaching schedule.'

Brushing a stray dark hair back, Rachel sighed. 'I know what that's like. It's hard to do everything. My husband pushes against the inevitable. He teaches fulltime, but somehow manages to help run the Kunanyi Folk Club and a sea-shanty group. I have my fingers in heaps of pies too. But at least travel isn't so much of a problem for us, being closer to the city.'

Haley simply nodded as Rachel continued. 'You could try the folk and jazz sessions. I'd go to them if I had the time.'

'What are the options? Trying some less formal community music does appeal to me, but I'm not sure where to start.'

'Well on Wednesday nights at the Cascade hotel they have a Manouche session; you know gypsy-jazz, like Stefan Grapelli and Django Reinhardt repertoire! They give out charts to newcomers. Very welcoming and a good way to practise a largely improvisational style.'

Haley smiled from behind her glasses before turning up one side of her mouth. 'Getting there and back on most Wednesday nights would be the same problem, but I'm keen to give it a go.'

Rachel nodded, thinking carefully. 'There's an Irish tune session every Saturday at the New Sydney. Oh yes, then there's the Old Timey Session that a guy called Rusty runs, but I'm not sure when and where they meet. Down your way the Gadds at Franklin have a house session once a fortnight. And there are folk clubs if you want to play a tune or network.'

'Thanks so much, Rach. Nice running into you. I'll try the New Sydney sessions. See if I can be regular. Will also give a look-in to those gypsy sessions during the semester breaks. Food for thought and much appreciated.'

'Nice to catch up with you, Haley. I'd been hoping you weren't feeling too deflated. Let me know if those suggestions help you get your musical fix!'

'Will do. Tell Julia to keep me on the books for VDB spots if they should arise though. I love playing with you guys.'

'Same. All the best.'

So it was that, following Rachel's advice, Haley had begun to frequent the New Sydney's Irish music sessions. She had always kept Saturdays free from teaching or preparations, so the new routine proved convenient as well as fruitful.

Haley found that the tunes played there were mostly simple, monophonic, with apparently arbitrary chords used in accompaniment, and, while the tempos could sometimes be a challenge, the hardest thing was the collective expectation that participants play only by ear or from memory. To her amazement she discovered that some of the established players seemed to hoard hundreds of tunes in their memories, any of which might gurgle to the surface at any time to confuse and bemuse those trying to play along.

For the most part, however, the standard repertoire seemed to comprise around thirty favourite reels, jigs, hornpipes, and polkas. These were played repeatedly, until the group sound settled, and the old pub's mural-covered walls echoed with the shamanic sorcery that this type of playing can conjure up. Once in a while, much to Haley's delight, a musician of greater virtuosity such as 'Brian the Flute' might exploit a break in the cacophony to launch into a haunting, plaintive solo air on his wooden flute.

At such times most of the musicians around the long table would fall to silence, rather than try to play along and follow the magical but idiosyncratic phrasing and ornaments that characterised these slower tunes.

Haley had prided herself on absorbing most of the more oft-played tunes. She had done memory work at the conservatorium and, in her early twenties, had two whole concertos under her fingers and a few others that required the occasional prompt from the score. For the most part, however, she had spent years playing off the notation, attempting perfect fidelity to the intentions of this composer or that. Folk music had proved a liberating forum, where the standard of rightness for a piece depended on one intuitively plugging into the group-mind and into the essential lilt of each tune.

She had been drawn particularly to the slip jigs such as 'The Butterfly'. As a classical player she had not much experience of 9/8 time outside of some Bach. The Irish 9/8 swung differently though. With an accent structure that was both enchanting and confusing, each melody seemed a perfect gem, added to, and consequently trimmed down by generations of fiddlers, flautists, and uilleann-pipe players, until its essential *Platonic form* was revealed.

Like the gypsy-jazz jams that she occasionally managed to get to at the Cascades hotel, the Irish sessions at the New Sydney offered an insight into a uniquely different musical culture, with its own protocols, imperatives, limitations, and standards of excellence. In both cases, however, it was the social engagement, as much as the musical, that inspired the drive into Hobart and back.

She had met some characters at the sessions. A few in their thirties and early forties were close to her own age. Some were younger, others older, a few were fellow travellers, but each had their own story.

Sometimes, Haley's red curls, lively eyes and open smile would attract the attention of one man or another, attentions occasionally flattering but mostly unwanted. She missed the warmth of physical proximity, but her ambivalence about relationships hinted at old hurts and the remnant insecurity they leave in their wake.

Haley had been ensconced with Richard since their days at Brighton High, bound together by comfortable familiarity but never married. Tall and conventionally handsome, over the years he became more and more engaged with his own career and hobbies and betrayed a decreasing interest in Haley's dreams or in her pursuits beyond the domestic realm. He had an annoying habit of leaving her waiting and of not answering calls, as if to keep Haley insecure about his affections. He had gradually become the classic absent-presence; their lives together reduced to parallel play. In truth they had already been drifting slowly apart for years, lives going in different directions, hanging together by the threads of habit and a fear of starting anew, given that such a long relationship had excluded any exploration and experience of alternatives. Nevertheless, when she accepted the only music teaching job that seemed available anywhere at the time, she had asked Richard if he would join her in Tasmania. It was a stretch; deep down she knew already that he had no intention of moving and leaving his own career behind. The pain that comes with such an ending of things could not simply be shrugged off. Haley knew though, that it would fade in time and so threw herself into her new life.

She had only recently come to recognise that her own gregarious side had been dampened down by the routine expectations of her long-term relationship with Richard. In Tasmania, a place of interlocking networks, her circle of close friends had begun to expand. Now, living alone in her cottage in the Glen, she valued her social engagements more than ever.

When Haley arrived at the New Sydney the session players were already packing up for the day. An elderly singer she hadn't seen before was bringing things to a close, with an understated unaccompanied rendition of 'The Parting Glass', sung in a gentle tenor. She found herself oddly moved by both the melancholy of the song and the quavering fragility of the voice. *Who was that?* she wondered.

Looking around, she saw that her mates, the Fiddlers Three as she called them, had reserved a table for dinner. 'G'day Hales!' said Charlie Dempsey, a thin, dark-haired, fifth generation Tasmanian man, who despite his heritage, always wore an idiomatic cheese-cutter hat in order to present as even more Irish than the Irish who attended the session. Rose Murphy, adorned in plain cotton slacks and a woollen top, simply smiled and called out, 'Hey!' The pastel colours she wore set off her perfect complexion and her soft grey eyes. Between Rose and Charlie sat Michelle Pearson, an assertive no-nonsense brunette in jeans and an old leather jacket. Haley greeted each in turn as she took one of the two vacant seats at their side.

'We missed you today, Hale!' said Michelle. 'We were a bit down in the fiddle department, and some fellow brought along his highland pipes, so you can guess the rest.'

'Ooow, I can at that!' replied Haley. The others shared a brief giggle.

What followed was an animated discussion about session etiquette. They debated the eternal question of how to find that sweet compromise between a homogenous sound, and the need of different instrumentalists to be heard and to hear themselves. In the light of the comments floating around, Haley began to think that perhaps it was fortuitous that she had missed today's cacophony.

Retracing her recent arrival there, a remnant curiosity surged in her, and she changed the subject. 'Who was that gentleman singing the last song just as I came in? I haven't seen him at the sessions before.'

Rose smiled wryly. 'That's because he lives at the other end of the island, up at George Town. He still makes it down here once every few months. Less and less these days though.'

Charlie butted in. 'He used to live down your way. Had a cottage in Franklin. Started the folk club there with some friends way back in the seventies. Michael Flanagan 'tis his name.'

Haley's eyes flashed with a vague sense of recollection at something Kerry Flakemore had mentioned. She was about to nod when Michelle cut across Charlie's mock-Irish brogue.

'Did you know it was Mick and his wife that started up the Cygnet Folk Festival, then later the Tamar Folk Festivals, after he moved up north? Lovely people too! Mick's not been so well of late. Nice that they still make it down here once in a bit, but it may well be his last time.'

Charlie, seemingly impatient, broke the rhythm of the conversation. He tapped Haley on the arm, nodding in the direction of the specials board. 'Do you want to look at the menu? We've already ordered. The roast of the day is looking good.' He gestured to the meal just delivered to the adjacent table. 'Pork with crackling and apple sauce.'

'I think I need something a bit lighter, is the trevalla

and Greek salad on today?' Haley turned to scan the board displaying the day's specials, just as a very tall wiry fellow wearing a coloured headscarf, and clenching two fists replete with glasses of Guinness, sat down next to her.

'Haley, meet Brendan, our friend from Belfast. And Brendan, meet Haley, a lovely fiddler and normally a regular at the session,' said Rose Murphy.

Charlie elaborated. 'Brendan is an excellent guitarist, as eclectic as he is eccentric. Plays traditional Irish, blues, jazz and even writes songs. Does it all well.'

Brendan had seen Haley arrive and had already factored her in to the order of five pints that he had brought from the bar. She couldn't help but wonder how he had carried all five without spilling a drop.

'So how are you finding life down here on this other emerald isle, Brendan?' she asked.

'Loving it! Travelling around with my caravan from here to there, wherever the gigs arise, but mostly spending time in the Huon, at the Ranelagh camping ground.'

'Oh, that's just over the river from where I am based. Are you getting enough chances down here to satisfy your musical needs?'

'Well, work is a bit thin on the ground, but I go to the blues jam at Dover, I come here to Hobart for the Irish craic whenever I have a free Saturday, and every second Sunday I go to the Trad Tassie session at Gadds' Cottage in Franklin.'

'I've heard about the Gadds but haven't met them. In fact, I took over a few of the students left teacherless when Marjorie Gadd retired. But is there really such a genre as traditional Tasmanian music?' asked Haley. She mused that apart from some old brass *Oom-Pa* players of German descent from the Barossa and Hahndorf, there seemed not to be any music that was regionally specific to her old state, South Australia.

Charlie sniggered, giving his own opinion of traditional Tasmanian music. 'Old country dance music that sounds to me like a mix of bastardised Irish and British music and badly played nineteenth-century ballroom music.'

Rose suddenly became animated. 'Come on, Charlie. I've seen the Tasmanian Heritage Fiddle Ensemble blow audiences away at the National Folk Festival. Some of the players that came out of that group are among the best fiddlers around. Have you heard "As The Crow Flies", "Wolfe and Thorn", "Lomond", "Frumious"? The list goes on. And then there's that young woman whose dad was from Cape Barren Island who came along today, she was brought up on the true Tasmanian stuff, doesn't stop her playing Irish tunes though, and why should it?'

'Well, I love that Tasmanian stuff!' Brendan elaborated. 'Everywhere in the diaspora the Irish sessions usually replay the same tunes, mostly the jigs, polkas, hornpipes, and reels. And fair enough, that is how it should be! You can go to a session in Clare, or Chicago, or London, or Hobart, and know that the other players will share repertoire and that you will be able to join in. But the Tassie stuff! It's like you are suddenly in some whole alternative universe where the music took a different turn, and mazurkas, varsoviennas, schottisches and waltzes became the core tunes; while the reels, polkas, and jigs all came with new names and strange new twists. It is refreshing to me; different tunes, different playing style and different feelings I get from it all. Won't ever be a style I master, or would want to focus on, but it has its place, and Tasmanians should value it for what it is, not diss it for what it's not.'

Between Rose's comments and those of Brendan, Charlie had begun to feel like he was being neatly put in his place, and so changed the topic. He asked Haley why she had brought in an instrument case when she knew that the session was likely to be over.

'Didn't want to leave it in the car, just to be on the cautious side.'

Michelle interjected, 'That's only sensible given your beautiful violin, Hale!'

'Oh no,' Haley replied. 'This isn't my good fiddle. It's an old beast that I took possession of just this morning. It's loud, but with a terrible action. Not sure if it's worth anything. I had hoped to get a recommendation from one of you, as to the name of a Hobart atelier or luthier who might have a look at it. Whatever it is, it needs some serious repairs. Given that it spent forty years hanging on a hay-shed wall it seems a miracle to me that the soundpost hasn't collapsed!'

'You're in luck then, Hales,' Charlie enthusiastically pitched in. 'When you go up to the bar to order your fish, introduce yourself to the blonde-haired bloke with the ginger beard, the one in the blue shirt who's waiting to be served. He's Aaron Larsen, one of only three or four decent violin makers and repairers in town. He has a workshop up in Bathurst Street, just a few blocks away. Mostly into making cellos and experimenting with local timbers these days, but he trained in Denmark, and seems to know his stuff when it comes to fiddles. He did a great fix on mine, after the cat knocked it onto the kitchen floor and split the scroll work.'

Aaron proved friendly enough, though initially he seemed disappointed that Haley's attention seemed solely work-related.

He was curious enough, though, to want to have a look at the violin in question. He asked if she would come around to his workshop after dinner. She took his directions down and agreed to make it there by 8 p.m., after determining that it wouldn't be too late, given the looming drive back home to the valley.

When Haley, Brendan and the 'Fiddlers Three' had dined, talked, laughed, and drank, she farewelled her friends and drove around the corner, and up the steep road to the Bathurst Street address. Aaron's house and workshop were conjoined, an old timber building on sandstone foundations, tucked in behind some trees on the lower side of the road. Arriving before her, he had turned the lights on, and she found the workshop door was already open.

Looks like the real deal! She scanned the long workbenches, the wall arrayed with specialised tools, each of a purpose and kind she could not identify. At one end, stands held expensive-looking sheets of exotic timber, supported upright so they would not warp. Near the far wall she saw the embryonic form of a new cello, a few recently repaired violins, and a viola da gamba yet awaiting repair. The room was fragrant with the smell of fresh wood shavings and the disparate odours of spirits, varnishes and glues.

'*Velkommen til mit ydmyge hjem,*' said Aaron by way of greeting.

'Say what?' returned Haley, more than a little confused.

'Ha. It's Danish, for welcome to my humble home.'

'Oh, the name! Should have guessed.'

'Well, I was born here, but my father was a Dane and I lived there for a while. Would you like a fresh coffee? I have a 1960s espresso machine that I restored. It lives over there.' He pointed to a small bench at the side wall near the workshop door. 'I insist that you have black, no milk and sugar here I'm afraid, and all the better for it methinks.'

'A purist,' exclaimed Haley, musing to herself that an anal-retentive character was probably a good thing for a person in such a profession. 'Black is okes by me!' she added, and with that Aaron got straight down to grinding the beans.

'Well, here it is, warts and all.' She placed the case on the near bench and removed the Flakemore fiddle. While his eyes did not light up straight away, Aaron was clearly curious. Haley raised an eyebrow as she noticed that he checked the coffee's temperature with a thermometer before pouring it into some delicate china cups. Leaving the cups to sit a while, he came over and picked up the violin. Straight away he could feel the warp in the neck and grunted. 'Warped!'

'Well, I guess it may have gained a twist in its forty years hanging on the shed wall,' Haley proffered.

'Nope.' Aaron disagreed immediately. 'See those grain lines? This neck was never quite true. I can't even identify the timber. The maker probably had only a leftover scrap of some hardwood and this irregularity already came with it. If so, he probably did his best to straighten it. I don't know why he didn't use maple, or even one of the harder varieties of pine, to better match the timbers used on the belly and sides. Could even be apple wood, but I have never seen that used for instrument-making before. Look at this finish! Amazing, there are only a few places where the original French polish hasn't been damaged, stained or completely varnished over.'

He raised the violin towards the light and placed his phone camera up to the f-hole, changing the angle slightly while taking a few photos. 'Can't afford a maestronet, so I have to do it this way for now.'

'Maestronet?'

'A tiny camera on a stem. Like an endoscope for violins,' he answered without intending any humour.

Magnifying the photos on his phone to their maximum, he laughed as he drew her attention to what he saw there. 'The soundpost has been glued in, for starters. No wonder it survived a geological age of hanging. But oh, look at this!'

He handed her the phone, his shoulder touching hers as he leaned in to touch his finger to the screen.

'The insignia you mentioned ... there! ... It has so obviously survived a rather violent attempt to scratch it away. That usually implies some ploy to remove a logo from a cheaper make, and to pass the instrument off as an antique. Not this one though. See what's left of the original image. It looks like a bird of some kind, a raptor maybe. I admit that I haven't seen this before, but the description rings a bell for me, something my teacher mentioned back in my apprenticeship days.'

Aaron walked over to a bookshelf and pulled out a hefty codex that Haley imagined must contain some secret luthier lore. He looked at the index before arriving at a chapter that apparently contained illustrations of four centuries of insignias, labels, and brand markings. He started at the twentieth century examples, then moved progressively backwards, not finding anything until he reached the entries for the eighteenth and seventeenth centuries. Then there it was.

'Holy shit!' Aaron gestured to Haley to look closer. 'What we have here is a Testore! Maybe a *secondi*, that is, a reject, but still a Sign of the Eagle violin from the Milan workshop!

In all her time as a classical player Haley had not heard more than a brief mention of Testore violins, and she couldn't recall the context or the player involved. Not sure of how to respond she simply asked, 'Then is it worth saving after all?'

Aaron gave her a sober look, stepped back from the bench and crossed his arms. He paused to consider his words carefully before answering.

'To be perfectly honest, this instrument is a wreck. At first, I was going to suggest scrapping it, as the repairs required would end up taking months and possibly costing you thousands. It may never have been a good violin, but given that insignia I am now in danger of changing my mind. I will definitely need to do a bit more research. I don't think we will ever determine its provenance completely, but I think I may be able to determine where it was made, and when, down to the decade.'

Haley raised her brow and simply asked, 'And?'

After another moment of deliberation Aaron sucked in a slow breath then replied, 'Restoring it would be a challenge, but I'm willing if you want me to try. Can you leave it with me?'

Haley hesitated. The cost sounded prohibitive and the outcome uncertain. Nevertheless, she found herself being influenced by Aaron's understated enthusiasm.

'Okay! Why not? Just do the research and tell me what you find before I commit to forking out for a full restoration rather than a quick fix.'

Driving home, Haley wondered whether she had made the right decision, considering the decrepit condition of the old beast.

Back in his workshop, Aaron took one last look at the beast before turning off the lights. 'You old monster, I'm worried that my skills might not be up to fixing you. I hope Haley didn't pick up on that.'

Chapter 6

Milan, 1700

Giuliano Geminiani had reluctantly acceded to his son's wishes. What else could he do? Without an excellent replacement violin, Francesco's lessons with Lonati would amount to nothing. Further, as much as he despised the thought of his son playing peasant music in rowdy taverns, he also admitted that it was good for the boy to make some money for himself. This presented a quandary for him. He had no desire to secure another fine instrument for Fra only to have it damaged by some tavern drunk, a situation close to inevitable.

Maestro Giuliano had somehow convinced the patron of the Palatine Orchestra that Fra was worth the investment. Francesco's promise to return to Lucca after his three years of training in Milan, to play with the orchestra and possibly score parts for it without asking payment, was all that it took. The *funzionari della città* of Lucca were proud of their orchestra. They often had trouble, however, attracting and keeping musicians of a high enough standard. Francesco, even as a child, was on his way to musical greatness and was without a doubt an asset worth investing in. But in his father's eyes he seemed to lack focus and could frustrate to the point of exasperation. Even as a child he would some-times put down his violin in the middle of a lesson, walk out, then just stand in front of one of his patron's Paolinis or Caravaggios and stare into the painting, silently, for an hour or so. Giuliano had even considered the possibility that Francesco might be more suited to painting or sculpture than music, but after a month of trial lessons it was clear that he had no aptitude for the visual arts. It was simply that he was entranced by great paintings, almost to the point of awe.

Francesco was truly fond of his father, and mostly intended to please and impress him, hardly surprising given that Giuliano was both the family patriarch and his first music teacher. Fra usually ended up making a mess of it though. He was who he was. He felt that his life was slowly attaining its true *telos*, moving in its own way, a way just not quite in accord with either his father's expectations or his father's timetable.

Francesco was, this time, very glad that his father had agreed to visit Milan, and it was especially convenient that Geminiani senior had found lodgings for a few nights, not so far from Maestro Lonati's apartment and studio. He was less happy about his father's timing, however. Geminiani senior had walked into the studio just as Francesco was practising a tarantella currently popular among the drinkers in the tavernas. At that moment Maestro Lonati, obviously not impressed, had walked up to Fra and clipped him forcefully behind the ear, saying, 'How dare you play that crude peasant noise on the good instrument that I have lent you! If you must indulge in that rubbish please save such acts of musical sacrilege for when you again take possession of a violin of your own.'

Francesco had been embarrassed in front of his father. Lonati was not usually this harsh in his approach, but Francesco took it in his stride and thought it best to play the game and so defuse the situation. 'Sorry, Maestro. I sought only to elevate the music of the streets to the standards demanded by our craft. But fear not, before the day is out I should have a new instrument. Thank you again for letting me use this very fine one until then.' Stretching out his arm, he handed the valuable instrument back to his teacher, who despite grunting at the gesture, was feeling ashamed at being caught mid-outburst.

In a few minutes father and son had left the studio and ventured out into the maze of ways and byways. For a short time Francesco amused himself by transcribing the rhythms of their boots on the cobblestones into notation in his mind. However, distracted by the sounds and smells from houses, kitchens and workshops, he soon tired of the exercise.

As they walked together through the web of narrow streets that led to the Contrada Larga, Fra asked his padre what he took to be a reasonable question. 'Why a Testore in particular? I heard a beautiful violin, a Landolphis instrument, and its owner was willing to sell it at a reasonable price.'

His father answered briskly, 'The Landolphis violins are inconsistent. Some are wonderful, but others, made from flawed timbers, sound great for a few years but won't last out a musician's whole career as a real violin should. I don't think we should risk it. On the other hand, the violins of

Antonio Stradivari are so popular that we would have to commission one, years in advance, and even then, given the price they can fetch, it could bankrupt the Palatine Orchestra. The Testores come from the same lineage of craftsmen. The Eagle Sign instruments that I have heard are certainly good enough, even the ones made from cheaper woods still sound good, and their glues hold together well. Importantly, most are well within our price range. The violin that I commissioned was made by Carlo Antonio Testore, Carlo Giuseppi Testore's oldest son. One instrument merchant also mentioned a younger son, Paolo, but warned me that his instruments were not always appropriate for a concert musician.'

They found the workshop, nestled modestly between a cluster of houses and shops. Holding his second-favourite bow in his left hand, Geminiani senior knocked loudly with his right upon the large oak door. They were promptly greeted and led in by a boy, who announced their presence to Testore senior and his sons. Testore senior had been expecting their arrival.

'Maestro Geminiani, well met *mi amico*! And this must be the young Master Francesco! Come in, gentlemen. These are my sons Carlo and Paolo. Carlo has finished your new violin and it is a beautiful piece of work. I am assured that it will suit the young savant perfectly and that it will serve as a trusty companion through many an illustrious performance.'

Francesco thought that Signor Testore was himself putting on a bit of a performance. Though he was genuinely excited about his new instrument he didn't feel a need to hear assurances of its qualities. *Let him play it, and it should speak for itself,* he judged, but was polite enough not to say so out loud.

Looking towards the younger son, Paolo, Francesco quickly recognised his face, having seen him in one or two of the taverns in which he had fiddled for the drinkers and dancers. They exchanged a wink and a nod of acknowledgement, while their respective fathers talked business.

When Signor Testore led them to the table of finished instruments on display, Francesco nearly quivered with excitement. One had been prepared for him and was sitting beside an open case made especially for it. He noted the case's strong wood, riveted onto metal ribs that could protect the precious violin through whatever trials and turmoils that might befall it.

The violin itself was elegantly formed and flawless. The back and the belly were maple, the back being made from two pieces, each the mirror image of the other. The varnish was golden, while the purfling was just a shade darker and had a slightly discernible reddish tint. The scrollwork was as ornate as one would expect, and inside, the eagle insignia showed itself, clearly visible through the f-holes.

Carlo senior looked on in anticipation, waiting for the boy to play and to acknowledge the mastery manifest in the instrument. Carlo junior, however, just stood by, looking serenely confident that his work would more than meet the standard required.

Giuliano Geminiani touched Fra firmly upon the shoulder, arresting his son's movement towards the table. Instead, he politely insisted that given the huge investment his patron had made in all of this, it should be he himself who first tested the instrument. Fra relented as his father fine-tuned the instrument then proceeded to play it, one tune or étude after another, smiling, nodding, or gasping between each. After some not inconsiderable length of time had passed,

Francesco became less patient and scowled, gesturing for his padre to hand the new instrument to him. Opposite, Paolo signalled to Francesco and pointed, clandestinely, in the direction of his own father, while mouthing the words *Mine is even worse.*

The two older men didn't understand why their lads had started giggling. The sound of choked-back laughter was insulting to Giuliano, who stopped playing for just long enough for Francesco to finally take the violin from him.

While the father was a virtuoso by reputation, it was clear, to any who might hear, that the son had already surpassed the father. A few years earlier Carlo junior had heard the then twenty-year-old Venetian prodigy, Antonio Vivaldi. He had started to imagine making a violin for such a player and hearing the sounds that they would bring forth. In his mind, at that moment, he realised that the young Geminiani had a comparable talent and, even at his tender age, might soon equal Vivaldi in skill.

Francesco tried slow pieces, sombre pavanes, a gigue, some sacred pieces, a galliard, then improvised a showpiece in the moment with improbable cadenzas, polyphonic string-crossing and ringing harmonics. While everyone in the 'Eagle Sign' workshop stood in deep amaze, Fra had fallen in love, knowing that this violin would go with him throughout his days.

Before he finished, however, he paused, wrinkled his brow, then launched into a fast and frenetic tarantella. At that moment Geminiani senior and junior both broke into frowns of disappointment. Fra's father, because it sickened him to hear crude village dance music played on such a perfect instrument. Francesco was disappointed for the contrary reason, as he had determined that his new violin was never going to be suited to the brash and strident demands of the folkloric dances that, for now, were his bread and butter.

With neither Testore senior nor his brother noticing, Paolo met Fra's eye, making a subtle gesture towards the instrument table and to another violin secretly sitting in shadows behind the others. When Francesco reached for it, Testore senior was about to cry out *Not that one, that is rubbish, a reject!* But it was too late. Francesco had launched into the same tarantella that he had trialled on the better violin, and out it came, loud as a siren, wailing, laughing, and almost driving some of the workshop attendants to start dancing. He then tried some position work and abruptly realised the limitations of this instrument. It was good for one thing, peasant dances in first position, even perfect for them in fact, but it could never deal with the complex composed music demanded for the concert halls and the parlours of prospective patrons. He placed it back where he had found it, but with a sad reluctance.

Giuliano Geminiani had already paid the considerable sum for Carlos's wonderful creation, which had now been carefully placed in its case and was ready for the walk back to Lonati's. Remembering then, that there was no alternative to allowing Fra to continue playing for money in the tavernas, he realised that his son was still in need of a second, rough-house, violin. He had spent all the money his patron had donated and some more of his own, but still he asked Testore senior how much he wanted for the flawed, *secondi*, violin.

'Just take it. Selling instruments like that one only brings shame upon our name. Just don't tell anyone where it is from. See that neck? It is a piece of apple wood that Paolo found in an orchard after the thinnings had been cut. It wasn't even dried properly, and that warped grain will continue to twist the neck until it is fully dry. When Paolo presented it to me, I nearly spat in his face! See there, I have already scratched out the eagle. Just make sure no one thinks that it is a real Testore! Just take it... and promise.'

Francesco was delighted with this turn of affairs. He now had both of the tools he needed to ply his trade and advance his income! On the way out he quietly thanked Paolo, who winked before whispering, 'Maybe I'll see you again sometime in the Inn of Three Swords.'

Though he had other fine instruments that came into and passed from his possession, throughout his life Francesco Geminiani retained a deep affection for both of his Testore violins. They were two brothers, as different as their makers, one being gentle, nuanced, and elegant, the other raucous, careless, and wild. The first he called his '*dolce angelo*', the second his '*bestia arrabbiata*' – respectively, the gentle angel and the angry beast. After his three years under Maestro Lonati, Fra left Milan and returned home to Lucca, Tuscany, where, as he had promised, he served his time playing with the Palatine Orchestra. After working off his debt for the first twelve months, he was then contracted, at full pay, to play and arrange for the orchestra for another two years. In that time, he became as enthusiastic about composing as he was about playing. He yearned to do a second musical apprenticeship, this time focusing on composition. He had already saved up enough money to fund his aspirations.

The patron of the Palatine had suggested that he wanted to give Francesco tenure, as second violin in the orchestra. The thought of being stuck in his home town, sharing a chair next to his father in the first violins, horrified him. He contrived to deliberately play badly, inserting unscripted rubato into pieces, or pushing the tempi of pieces until he was at odds with the concertmaster.

The tactic worked. When he eventually left the Palatine, he then studied composition under his hero, the great Corelli, and so emerged as both a violinist and composer to be reckoned with.

He would go on to lead orchestras and chamber groups in France, England and eventually in Dublin, Ireland, where the city was emerging into what would be its Georgian glory. Even then, the tavern fiddle of his youth, his '*bestia arrabbiata*', would go with him, for it was reputed that Irish pubs served the best whiskey, and the patrons were always up for a jig.

Chapter 7

The Huon Valley, Tasmania, 2023

Friday had been a stressful day for Haley. The private lessons she gave, teaching at home, were always a mixed bag, but yesterday it was a shambles. A Zoom lesson had been scheduled, then cancelled without warning because the student's family decided to go camping for the weekend without telling her. When she rang the boy's father to ask what had happened, he was already on a wharf fishing. Taken by surprise, he came across as formally apologetic but a little too distracted to sound like he meant it.

'Sorry, Haley. Kevin's mum was supposed to ring and tell you. I just forgot that he had a lesson and didn't check if she had. Wanted us to take advantage of the weather. I'll still pay for the missed lesson, don't worry. See ya.'

Then there was Anthea, a gifted girl in her mid-teen years, who played beautifully, but who cursed herself out loud, nearly bringing herself to tears, every time she got a passage wrong or a note out of tune.

I guess perfectionism is always going to be a mixed blessing in a young musician, paralysing as much as it motivates, Haley thought, recapitulating her long-held philosophy for teaching music. Haley was a firm believer in making it fun, and that sometimes meant 'fake it until you make it'. Better to start finessing a piece later, when you already have a sense of the whole in your memory, and the rough template of the fingerings in your hands. She felt strongly that the theory that all bad habits must be eliminated right from the beginning, and that each bar or phrase must be perfected before one moves on to the next, was just bad pedagogy. She had seen too many aspiring players lose heart before they really got started. In the case of Anthea, Haley had yet to figure out the best strategy to encourage her to relax, have fun and to enjoy the process. *There will be a way,* she thought. *It's trial and error on my part at this stage.*

There were a few other lessons that day, but not a lot that brought her any satisfaction. Karen, an easy-going local girl who had just turned eleven, was a breeze. But while she had been in good spirits, as she always was, she had clearly done no practice, and so the lesson had to be a rerun of the previous one.

Then there were the twins, Cable and Seth, eight-year-old boys who were more interested in having sword fights with their bows than actually playing.

The only bit of light for the day was her last student, a friendly but slightly nervous adult called Lucy. Lucy had mentioned that she had recently started attending the Huon Heritage Ensemble sessions, and she had brought a few scores along for Haley's guidance.

'Do you think you might be able to help me with these, Haley? They're tunes the Sunday group plays.' Without waiting for an answer she passed the photocopied pages to Haley.

One page was titled the *Barn Dance Set*. It contained three short tunes. Each was a schottische, a form that Haley had not come across before.

'Hmmm.' Haley read down the page. '"The Mountain River Schottische", "Lyall Mansfield's Schottische", "The Old Huon Schottische" ... So what are these?' – the question directed more at herself than at Lucy. 'On the page they look a bit like Irish hornpipes, given the plenitude of triplets ornamenting the melodies.' She played through one on her fiddle before asking Lucy, 'Is this how you remember them sounding?'

Lucy shook her head. 'Well, not quite. The group played them at a slower, march-like tempo. But that bouncy lilt is right. They're not fast tunes, really. Apparently they have to fit the tempo for the progressive barn dance.'

Haley was struggling to remember if she had ever seen the progressive barn dance, so she resorted to the web and did a quick Google search on her phone.

'Oh, so the schottische is originally Polish!' She discovered that it turned out to be a variant of the polka influenced by the Scottish slide that was danced by the highland regiments stationed in Poland during the Napoleonic wars. She quickly formulated that, if a hornpipe is like a reel, slowed down a bit and swung, then a schottische is like a polka, slowed down a bit and swung. With this insight in mind, she proceeded to play through the tune set, using the light hornpipe bowing that she had picked up watching Rose at the New Sydney Irish session, but adding just a few longer classical bowings here and there for emphasis, all the while entertaining a vision of women in floral dresses and men dressed in archaic suits, dancing progressively around an old country hall.

Once she had played the pieces through this way she looked up at Lucy, eyebrows raised. Lucy nodded enthusiastically. 'Yes, that is just right! That sounds exactly like the way the ensemble was playing them last Sunday.'

'Thank goodness. The style's not something I've heard before, but I think I get it,' said Haley.

Eagerly, Lucy asked, 'Now can you show me how you get that light touch and the steady bounce? When I play that, it just sounds like this note, then that, stiff, with no dance in it.'

What followed was an extremely constructive lesson on the difference between various folk-bowing styles and Classical and Baroque bowing styles. Lucy left that evening, a bit overwhelmed by the different motor skills needed to cover the whole gamut of fiddle genres, but with the confidence that she could now play the *Barn Dance Set* with just the right feel.

Haley had taken a copy of those tunes, and a handful of others in different rhythms, that Lucy played with the Huon folk ensemble. She played through the *Barn Dance Set* once more after Lucy had gone. They were really quite delightful! Three collected tunes, all with local provenance, and they did so evoke the gentle, unassuming, village life of this valley. Haley felt some uncanny affinity with the musical mood that they conjured, as if there was an hereditary memory buried somewhere deep that she was accessing. She decided that one day she would investigate their provenance. This kind of music was new to her, but her ancestors were from down this way, after all. It would be good to know more.

Saturday

Needing a distraction from the events of the day before, Haley drove to the Saturday Market at Judbury, about five kilometres west from the Glen, just over the second bridge across the Huon River. She parked under a pine tree for shade, disturbing a goshawk in the branches above when she slammed her door closed.

The morning scene around her was all colour and movement. A medium-sized throng circled around the grounds inspecting the craft stalls, and the produce stalls, and the recycled-clothes stalls, and the second-hand book stalls, and the rest. All the while a lone guitarist played a sweet fingerstyle melody somewhere in the background.

The music stopped abruptly. She looked up, surprised to hear a voice calling out in her direction.

'Hey there Haley! Did you bring your fiddle?' By his head scarf, brogue and beaming smile, she recognised him as tall Brendan from Belfast, whom she had met in the pub the previous Saturday.

'Good morning to you, Brendan,' she called back, approximating what she imagined might be a whimsically Irish mode of greeting. She then gestured in the direction of the parking area. 'Sounding good! My second fiddle's in the boot of the car where I keep her just in case. No pun intended. Won't be long.'

She returned shortly, joining him for a set of well-known Irish tunes. Next, she did her best to improvise harmony parts to some of his original ballads. When they had finished, they smiled and thanked each other for the play.

'I guess you won't be at the session in Hobart this afternoon, Brendan?' she asked.

'Not a chance,' he replied, half laughing as he spoke. 'I have to play here until four o'clock. Market gigs go on for hours. You've got to be boned up on so much repertoire just to avoid repeating yourself. I'll be totally knackered when I'm finished. But I'm due for a short break about now. Will you be joining me for a coffee?'

They found a table and both ordered flat whites.

Brendan asked her if the luthier she had met had been able to offer any advice with regards to the ancient fiddle that she had brought to the pub the week before. She told him that Aaron had discovered that it truly was ancient, well over three hundred years old in fact, and from a famous Italian maker's stable. She informed him that Aaron had also guessed that it was a reject.

'That it survived at all was itself unusual. The foremost violin makers in eighteenth-century Italy were all proud of their standards for excellence. So generally, they were in the habit of smashing or scrapping sub-standard instruments. They had reputations and livelihoods to protect you know. Somehow this slipped through, and somehow ended up down here on a shed wall amid chooks and sheep and old apple crates!'

'Interesting,' said Brendan. 'Do you plan on getting it fixed up?'

'I had told Aaron to go ahead, but I've spent the week pondering it all, and now I'm having second thoughts.'

'Why is that?' asked Brendan.

'Well, I was hoping to pass it on to a girl from Dover way. It's her mother who wants me to find a good violin for her really. The lass, Jesse, loved the music and apparently showed a lot of promise. Then three years ago, after one unfortunate experience, she gave up violin altogether, announcing that she would never play again. For a variety of reasons, she now suffers badly from depression and has other anger issues as well. Her mother thinks, optimistically, that a new violin, just the right violin, might inspire her to start playing again, and so help her find whatever part of herself that has been lost.'

'D'ya think that will do the trick then?'

'I'm not sure if she can ever be won around to take up playing again. Nor am I sure, even if she could be, that the old beast of a violin is the one that will turn things around. Another consideration is that Jesse's mum is a single parent, with a modest income, and even if she and I both throw in money, we're unlikely to cover the cost for repairs. Perhaps I can find another fairly priced quality violin. Whether that would help, or whether I can source one before Jesse's fifteenth birthday, I just don't know.'

'Oh my! The burdens of being a teacher! Good luck, Haley. Let me know how it all unfolds. I better get back to playing before the market organiser notices!' said Brendan, and they departed and proceeded to go about their business.

Larsen's Workshop, Bathurst St, Hobart

'Very good, Mr Larsen! I can't even see a trace of either the damage or the repair.' Aaron's customer, Rosemary, seemed very happy with his work. It had taken him the better part of a week to finish the repairs on her viola da gamba.

'Thanks, glad it passes muster, Rosemary,' he shot back, beaming. Aaron had learnt to savour every bit of praise his workmanship garnered. He had really only one year of specific training in the field in which he worked, and though he prided himself on his attention to detail, he knew that some of the other luthiers in Hobart boasted rather more stellar credentials.

After Rosemary had paid, taken her prized instrument, and left, he mused that he might now have time for some other projects. The battered Testore, that had lain untouched on his second workbench all week, was playing on his mind. It was a wreck, and even if it could be repaired, it must always have been a beast of a thing. He groaned with indecision. Repairing it would require every skill he had. It would tie him up for weeks, and even so he might not end up with an instrument worth playing.

There was something about it, however, that still intrigued him. Perhaps it was the myriad scars, the signs of mistreatment, the odd markings here and there, or even the many indications of desperate and rudimentary attempts to repair it that maintained his attention. Its sheer age and the fact that it had so many layers of injury and repair indicated that numbers of players had valued it enough to try to keep it serviceable across several centuries. He pondered upon the mysteries of its provenance. Picking it up, he spoke directly to it. 'Where have you been since your difficult birth back in Milan in the early 1700s? What happened to you in the epochs between then and the time Haley McGribben found you hung out, to rot away, on the wall of a Huon Valley hay shed? If only you could talk, I know you would have some stories to tell.'

Aaron looked over the violin's layered patina, noting someone's crude attempt to use deck varnish to fix the finish. They had succeeded in covering some cracks, water marks and the remnants of the original French polish without rubbing the violin back and doing a proper restoration. In fact, the crass deck varnish just made his task even harder.

It was a mess. He'd just have to be honest and tell Haley it was hopeless. But hang on! Just there ... he managed to get his blade under a little bubble in the varnish. At some point water had worked its way under the surface and had almost lifted the varnish in a few places. If he had just the right tool, and worked very carefully, maybe he could remove the surface gloss in that area, without taking everything beneath it. As for the rest of the belly plate he had no idea. The varnish-removing gel that he had in the cupboard was probably too harsh for such a delicate project, and was likely to take the good with the bad.

Aaron considered. This work would require a huge time commitment over the next few months. *Well, there goes my social life, yet again.* It was solitary work and though he loved it he knew that it imposed an isolation upon him. He found himself reflecting stoically, but sadly, on his record in matters of the heart. Janice's words came back to haunt him as they often did. *You spend too much time in the workshop, and I've had enough of competing with whatever latest work project has grabbed your attention.*

Aaron had reminded her, *Well Janice, I have to make a living and this is what I do. What's more, my passion to do it well and to perfect my craft is part of who I am, like it or leave it.* Consequently, and without much hesitation, she chose to leave it, and to leave him. Aaron, at the time, not sure if he was sad or angered, had responded in his usual manner by burying himself even deeper into his work.

The New Sydney Hotel, Hobart

Haley had met up with Michelle and Rose, and together they fiddled their way through just about every set of standard tunes the gathered players had conjured. Every Saturday it was different. One was never sure who would turn up. Today there had been some moments of real beauty, as could happen when some really experienced players graced the session. That flute player with the white hair had brought along his harpist friend, and together they somehow lifted the throng into a higher realm of musicality. Haley, however, was distracted. The painful indecision as to whether to take the gamble and pay for the repair of the Flakemore fiddle was taking away from her pleasure of the music.

Rose had noticed. 'Earth to Haley, you missed that last section repeat. That's not like you, not with your sharp ears.'

Haley put down her instrument for a while and told Rose what was weighing upon her mind, adding a brief synopsis about Jesse and her backstory. Rose, possessing a prudent, no-nonsense nature, looked her in the eye and said outright, 'Nope, Hale! It's going to be too expensive. Work on paying your mortgage and building your student base before you start handing out money on a violin that isn't worth it, for someone who probably won't play it.'

'Fuck it! You're probably right Rosey my dear. I'll just focus on the music for now. If I don't, what's the point of being here?' Haley had only needed someone to say what Rose had just articulated to tip the scales in one direction. She determined that, rather than driving directly back to the Huon, she would drop in on Aaron Larsen and tell him not to embark on the evidently fruitless attempt to redeem the beast.

Larsen's Workshop, Hobart

Looking at the battered Testore made Aaron think about Roberto plying his trade in his workshop in faraway Cremona.

Old friend, I would love you to see this beast, and to ask your opinion.
Aaron had not heard from his old friend Roberto for nearly
a year. Prior to then they had stayed in touch regularly just
as each had promised before they left Copenhagen over ten
years ago.

Roberto had been, at least for a time, the closest thing
Aaron had to a brother. They were brothers in the craft,
bound by the chisel, the workbench and the wood, and they
shared that kind of love that brothers can have, looking out
for each other, but always nudging upon the edge of gentle
competition. Aaron's bond with Roberto had been tested
when Aaron's Danish girlfriend left him for Roberto, before
in turn, transferring her affections to a German backpacker.
This one blight upon those otherwise benign memories
still ate away at Aaron's confidence in affairs of the heart.
It had, however, done nothing to put a wedge between the
two friends.

Aaron was born in Tasmania, but having a Danish father
meant that he had dual citizenship. He had begun a wood
design course in Hobart in the early 2000s but, being unin-
spired by the senior tutor, he eventually lost interest. Rather
than completing the course he decided, instead, to take a
gap year and travel to Europe. Ending up in Denmark, he
found himself staying in Copenhagen for more than two
years. There he was living in Freetown Christiania, a squat
on an island in the bay. Christiania had once been a military
base, but since the 1970s it had been occupied by a community of bohemians, hippies and anarchists. The community
had resisted decades of government attempts to drive them
from the island by legal means and by force. The community, however, endured, at one stage even declaring itself an
independent micro-nation. By this stage it had become one

of Copenhagen's most important tourist drawcards, and later governments passed legislation to more or less legitimise the commune. It was in Christiania that Aaron met Roberto when they found themselves staying in the same apartment.

Roberto had studied to become an atelier and luthier in his home town of Cremona in Italy, arguably the current global centre of violin and cello making and restoration. Somewhere along the way he had begun to look for a niche not filled by Cremona's many fine luthiers. First delving into early music instruments, he had soon become fascinated with Scandinavian folkloric instruments. Thus, he sought out a master in the field with whom he could learn to craft such instruments as the Swedish hardanger fiddle, the Norwegian *nyckelharpa*, the Finnish *kantele* and the Danish bowed dulcimer.

While first exploring Copenhagen he had passed by a store that had a wonderful display of such instruments for sale. When he enquired, he was told that the luthier's workshop was just out the back of the shop. It was then and there he was to meet Aksel Frederiksen, to whom he became apprenticed for eighteen months.

It did not take much for Roberto to convince Aaron to come and study with him under Master Frederiksen. Aaron made it clear to Aksel Frederiksen that, unlike Roberto, who already had such skills, he hoped to focus mostly on violin, viola and cello repairs, as this work could secure him an income back in Tasmania.

In exchange for learning the basics of the luthier's trade, Aaron was required to serve at the shop's front counter, to sweep the floors, and to cut the component timbers in accord with Aksel's pre-set templates. Aksel Frederiksen's words still resonated. *You pay your dues around here, Ozzy boy, and I will help you learn the gentle care for broken things that is the key to all you wish to know and do.*

When their time as his students had elapsed, the two young men left Aksel's shop and studio, both forever in his debt. Roberto returned to his family workshop in Cremona, while Aaron began the journey of building a luthier's business from scratch back in faraway Tasmania.

Taking a break from the arduous attempt to clear the crude varnish from the body of the wrecked and wretched Testore instrument, Aaron poured himself a beer and sat down at his laptop to check for any new emails.

He was delighted to see a message from Roberto, the first in many months.

Roberto had simply written:

Dear friend,

Sorry for not keeping in touch. Long covid has had a crushing effect on our workshop, with my father and all our apprentices taking more time off than not. I have been lucky. The disease had little effect on me, after an initial day or two of coughs and sniffles. But that left me having to do the work the others would normally do. I hope that you are doing well. Have you come across any repair jobs of special interest? I just made a replacement bridge for an Amati. It was amazing to work on such a piece of Cremona's history, despite the simple nature of my contribution!

I have attached a file that may be of interest to you, my brother. Good luck to you, my brother.

Your Friend,

Roberto.

Aaron was happy to hear from his friend at last, but his mind was still on the Testore. Before opening the attachment, Aaron returned to his workbench. There he continued to try to lift the varnish from the sections of the belly and back where it had bubbled due to the long-term effects of sun and water. Miraculously, he was able to lift off a large film of the crude lacquer from a quarter of the belly. Revealed beneath the removed layer he noticed that the original French polish had been rubbed almost off, as if it had been drenched in a strong spirit that someone had tried, vigorously, to remove with a rubbing-cloth.

He wondered at this. It was clearly not an attempt to restore the polish or even to remove the original finish. Rather, it seemed to indicate some arbitrary action or even an accident.

Around about then Haley turned up, unannounced, at the workshop. She was looking as pretty as he remembered from their previous encounter, but he could tell that she was a little distressed. Aaron was pleased to see her but had already guessed the reason for her visit.

'Hi Haley. I'm guessing you are here to tell me not to bother going ahead with the restoration?'

'Oh Aaron, I'm sorry,' she replied. 'I've done the sums, and even together, the mother of the girl I wanted it for and I just cannot afford it. And nor can I know that it will be any more playable even then, and what if young Jesse still won't play it? It's all too much. The risk I mean.'

Aaron had anticipated this. 'I totally understand. I thought that, as a restoration job, it was touch and go anyway. But would you really mind if I hang onto the beast for another week or two more? I have never had a 300-year-old Italian violin to look at before. I would really like to pull it apart in order to get a better idea how the Testores were made.'

Haley was fine about this; it was a give-away in the first place, after all.

She left Aaron with the beast and thought, *After that false start I need to start really looking for a half-decent cheap instrument that Diane can give Jesse for her birthday. Good luck to us both on that score.*

That night the drive back to the valley through the gloaming and the drizzle seemed to Haley to be longer and touched with melancholy. When she finally pulled up into her driveway, she had a feeling of being watched. Raising her head, she saw a masked owl staring at her from the branch of the blackwood tree beside her cottage.

Aaron Larsen's Home

Aaron decided that he might need a second beer after all, before settling back at the computer. He returned to Roberto's message, then saved and opened the attached file. And there it was, an outline of the Master's Program in Traditional Violin Restoration offered by the Academia Cremonensis.

Compared to Roberto, Aaron always considered himself a beginner. Even when his work clearly pleased his customers, the inner gaggle of 'imposter syndrome' never quite diminished. Once Aaron had asked his Italian friend if there was somewhere in Cremona that he might go to advance his own skills to the level Roberto had attained. Roberto had told him about the Academia Cremonensis. The Academia was an academy of violin-making and bow-making located in an eighteenth-century palace, the Mina-Bolzesi. Looking into what was offered, Aaron did the sums. The fees were very expensive, and then there was the plane ticket on top of a whole year of living expenses. He had determined, with some disappointment, that his dream was out of his reach for now and perhaps forever.

But this time, Roberto had attached an application form for a scholarship that would cover all tutorial costs for the one-year course.

Aaron knew well that a handful of such scholarships went out each year, and hundreds of luthiers from all around the world applied for them. It seemed like just another recipe for disappointment and eroded self-esteem. Nevertheless, he read through the various criteria the application specified.

The scholarship would be awarded to a candidate with at least four years of professional experience in the fields of violin making and restoration. References from customers and fellow luthiers were required. Most importantly, the candidate must show an example of their work in restoration by sending in extensive photos, taken from at least five angles, of an instrument at all stages of restoration and including close-ups showing the restored instrument. Also required were videos and audio of one or more orchestral-level violinists playing upon the instrument. The academy specified that some unaccompanied Bach and any extract from a Vivaldi concerto must be among the recorded pieces.

The Testore! It seemed like perfect timing. Aaron's self-doubts were as persistent as ever – did he have the skills to make the beast sing? But then he thought of Haley's disappointment that afternoon and knew what he must now do. Hoping that he had found that window of opportunity between Haley arriving home and her heading off to sleep, he rang.

'Haley. Aaron here. It's not too late, I hope. I just wanted to say' – he hesitated, realising how much of his income-generating time this would erase over the next few months – 'I'll do it for free. And I promise it won't be a dud, even if I have to rebuild it from scratch.'

Haley had no idea how to respond. To her, such an offer seemed impossible. 'How? What?' was all she could muster.

'One proviso,' said Aaron. 'I need your permission to use it as an example of my work for a scholarship I hope to apply for.'

And with an 'Absolutely!' from Haley the deal was sealed.

Aaron now considered that he should start treating the beast with more respect. Before packing it away in the safe-cupboard this time, he took one last look at the rubbed-off section of the original French polish and wondered again as to what had occurred.

Chapter 8

Ireland, 1733

The Harp

Healer of each wounded warrior,
Comforter of each fine woman,
Guiding refrain over the blue water,
Image-laden, sweet-sounding music!

> – From *The Book of the O'Connor Don*

Lord Inchiquin's Residence, Dublin

The Governor of Kinsale, who preferred to be addressed as William O'Brien, Lord Inchiquin, was back in his Dublin residence. This was a grand manor which he rarely used, apart from those times he felt the need to display largesse towards diplomats or other esteemed visitors to Ireland from Britain and the continent. On this occasion, he was taking advantage of the visit to Ireland by the London-based Italian maestro Francesco Geminiani and his chamber ensemble, to host a special concert for his peers and their families. He had long been infatuated with the ornate quality of Italian music and yet he retained a special pride in the simpler melodic music of his own country. This time, he would present his guests with a unique combination of both.

Years ago, before he had been burdened by his current governorship role, he had commissioned a piece from the famous blind harpist Turlough O'Carolan. O'Carolan, as usual, composed a melody of perfect form and almost other-worldly charm. He had named the tune 'Lord Inchiquin' in O'Brien's honour.

O'Brien had determined what he felt would be the perfect formula for a night's entertainment. This would consist of a recitation, to be held in the grand hall, of works by Maestro Geminiani himself and by Geminiani's teacher, the late great Arcangelo Corelli. Then, after the performance, he would treat all to a special supper in the dining room before his guests retired to the little garden palace. The latter was in fact a spacious studio, of the kind the French termed a 'Solitary'. It was located in the garden among the rose trees. This had been only recently completed, and O'Brien was interested to see what visitors thought of its unique interior. In the little garden palace his esteemed guests could sit, enjoying imported wines or Irish whiskey, while taking in the serene harp playing of O'Carolan.

County Kildare, on the way to Dublin

A fine rain fell upon the vale, upon the sad fields, the rocky roads, the neglected hedgerows, and upon the two-storey stone farmhouse in which they had lodged. Keeping them tethered for now, Ciarán saddled up the master's horse and then his own. Next, he lifted and secured the precious harp, in its leather and wood carry-bag, onto the little mule along with their tin pot, their blankets, water jugs and some supplies. *How many times have I played out this ritual?* reflected Ciarán. The 'Little Lady', Aoife the mule, merely snorted quietly, unfussed by the familiar proceedings.

It had been a particularly hard year for their hosts the Cleary family, and for all Kildare, and in fact most of the country. The Clearys, like many others, hadn't fully recovered from the failure of the oats in the previous year; a failure that had devastated the principal crop on which they depended, both for their own sustenance and as feed for their animals. The cows, horses and sheep were stabled in the bottom storey of the farmhouse through the bleak winter. Ciarán, who had bedded down among them, saw at first glance that they were in very poor condition this year.

Their hosts had been sincerely apologetic, but they had little but gruel to offer Ciarán and his master, Turlough O'Carolan. A far cry it was from the abundance they had been able to put on the table during previous visits.

Ciarán had put it to Turlough that they could reach the outskirts of County Dublin if they left early. His master, however, was never an early riser and after nearly fifty years travelling the roads from one patron and one performance to the next, he found it progressively harder to stir his aching muscles and joints into motion.

Back on the stony and winding road from County Kildare to County Dublin, Turlough was sitting firmly in the saddle, complaining more and more about his aches and pains with every mile. Ciarán was at his wits' end. The rain had eased, the sun was out, the wind was at their back and they were on a downhill stretch heading to a place where they would get paid good money for not a world of effort. Money enough it was, to feed, generously, their wives, children and at least some of their growing horde of grandchildren back home. Ciarán could not stand another minute of O'Carolan's grumbling.

'For the bleeding heart of little baby Jesus will you never stop complaining, man? I have travelled every path at your side for fifty bloody years and I wager that my aches and pains can match yours any day. But is there any value in moaning about things? There are little flowers by the road, the first sign that winter will soon relinquish its grip to spring, and then there are those beams of light coming through the clouds and turning that field and the glade ahead into a wonder of greens and gold.'

Turlough's response was just as irascible. 'Do you not remember that I am blind, you insensitive bugger. I remember well the colours of the world from before the smallpox robbed me of my sight when I was eighteen, and I still grieve each day for it. There are no consolations of the eye for me, along this road, or any other. Do you know what it's like not to be able to see your own wife's face?'

Ciarán was prudent enough not to try and reply to his master. If the old bugger hadn't spent all night sitting under moon and stars with a head reeling from whiskey – as he did on way too many nights, in fact – then perhaps the gout of the joints would not have stricken him so badly. But best not say that either. Instead, Ciarán changed tactics.

'Thank Saint Brigid that your fingers remain as supple as they were when you first completed your harp studies under Blind Mary. If not, I hazard to think what kind of income either of us would be able to make.'

Without hesitation O'Carolan retorted, 'I do thank the blessed Saint every day, but more than that, I thank the ever-lamented Mrs MacDermott Roe, may she sit beside the angels in heaven. For it was she that understood that the smallpox ending my sight meant that blacksmithing was a closed door for me. It was she that paid in full for Blind Mary to teach me, one blinded soul to another, until I had perfected my craft. It was she who set up the trust that gave you a life's tenure as my companion. It was she, not the blessed Brigid, who found the money to get us our first horses, riding gear and our pack mule.'

Ciarán chuckled to himself. He'd heard about the sainted Mrs MacDermott Roe many times. As they rocked in the saddle with every pothole, the familiar retelling served to soak up the hours and to distract the blind harp master from his litany of discomforts.

O'Carolan had been the most beloved harpist and tune-smith in all Ireland since his twenty-first year, and was famed for his intricate melodies. Though Turlough was not able to write his compositions down, he had funded formal music lessons for his eldest son, who, becoming musically literate, had transcribed several hundred of Turlough's most admired compositions. Consequently, others had started playing his planxties and various other pieces, but it was said that none could evoke that other-worldly magic that inhabited the tunes when Turlough performed them.

Lord Inchiquin's Residence, Dublin

Turlough and Ciarán came, finally, to the turn that led to the mile-long coach road to O'Brien's mansion. It was dead straight, lined with Lombardy poplars for the first stretch and manicured hedgerows closer to the residence and the stables. Over a rise, and a few miles to the east, was the port city of Dublin, with all its comings and goings. By contrast, Lord Inchiquin's home away from home was a regal island, seemingly separate from the rest of the world.

His Lordship was there to meet them in the carriage circle. A groom was there beside him, standing ready to stable the horses and unload the mule.

'Turlough! Welcome, welcome my old friend. Come, Maestro O'Carolan, let my groom help you alight from your saddle.'

When the old harpist found his feet, O'Brien embraced him in an informal manner, as if greeting a comrade or peer. Turlough feigned discomfort with this action and spoke in mock-query, 'So, young Billy, what is it I am to call you now then: Master O'Brien, Governor of Kinsale, Governor O'Brien, or Lord Inchiquin, your excellency? The gravity of your titles must be beginning to weigh down that spirit of yours. Even trying to remember all of them sends my mind into a spin.'

Ciarán elbowed his master, concerned that O'Carolan's overt disrespect for a noble, who had long been a very generous patron, was getting out of hand.

Lord Inchiquin noticed and laughed, announcing, 'My dear Master O'Carolan, Will or William will suffice for you as always, but I insist that faithful Ciarán here simply calls me God.'

Though he knew it was meant as a joke, and he took it as such, Ciarán could not help but blush at the jovial blasphemy of it all.

After they had rested in their rooms for a while, O'Brien

took O'Carolan to show off the preparations for the next evening's concert and dinner. Extra seating had been moved into the great hall, and a space at the head of the room, beneath a rich tapestry depicting the muses, had been cleared for Maestro Geminiani's ensemble. Surrounding the seating provided for the quintet were high-stemmed candelabras, set up at the front, to illuminate the musicians, and at the rear, to allow them to read their scores. Next, Turlough was taken to the dining room, where long tables had been arrayed. In the kitchen cooks were cleaning, plucking, preparing, and stuffing a quantity of quails, pheasants, and turkeys, for the roasting scheduled for late the following afternoon.

'Now, Turlough, I cannot wait to show you the Garden Palace. When I commissioned the design, I was already imagining the sublime strains of your harp music filling the rounded space within!'

Turlough was led through the garden. There he was sure that he could smell each early blooming rose-flower as he passed. Hearing the sound of their footfall as they entered the garden parlour-room, the harpist immediately noticed the unusual acoustics of the space. He brushed against one of the curved walls and felt something unusual about the texture. 'A curved wall in a circular building, but what are these on the walls?' He ran his hands over the walls, left to right, then up and down. 'Shells!' he cried out in surprise. 'Here is a row of cockles, and there a row of scallops, but these conches I feel that some are turned back to the room while every second one is hollow-side out!' He put his ear to one and delighted at the sound of the sea within.

'I told you that you would love this place,' said his host. 'It is called a Shell House. A few of the great gardens of Ireland have them, though it is a recent notion. The patterns are ornate. The effect is like a Byzantine mosaic. Your harp will further adorn this place with its own magical patterns.'

'Ah, if only I still had eyes that worked,' said Turlough forlornly.

Later that day Francesco Geminiani and his four ensemble members arrived with their instruments and full baggage. Two of these were Geminiani's own countrymen, who had both been apprenticed to him at some time. Another was a Prussian who had followed Maestro Handel to London some years earlier, and the third, a violin-cello player, was an Irish-born Englishman, a third son of the Protestant nobility.

O'Carolan had been besotted with the music of Arcangelo Corelli from the first time that he heard it, a decade before. In Ireland, Corelli's compositions had become as popular as Meister Handel's were in England. Geminiani's reputation, as the foremost of Corelli's stellar pupils and a faithful champion of Corelli's compositions, was widely known to all lovers of good music.

O'Carolan was ecstatic to meet Francesco. Francesco, if anything, was even more excited to meet the legendary blind harpist about whom he had heard so much, and whose pieces had filled him with wonder.

'It is my absolute delight to finally meet you, Master O'Carolan. Do you know, I have several of your pieces? Your son's transcriptions I believe. Precious melodies, every one a gem. Back in Italy we know how to orchestrate, play with tunes, dance one against another; but I fear few of my lauded contemporaries would still know how to create a melody, pure and simple, that directly touches the heart. It seems that each wants only to take the melody on an ostentatious and extravagant journey to allow virtuosi to stun and amaze. And I am just as guilty as they, I am afraid.'

O'Carolan was a little embarrassed by Geminiani's compliments and his extravagant Italian manner. 'I am amazed and honoured that you have even heard of me, let alone that you are in possession of some of my humble tunes.'

'I found them delightful. They felt somehow familiar but at the same time strangely different, like a marriage of the new music coming out of Italy and the ancient music of old Ireland.'

'In Ireland we do not play with melody as you do on the continent. It is up to the accompanying parts to weave their threads around it.'

'Yes!' Geminiani nodded in agreement. 'In Irish music the melody, and not the bass or harmony, is sovereign. The melody can be dressed in ornaments, mordents, trills, glissandos and the like, but it must always be respected, its essence preserved. On the other hand, the bass, the harmony and even the key can be changed. The melody must remain, for it is the setting – all that surrounds it is improvised upon. It was not until my first trip to Dublin, with Lord Essex some years earlier, that I heard a fairly competent young Irish harpist and grasped what was going on.'

He turned to a somewhat confused-looking Ciarán and began to explain. 'On the continent we call the new music Baroque, from the Portuguese *barroco*, meaning the "oddly shaped pearl". At first it was used by our critics to laugh at our music. But now it seems a fair enough name. We Baroque musicians – Corelli, Handel, Vivaldi, Meister Bach, my humble self – insert various catchy passages of melody against a fixed bass that, for the most part, sets the harmony and informs the part-writing. But while the bass is fixed the melodies are deconstructed, fragments or whole passages overlapped, one against the other to create playful polyphonies, acceptable as long as the counterpoint pays homage to the bass and the deeper harmonic structure. Once he is presented with the bass part, any reasonable composer or player can improvise more than one overlapping melody, taking material from familiar tunes. I have even heard that Herr Bach senior can improvise up to six interlocking melodies at once over almost any bass progression!'

Turlough pursed his lips as he tried to imagine such a process. 'Now that would be a miracle to behold, I'd say!'

Francesco nodded, eager to continue, forgetting for a while that Turlough would not see such gestures.

'At first, Master O'Carolan, when I studied the simple monophonic perfection of your compositions, I assumed that the Baroque had passed Ireland by. Yet after hearing two of these tunes being recited by that young player on my first trip here, I understood.'

'Have you endeavoured to play them on your violin?'

'Oh yes, and my little guitar!'

Turlough looked puzzled as he had neither heard, nor heard of, such an instrument. Francesco saw the old man's confusion. 'The guitar is a kind of cousin to the lute. It is suitable for rendering delicate instrumentals, but is now coming into popularity as an instrument for accompanying the fiddle and the voice. My first teacher made me learn it so that I could better explore the harmonic possibilities of pieces. I am currently writing a guide to its use as a support instrument in the ensemble setting, largely because I noted that this had not yet been done.'

With some surprise, O'Carolan had noticed Geminiani's use of the colloquial term 'fiddle', and he asked the younger Italian why he had used that word, rather than calling it a violin.

Francesco dropped his voice as if he was whispering an intimacy.

'I confess that I mostly paid my own way during my early years apprenticed to Lonati in Milan. My stipend barely afforded me food and board, so I learnt to play all the tavern-dance tunes, and village-dance tunes that were the fashion in the taverns and rough-houses. I was given, along with my treasured Testore violin, a *secondi* fiddle, one seemingly made for purpose, loud, brash and bright, that could rise above the rowdiest crowd. During that time, I came to appreciate that the music of peasants and of menial workers can have its own simple beauty. Now, when I hear the kinetic playing of the street, a playing that draws you from your seat and coaxes you to dance like Dionysius, now when I hear that, I call it fiddling. For, is not fiddling the people's own word for it?

Turlough nodded towards the maestro. 'It's certainly what I would be calling it too.'

Geminiani winked then pursed his lips before his face took on a more serious set. 'What we will present tomorrow evening, as you might know, will most definitely not be fiddling. My string quintet have been well trained to create the ornate, the intricate, and the gently ecstatic. It is not our business to stir the body into frenzy, be it with an Italian tarantella or an Irish jig. That was another life. I treasure the memory, but now I am older and shackled by my own repute.'

'Then I pity you, Maestro,' said Turlough in sincere response. 'It was never so here in Erin. The story is that the harp was brought to Ireland by the Tuatha De Danann. They were a race worshipped as gods, before Christian prayers and curses forced them to devolve into the fairy folk.

Legend has it that the harp of the great god Dagda could fly through the air, slay his enemies, make the sick, crippled, or dying rise from their beds to dance wildly, and it could also calm the storm or quench the fire. I had to give up my first trade as a blacksmith after succumbing to a pox in my eighteenth year which left me blind. When I first began to learn the harper's craft under Blind Mary, she told me that I was already too old to ever become a master harpist. I was distraught. Thus it was, that one moon-kissed night, guided by my hound, I ventured, with my harp, out onto the fairy mound beyond the steading. There it was I prayed to, and called upon, every angel and saint that the priests had ever mentioned. I prayed that I would be able to conjure some real magic from the strings. I tried, but my poor playing simply increased my sorrows. Warming myself with some poteen whiskey I then, out of sheer desperation, called on the old gods, the fairy folk, the Shee, the spirits of the mound – and before long something happened. The cold earth warmed and shook, and the voices of the small folk sounded all around. They called my name, they sang to me, sweet lullabies that sent me almost to sleep, then they sang me to tears with the terrible melancholy of their lamentations. Then, to turn my humours around, they brought out their own harps, their pipes, and their fiddles and played, and played, until I jumped from my very own skin and felt my soul dancing across the very moon-lit sky. I awoke on the mound the next day, hung-over for sure, but with my mind brim-full of the fairy music, and a knowledge that, were I to play every day of my life, I would never run out of the tunes they had embedded in my mind. For my cup was now full.

'And so, as any decent Irish harper should, I learnt the

three forms of music. These be the *Goiltai*, or sorrow strain, that which can cause even the hard of heart to weep; the *Suantri*, or sleep strain, that calms the beast in us and lulls us to repose, and finally, the *Geantri*, or joy strain, that brings immediate happiness to those who hear it, and drives even the broken of body, to dance. It is the latter, were you to play it on a violin, that you might call fiddling. If any harpist, piper, or flautist was to master one or two of these forms but not the other then we would not call him a master, however dexterous be his hands and fingers.'

Francesco was not sure if he was being admonished, instructed or both. Either way he was transfixed by the older man's story. 'Oh, this is so interesting! Your musical cosmos is so unlike mine, dear Turlough!'

'Not so different in the heart of it, Maestro,' replied Turlough. 'For have you not played the frenzied fiddle tunes, and commanded the dance, as well as performing the stately pavanes, the melancholy requiems, and the serene meditations?'

These words spoke to something deep within Francesco. It was something, an explanation, and a licence, that he had waited a lifetime to hear. At this moment, the renowned master of the art-music of his age suddenly made peace with the mad young man within. The lad he had left behind, forever haunting the streets of Milan and the tavernas of his memory, drinking alongside the young Paolo Testore while driving the throng to dance with his '*bestia arrabbiata*'. He had, he realised now, kept the beast for a reason. It was a reminder of something he had almost forgotten. From that moment he considered Turlough to be a wise elder brother and fellow traveller.

⁓ᴐ⁓

O'Carolan was going to insist to Lord Inchiquin that Ciarán be allowed to sup with them all that evening. Consequently, he was both delighted and surprised to find his lifelong companion already at the table and exchanging tall tales with the players from Geminiani's ensemble. The blight that had taken the food from the tables of the farming folk did not seem to have weighed at all on O'Brien's kitchen. After supping on roast beef and all kinds of vegetables, a fruity pudding covered in a honey sauce was served, and drinks for all were poured.

It was then that O'Brien put up a wager to the two visiting maestri. 'I challenge my esteemed guests, Maestro Geminiani and Maestro O'Carolan, each exalted in his art, to improvise tonight a single movement of a concerto for their favoured instrument. Just one instrument, with no accompaniment. Improvised from any original themes you may have floating in your minds. Each has just one hour to prepare some ideas and to warm up his fingers. Further, I promise to double the payment for he who wins. I have one other criterion reserved, for final judgement, but that I shall keep that to myself for now.'

Geminiani was about to protest that he needed the remains of that evening, as well as the following morning, to rehearse the music for the program that the quintet would perform for the guests arriving for the events of the next night. Before he did, he glanced towards O'Carolan to register whether the old harper seemed reluctant or willing to participate in such a tasteless wager. A wager that seemingly sought to pit oranges against apples.

Turlough, like Francesco, had long understood that competition was the enemy of true musical expression. Instead, he considered that good music must always flow from a pure source, and that it is meant to soothe, heal, awaken but never to beat down and defeat a fellow bard. He was just about to refuse O'Brien's offer, but before he could utter a word, the point of Ciarán's elbow struck him in the ribs.

'Master,' Ciarán whispered in his master's ear, 'think first. Twice our fee! Can we afford not to play the Lord's silly game? You have nothing to lose. Remember how many mouths we both must feed back home. These are hard times.'

'What do you say, Maestro Geminiani?' asked O'Carolan, reluctant to be the first to make a decision.

Francesco finally shook off his reservations. 'All right! If it be done in a playful spirit, let us do it! And we should dedicate whatever we come up with to each other, and to our muses, whoever they be.'

After dinner the two men retreated to different rooms. Geminiani took his violin into the great hall, while O'Carolan went outside, to the Shell House in the garden, with Ciarán hauling his harp.

Francesco looked around the hall. He found it an effort not to be distracted by Lord Inchiquin's fine gallery of oil paintings. Art had ever intoxicated him. Returning to the matter at hand, he decided that he would dedicate his own improvisation to Turlough. He took those fragments of the harpist's melodies that he could remember and inserted modulations, octave jumps, spiccato bounces of the bow, and florid cadenzas. He then morphed these into a theme from Corelli, before returning to a final passage from an O'Carolan tune, the name of which he had forgotten. Each time was going to be different, but the basic form was set in his mind.

In the garden palace, Turlough tuned his harp, before taking his seat and closing his eyes. Unsure of what to play, he called upon the Shee of the fairy mounds but felt only their absence. They had always brought him the music when called, but this time he received no answer. No ageless tune of old Erin rang out in his mind. He was beginning to think that he would fail the little test that O'Brien had set him, when Ciarán broke the silence. 'Turlough! Come over here. You must listen to the echo of the ocean waves trapped in this particularly large conch shell.'

Turlough edged closer to the wall, finding, embedded in it, the large shell that Ciarán had mentioned. He placed his ear against it, and heard there the sound of waves and winds. Then he began to hear other sounds – sea birds, the fluttering sail of a ship, stevedores working in distant ports, and finally, the siren call of a great spirit, one that traversed the ocean currents, flowing from the Irish Sea to the Mediterranean and back. *Perhaps it is one of the old gods that I have just heard*, he thought. *Or is it the same muse that lays its touch upon Corelli's music and Geminiani's music too?* Whatever the answer, he knew that the shell's song had given him just the gift he now needed. He returned to the harp and out it came, fully formed, a single movement of a concerto, in the Italian style, but laced too with the touch of the Tuatha.

When Turlough joined the others in the great hall, Francesco was already warmed up and ready. Turlough had no words to describe the glory of Maestro Geminiani's improvised piece. His technical skills were awe-inspiring, but the subtle homage to Turlough's own tunes completely charmed the old harpist.

Turlough was moved to tears of joy, and when Francesco had finished, he was the first among the small group of listeners to rise to his feet and shout 'Bravo!' The others all followed, clapping loudly. Lord Inchiquin was most delighted. After Geminiani had put away his violin, Ciarán moved a chair into the performance space, before guiding O'Carolan to it.

For a while O'Carolan simply sat in meditation. Somehow, as if directed by his example, the listeners also fell to complete silence. So it was that O'Carolan's concerto began. It emerged fully formed, like Athena from the head of Zeus, sounding to the ear less like an improvisation and more like a fully settled and well-rehearsed composition. In it the melodic line was strong, but always followed the development in the bass line, in a way more like the Baroque composers of Italy and less like the harpists and pipers of Ireland. Still, beneath its ornaments and winding development, it maintained the directness of the pure and ancient airs on which Turlough had been raised.

Francesco Geminiani smiled with pure joy. 'Oh! The delight of it. Turlough has not played flashy cadenzas or gratuitous glissandos. He has got to the core of it all. There is something Baroque here and something belonging to the folk.'

O'Brien had, in all honesty, been more impressed by Geminiani's violinistic fireworks than by the perfect melodic formalism of Turlough's piece, but he turned to his valet, to Ciarán, and to the members of Geminiani's troupe and announced, 'We have all been truly blessed tonight, for we have been graced by two wonderful performances by two great masters. I would ask you all to raise a toast to these maestros.'

Then he spoke directly to the two musicians. 'I mentioned I had one further criterion. Before I can make my decision, there is one more test. I will now ask each of you to repeat his performance.'

Francesco was staggered by the sheer foolishness of this request. 'Your Lordship, with sincere respect, I am not sure that you understand. An improvisation is just that, an impromptu composition that lives in the moment of its performance, ephemeral and unrepeatable.'

O'Brien looked at Turlough. The old harpist picked up his instrument, and without either fuss or words, simply repeated his concerto, note for note, changing only one or two ornaments, and even improving on the dynamics and phrasing.

Geminiani was not sure what he had just witnessed. O'Carolan, he now grasped, was not just an intuitive composer, whose pieces emerged fully formed from his imagination, or from wherever it was that such fairy music came. The old blind harp player had, indeed, a perfect musical memory – a gift so rare that Francesco had never come across it before.

Lord O'Brien stood up before those gathered and pronounced his verdict. 'Having heard music from two of the greatest masters ever to grace these shores, the time has come for me to announce my verdict. Maestro Geminiani's performance was unlike any I have witnessed, both in its brilliance of conception and in its execution. However, Master Turlough contrived, spontaneously, a composition that he then showed that he could repeat perfectly. Consequently, he has given the world a new harp concerto, one that is likely to be played again and again. Each composer thus brings a different standard of excellence, and so in all fairness I must declare that both are winners. I shall hereby instruct my paymaster to ensure that each is paid twice the amount originally quoted. What are a few extra pounds after all, when we have gleaned such riches this evening?'

Both contestants were buoyed by this outcome. Turlough thanked his host. He then bid a good evening to Francesco, before retiring to the Shell House. Ciarán looked at the dram of his Lordship's best whiskey in Turlough's hand and scowled. *Yet another morning of headaches and complaints looms ahead. Mother Mary preserve me.*

Geminiani's focus shifted to the musicians comprising his ensemble. In that evening's rehearsal he ran them through piece after piece, passage after passage, polishing and refining until each part fitted perfectly into the whole.

The next evening, though, seemed like an anti-climax. The guests were thrilled by the Corelli pieces, and by Geminiani's own suites. The dinner was delicious, though a little extravagant. Even the French ambassador, who rarely complimented the efforts of Irish chefs, found enough there to delight him.

O'Carolan, who lived almost entirely in an aural world, was in seventh heaven, listening to the finely tuned ensemble. When the performance had finished, he congratulated Francesco, clasping his hands in his own. 'What beauty you lavish upon us, my friend. I noticed that you made some changes to one of Corelli's works though.'

Laughing, Francesco whispered to Turlough, 'Shhh, my friend! No one other than you would have noticed. In rehearsal my cello player was struggling with the high part in one passage, so I rewrote the part down an octave for him. Do you know that composition well, Turlough?'

'Well, I heard it one time, some years ago, in Dublin.'

Geminiani sighed. 'Ahh! To have a perfect musical memory such as yours! What a strange genie you are, Mr O'Carolan. It has been a revelation to have met you.'

After dinner, Lord William O'Brien got to show off his

newly finished Shell House, with its ornate interior. His guests were amazed by the intricate folly of the mosaics of shells that were at once elegant and whimsical.

When Turlough played, he first lulled them with a lullaby, then gradually lifted the mood with a dance tune that could only have come from a fairy otherworld. His art took the crowd through laughter to tears, then through quiet melancholy. To honour his benefactor, he played his planxty for Lord Inchiquin, then he reiterated last night's concerto before ending the evening's entertainment with a solemn meditation.

The next day, Turlough took possession of his pay, placing it in Ciarán's safe keeping. He turned to his host. 'Thank you once again, my dear friend Lord Bill. I must say that you have outdone yourself this time. I leave here today having enjoyed many rare experiences, and heard such marvellous music amid the best company. Best of all I have now found that I have a young brother in Francesco Geminiani. I know in my old bones that I have only a few years left in me. Soon enough the Tuatha de Danann will come to guide me beyond the mortal line, and I will go with no regrets, having had days like these and friends such as yourself.'

Before Ciarán helped O'Carolan onto his saddle, Geminiani came running across the cobbles towards the stables.

'Turlough, Turlough! I have something for you. Please accept my gift. This fiddle, made by Paolo Testore, is my growling beast. It was with this monster that I played for money in the tavernas and the rough-houses of Milan. I came to be ashamed of my time playing such frenzied music, but I could never bring myself to cast the fiddle away. It was always the mad and bad sibling to my beautiful violin. Though I will never play tavern music again, you have helped me understand that all forms of music live within the true musician. I have been honoured to meet you, and now wish you to have this, so that you will always remember me as a friend.'

'Francesc—' began O'Carolan, but Geminiani interrupted.

'Please call me Fra, as all my true friends do.' The two men hugged and Turlough graciously received the beast, making certain that Ciarán had strapped it safely to Aoife, the mule. 'I will never play the fiddle, my dear Fra, but I will treasure the sentiments that you have conveyed, just as I treasure these few days we have shared. Perhaps we will meet again, should the fates let me still be alive, next time you grace Erin's shores.'

～

Back in England, Geminiani put away the O'Carolan tunes, thinking that one day he might try and use Turlough's beautiful melodies for a suite. He fantasised a piece where sections would alternate. The first section would be in the continental style, where the playfulness lay in the top voices, and then there would follow a movement in the Irish style, where the melody was simply repeated while the music of the ensemble wove complementary lines and shifting harmonies around it. He carried this thought for many years, but decades busy with commissions would find it pushed further into the background and further from mind.

Belfast, 1734

A full year after those days and nights at Lord Inchiquin's manor, Ciarán and Turlough again took to the winding ways. This time they travelled the long road north to Belfast

Town, Turlough having been invited to play at the home of Norman Hume, a wealthy Protestant. Hume was a trader, who owned three merchant frigates, a warehouse, and an emporium down near the docklands. O'Carolan was finding now that his age and ailments were making such journeys harder than ever. He had even given up whiskey for a time, but found that without it the aching of his bones only worsened, and thus he resumed his old ways. *This time will surely be my farewell to the road, and perhaps even to music,* he thought. *For in these twilight years the fairy-folk call upon me less and less.*

To remind himself of their friendship, Turlough often took Fra's old fiddle along on his journeys. Sometimes, in this farmhouse, or that tavern, he would find someone who could play it, fiddling along with him, on one dance tune or another. Such moments of folly lightened his spirits and distracted him from his perennial discomforts.

Arriving a day early, they lodged for one evening in an inn, a small building of freestone and salt-encrusted mortar, proximate to Hume's establishment. They had bedded down in this place several times over the years. The premises were owned by one Michael McBride. McBride served several brands of whiskey, but was well known for the famous dark ale that he brewed there on site.

Being short of cash prior to playing for Hume, Turlough was lodging, drinking, and ordering hot meals on credit. McBride, who had known O'Carolan for over a decade now, had no problem with this arrangement, at least in the short term. So it was that O'Carolan sat with his lifelong companion, Ciarán, at a table near the bar, the harp on the floor besides, and the fiddle upon the table. McBride had been a little reluctant to give Turlough a whole bottle of Bushmill's Whiskey on credit this time around though. The old harper seemed to have an insatiable thirst for the expensive liquor, and McBride's own stock of it was not inexhaustible.

Between drams, a nervous palsy came upon the old man, and in a jerking of his arm he knocked the bottle, spilling the precious liquid all over the violin sitting on the table. Ciarán reacted swiftly to steady his old friend until the convulsions had passed. O'Carolan's wits returned enough for him to register that there was a bottle rolling on the floor and a table dripping with the sacred *uisce beatha*. 'Ah Gobshite!' he yelled, uncertain whether he was directing the insult against Ciarán for not saving the day or himself for his own lack of control.

Attempting to limit the damage, Ciarán righted the now empty bottle and then proceeded to wipe the table. He then wiped Fra's violin with its own sack-cloth bag. His vigorous rubbing dried the instrument, but unfortunately served also to remove the finish from a section of its belly, exposing the pale wood beneath. Understanding the blemish for which he was responsible, he decided not to remark upon it to Turlough, consoling himself with the thought that in such moments as these, the master's lack of sight was a kindness.

Turlough, unaware of the damage to the fiddle, merely called out to McBride to bring him a replacement bottle. McBride had reached his limit, however. 'This whiskey costs me a good fortune, yet you drink it like a fish and spill it like a rain storm. Have you not some payment you can give me in return?'

By way of reply, Turlough picked up the beast from the table, waving the violin at the publican. 'Though it pains my heart to part with this, as it was a token of friendship from a great man, I will offer it to you now, provided you offer me another bottle of the god's sweet nectar.'

Ciarán knew that this decision, made in a haze of drunkenness, would be something Turlough would soon regret, but for his own reasons he chose to say nothing. His master was, for now, delighted to again have his dram-glass full.

Meanwhile Michael McBride understood that he had got the better deal, for such Italian instruments were as rare as hen's teeth in Belfast. Happily, he took the violin. He grabbed a bow from behind the bar and played a scale slightly out of tune, before launching into a truncated version of 'Black Headed Deary' that was so bad that O'Carolan cringed upon hearing it.

Having finished murdering the music, Michael hung the Testore violin on the wall, up behind the bar, beside another fiddle locally crafted and of no significant provenance. 'My son is still a child, but he can already play a tune or two. One day, maybe, we will use this and the other to perform duets for our patrons.'

Turlough was too distracted by drink at this stage to express an honest opinion. Ciarán looked at the state Turlough was in and was already worrying that tomorrow's harp recital was approaching all too fast.

The legendary Turlough O'Carolan would pass away before that year was done. His faithful companion Ciarán would only last another rotation of the earth before he too died.

Over twenty years later, an older Francesco Geminiani had left London and retired to a humble two-storey home in Dublin. This was a time when the Georgian splendour and new wealth of that city had begun to show itself in fine stone buildings, proud church spires and a host of new bridges over the Liffey. Geminiani's living quarters, along with his teaching and rehearsal studios, occupied the ground floor of his house. Meanwhile, he had made the top floor a gallery for the many paintings on which he had squandered most of his fortune. He had been working, for no one knows how long, on a final composition, dear to his heart. Some speculated that he had managed to achieve his ambition of setting some of O'Carolan's melodies into full orchestrations in the Italian style. The world would never know the truth though. Only a short time after he had completed the manuscript, his home and gallery were broken into, and the manuscript, of no value to anyone else, was stolen. Geminiani, devastated, passed away soon after on 17 September 1762.

Further north, at McBride's Inn, by the docks in Belfast, Geminiani's old *'bestia arrabbiata'* hung by a woven string from a hook on the wall, up behind the bar. Like its companion, it was brought down when Michael, then later his son Ryan, felt the urge to play it, or when a visiting fiddler, usually a Scot from one of the ships in port, stayed at the pub. Another generation later, and by the turn of a new century, it was Ryan's son and Michael's grandson, Arthur McBride, who had it in his hands more often than not. Arthur developed into a fine fiddler, at a time when the fiddle was becoming as popular in Ireland as the harp, the pipes, and the flute had long been. Hardly a night would pass when the two fiddles were not brought down from their hooks, while Arthur, his friends, and his cousins drove the guests and local drinkers to a state of frenzied joy with their reels, jigs, hornpipes and a 'highland' barn dance tune or two from Donegal.

Chapter 9

Dover, Tasmania, 2023

Haley had been left both enthused and astonished when Aaron had promised to restore the battered Testore, charging neither her nor its future owner for the labour, skill and care that would be invested in the project over the months ahead. Such generosity was, in her experience, a rare and precious thing.

On the other hand, prudence demanded that she could not, at this stage, inform Di Doolan as to what was happening and so raise her expectations. Haley was not convinced that the violin was completely restorable. Further, she thought, even if Larsen's repairs rendered it a beautiful-looking antique instrument, might it not still sound like a howling beast rather than a fine violin? Her final concern, and by far the greatest, was that Jesse would still refuse to play or even to resume lessons, and would thus render the project fruitless from the point of view of the girl's mother.

Today Haley arrived early on one of her visits to Dover District High. She assembled the marimbas, sanitised the recorder mouthpieces and tuned the school violins. Then, while she still had time, before the first class of music students would come through the door, she decided to take advantage of the acoustics in the large room and play some violin. She warmed up with 'Niel Gow's Lament for the Death of His Second Wife', a Scottish tune of almost infinite sadness. When her fingers were warm, and her musician's soul was soaring, she played the Meditation from *Thais*, by Jules Massenet. Near the edge of the door, she noticed movement. A group of three girls had come inside early from the morning recess. They were hovering in the corridor just outside the room. When Haley looked up, they did their best to act as if they had not been listening. Haley kept playing as two of the three dispersed, back to their home classes. One stayed, listening intently. Haley noticed that it was Jesse, and stopped playing for a moment.

'Come in, Jess, feel free to listen anytime.'

Jesse came near. 'Your violin has such a beautiful voice, Miss McGribben.' Clearly, she had more to say, but she reddened and went silent.

'Would you like to play it a while, Jess?' Haley offered. But it was too late. Jesse had donned the mask of teenage anger. She looked at the music teacher as if wrestling with an inner torment that was now threatening to surface.

'No. I don't play violin.'

She turned, departing the room abruptly, leaving Haley perplexed as to what had just transpired and how to proceed from here. On the other hand, she knew now that the sound of the instrument still retained that old allure for Jesse. It was there, somewhere deep, despite the wall of angst in which it was now enclosed. Perhaps, she considered, it was all a matter of timing?

In the afternoon, there was a slightly disturbing dynamic in her last class for the day. The year nine students could always be a handful. Today, though, a new girl joined the class – Wattle Darcy. Wattle bore an upright posture, straightforward gaze, and a confident manner, unusual among those new to a school and new to its particular regional culture. Her dark-brown hair, hanging in a medusa-like array of braids, gave her a slightly hippy look. Haley did her best to make her feel comfortable. The established clique of girls, however, made no effort to be friendly. One feigned a sneeze when Haley introduced the newbie to the group, while a friend beside her sniggered, making a little witticism. 'Wattle! Hay fever season already?' On the contrary, some of the boys seemed to be going out of their way to get Wattle's attention. Haley wondered if she could leverage this to get them to focus upon their marimba skills in order to better show off. This hope was forlorn. On the other hand, Wattle seemed impervious to both the bitching and the unsubtle flirting. She chose to play violin and showed that she could already play a little. She read through the score and had no qualms about asking for help when a section came around that she could not decipher. After the lesson Haley asked Wattle if she had taken any violin lessons.

'Just a few lessons, Ms McGribben. Bit less than a year with Karen from over at Cygnet.'

'Is Karen still teaching violin in the valley?'

'No, she quit with the teaching to build up her beekeeping and honey business. That's why I stopped learning the violin.'

'If you would like one-on-one lessons, I can do that. I

teach a few days and nights a week from my home studio back in the Glen.'

'I would love that, Ms McGribben! I would need my folks to do the drive there and back. Maybe they could drop me off while they do their big weekly shop in Huonville. But I'll have to ask them.'

After school, Haley stopped in at the Dover dock. Above, gulls spiralled in the cool southerly breeze. She was in luck. A fishing boat had come in, just that morning, and a portion of the catch had been bagged and placed, for local customers, in the little depot at the wharf.

There was whiting, cod and flathead, along with some impressive hunks of tuna, fresh in texture and brightly coloured. Seeing this, Haley recalled a holiday in Port Lincoln, during her childhood in South Australia. Her father had purchased tuna straight from the docks there. The red flesh had been cut into steak-sized pieces which her father later prepared and seared.

Some of the meals of childhood remain in the memory, catalogued by fond associations, and when brought to mind they fuel both nostalgia and visceral cravings. Served in white bread rolls, with pesto sauce, tomato, and lettuce, that tuna feast was one of those meals. This day, however, Haley was disappointed to be told by the attendant that between them, two of the valley's sushi chefs had reserved all of the tuna catch. She settled instead for a few pieces of flathead. This was not a fish that she had eaten as a child, but one her friend Charlie had introduced her to.

As she returned to her car with her purchase, another car pulled up. Diane Doolan, it seemed, was also planning to prepare fish for dinner that night. Haley felt a tinge of guilt when they met. Di greeted her warmly enough, before dropping the question as to whether or not she had had any luck sourcing a good but affordable violin. Haley hesitated before answering. She suspected that Diane had noticed that she seemed uncomfortable with the question.

Haley fudged the issue. 'I think I have a few possibilities, but none that I can say are sure bets yet. How long do we have before Jesse's birthday again?'

'Two-and-a-bit months, dear. D'ya reckon we can lock one in before then?'

'I'm sure one will come up before then.' Haley continued, perhaps a bit tactlessly, 'Maybe, if she really doesn't want it, when it comes, you could sell it on, and let her have the money instead.'

'Thought about that already. Still hoping it doesn't come to that, and that things will turn around for her,' said Diane.

Haley nodded and smiled. She had decided not to mention her interaction with Jesse earlier that day. It seemed premature to come to any sort of conclusion about what that might foreshadow, either way.

Driving home, she noticed out of the corner of her eye, a golden peregrine. The bird circled around an acacia grove, as if looking for the right wattle branch on which to alight.

Home at the Glen, Haley cooked up and ate the fish along with some refried potatoes and an avocado. She then relaxed on the couch with a glass of dry white wine, before picking up the poetry book. This time deliberately skipping over 'The Blue Violin'.

Larsen's Workshop, Hobart

Aaron had his friend and fellow luthier Harry over. He wanted a second pair of eyes to look over the old Milanese violin. Harry had never come across a Testore before and had been prepared to be impressed. Instead, after inspecting the beast he simply commented, 'What a mess! Good luck there, mate.'

Over the previous days Aaron had used gel, coarse paper and a scraping tool for the painstaking work of removing the glossy varnish that some silly bugger had covered the belly and back in. There was a remnant polish beneath that, scrubbed off in part but enough to allow the matching of a new French-polished finish, when he came around to it.

'I am glad it's you not me,' said Harry. 'You've done a good job removing that rubbish though mate. But you do know that those cracks and splits were only held together by the varnish. I suggest taking all the component plates apart, regluing them then reassembling them later.'

'Fully aware of all that, Haz! First stages now though.'

Harry turned the violin over. 'The neck has even more of the film to be scraped off. Looks like it might be a marine varnish not just a furniture gloss. Home brew repairs are the worst.'

Harry then brought Aaron's attention to a circle of lighter colouring on the rear of the neck.

Aaron had another look at the blemish his friend was pointing out. 'Yes. Hmmmm? I had seen that but thought it might be just a flaw in the grain. Notice that the neck is slightly thicker than a standard neck, and this timber, seems like it's some sort of fruit-tree wood. Pear was used in Milan in the eighteenth century, but not for the neck. This looks more like it was cut from a branch of apple wood while it was still green. Either it was an experiment or more likely it was the last of a batch and the maple or rosewood had run out. We can only guess. Yes! I see now that that little circle is not part of the grain or some natural discolouration.'

Using his scraper, Aaron removed the varnish from that area, flake by flake.

'See!' said Harry as the light circle now became plainly evident. 'Do you mind?' he asked, before taking a needle-fine chisel from Aaron's bench and scraping out the circle.

'So, this looks like a plug made from sawdust and glue, stained to make it less obvious then polished over.'

Fascinated, Aaron took over from Harry again. Further cleaning back the area revealed a neat hole going right into the neck.

'Holy shit, this is something I have never seen before!' Embedded in the neck, just beneath the worn ebony fingerboard, was a piece of lead shot of the kind once used in small muzzle-loaded hand guns.

'There are the ghosts of a hundred stories in this instrument, mate,' said Harry, who was coming to think that the restoration might just be worth Aaron's while, even if the violin ended up in a museum cabinet, rather than in a performer's hands.

Chapter 10

Belfast, Late December 1810

Alexander Laing, better known at the time as Sandy Laing, had been called back from County Cavan. It was clear to his superiors that Laing's effort to recruit the reluctant locals to fight with the British army, in yet another iteration of the war with France, had been less than noteworthy. Little did they know that the young Sandy had spent most of his time in Cavan frequenting public houses and sharing tunes with rural fiddlers. Sandy carried his father's precious fiddle with him wherever the British army sent him, entertaining comrades in the 92nd Gordon Highlanders or picking up Irish tunes to add to the encyclopaedic repertoire of tunes by Marshall, Gow, and others that his father had taught him.

When he was recalled to Belfast, his senior officer foreshadowed that it was likely that Laing's regiment would be called to fight in France before the next year was out. Laing would need to be ready for that, particularly as his work as a recruiting officer in Ireland remained so lacking in results.

Returning to the barracks, Laing lay upon his bunk. Disgruntled, he was beginning to come to grips with how things were likely to pan out. He determined that his father's violin, crafted over sixty years ago in Cremona, was far too valuable to risk dragging through the mud and blood of one European battlefield or another. He would arrange with the army postal service for it to be shipped back home to Tannadice in Scotland, there it would remain in safe keeping until such time he might send for it.

After the next morning's drill, he was again called before his commanding officer. *I'm not getting shipped off to France already am I?* he speculated. He need not have feared though. He was to be given a more routine task.

'Two of our recruiting officers, Sergeant Napper and Corporal Lamp, claim to have been assaulted while going about their duties on Christmas morning. There were no other witnesses, however they identified one of the assailants as the son of a publican. His name is Arthur McBride, and it will be your task to serve a warrant upon him. When McBride is questioned, those officers will need to confirm his identity, before we can take him to trial for any offences against the Crown.'

Sandy knew Napper and Lamp too well. He despised both, considering them to be the kind of men that join the army because they have neither skills nor talents, and so hope to compensate by lording it over regular soldiers and bullying recruits. He judged that his own self-interest in joining the army, in order to secure steady pay for a while, was far less perverse. He had drunk in McBride's and seen the young Arthur behind the bar cutting a handsome and gregarious figure. If this Arthur had got the better of Napper and Lamp, then all power to him! He liked the man already!

When Laing arrived at the dockside pub, he found Arthur cleaning tables in the empty bar room. He introduced himself but need not have.

'I know you, Mr Sandy. I was staying for a while with a cousin in County Cavan, and had the blessing of hearing you fiddle some fine Scottish tunes in the local hotel. That was a grand night, and one made even better by your playing.'

Laing was charmed by Arthur's earnest flattery and felt a natural reluctance to inform the man as to the purpose of the visit. So it was with some unease that he told McBride that he was there to serve him a warrant. 'I don't want to do this. That you gave those arseholes a good hiding is only to your credit in my opinion. A recruiting officer must be able to take no for an answer. Perhaps we can contrive a way out of this?'

Arthur was already at the bar pouring out a pint for his guest and another for himself.

'I'm at your mercy, dear Sandy. What have you in mind?'

Laing grinned, noting that the dark ale had a fine head. 'Well! I have word that the regiment that Napper and Lamp belong to is being shipped off to the battle fields in the Rhinelands in four weeks or so. Once they are gone there will be no witnesses to your assault on the British Army's finest, and then you can't be charged.'

With one elbow on the wooden bench, Arthur nodded before taking a slow sip of his ale.

Laing continued. 'Would it be possible for you to vanish until then? I can return to my commander saying that a man in your employ said that you are abroad in Scotland, trading one whisky for another, and have been for some time. What say you?'

'That is a fine idea, my new friend! I shall head off in

precisely the opposite direction. Perhaps I'll go to pay a visit to some distant relatives on Inis Mór, a sweet little island in the far west coast of Erin. There, even the tendrils of the British Empire have not yet spread. If you are right, a month away from Belfast should do it, and it is a lovely enough place to spend a while avoiding a whipping or the firing squad.' Arthur topped up Alexander's glass. 'But given that you have put yourself out, and perhaps in danger, by helping me avoid custody, is there some way I can pay you back?'

Laing gestured towards the two fiddles hanging up behind the bar. 'Well, you could join me in a wee duet or two, assuming you can play those things.'

Arthur quickly had them off the wall, and the two men coordinated the tuning of the instruments. McBride had only a few Scottish tunes under his hands, and he offered up one first, launching into 'The Mason's Apron.' Laing, who was well schooled, straight away played the harmony part until both violins were roaring away together. Laing was finding that the violin that he was playing had to be bowed with a lighter touch and a looser wrist, otherwise it would drown the other out. They then played 'St Patrick's Day in the Morning', 'The Irish Washerwoman' and 'The Soldier's Joy' before ending with two slow tunes, 'Mcleod's Lamentation' and 'O'Carolan's Farewell to Music'.

When they had finished playing, the Scottish soldier and the Irish publican laughed in unison, embracing each other as if brothers. Sandy handed back the violin to McBride, commenting as he did. 'Oh, she is a loud-mouthed beast! Good for the dance, I wager!'

'You must have it!' said Arthur. 'I insist. If we never meet again, I wager we will still remember today, you all the more so, with my grandfather's fiddle in your hand. You know it is rumoured in our family that it once belonged to the very person who composed that last piece that we played together?'

'What? The blessed O'Carolan himself?'

'So it has been said. Oh! But maybe that is just family stories getting out of hand, you know how it is?'

Sandy was delighted. The Lord above must be well disposed to him that day, given that he had just sent his own good fiddle back to the family home in Scotland for safekeeping. He now had a beast that he could take on his travels without too much concern as to its well-being or condition.

Laing's commanding officer seemed to take him at his word this time, but for one reason or another he was promptly given a new commission. Rather than being sent directly to the bloodied fields of Flanders or some other cursed battlefield, Alexander was sent back to Scotland, to resume recruiting, working this time in Banff and Paisley.

While recruiting in Perthshire, Alexander succumbed to easy temptation, and was caught dipping into the box of silver crowns from which he was to present new recruits with a coin each for signing up. Having been found guilty by the Perth Court of Justiciary, Laing was transported first to Sydney Town in 1814, and then on to Van Diemen's Land in 1815.

Laing in Van Diemen's Land

Embarking on the *Marquis of Wellington*, with other convict transportees, Laing had been allowed to take some limited personal items with him. One of these was Arthur's fiddle, as he had come to call it. By 1817 Alexander, now 27, found himself assigned as a labourer, stablehand, and clerk to a settler, a former ensign, T.A. Lascelles, on his farm overlooking the expansive blue of Pittwater, south-east of Hobart Town.

Sandy had managed to make a serviceable protective bag for the fiddle out of a green army-issue blanket. He would leave the instrument, so enclosed, in Lascelles's kitchen, where it would stay until such time as his master might call on Laing to entertain him, his daughters, or his guests.

Michael Howe's Camp, Coal River Valley, Early April 1817

A few men on horseback patrolled the periphery of the temporary camp in bush-covered hills behind the Coal River Valley. The colony of Van Diemen's Land was growing fast, and more and more land was being cleared for farms, towns and roads, but there were still plenty of places among the crags, hollows and forests of blackwood, she-oaks and eucalyptus where a canny gang of outlaws could hide.

Leaving his Palawa wife back in the north of the island, Michael Howe had reassembled his gang after a disastrous battle with the government militia in February, and set up further south. While others kept lookout, he engaged his second in command James Geary in a very private conversation.

'Jimmy, me ol' mate. I have seen my future, clear as day, and the way things are going my end will come soon enough.'

'Yes, Micky, we lost good men back in February and it is reasonable to assume that we will lose more, so what of it?'

'For fuck's sake James, all we have done for months is lose. I remember when that mad cunt Whitehead got shot, raiding that house, he made me promise to cut off his head and bury it so the bastards couldn't get the reward for killing him. Now I have an even greater price on my head, enough so that even old comrades are measuring whether it's worth killing me in my sleep, just for the bounty!'

'I know, Michael. There was a time when we all thought that we might win this war.'

Michael abruptly kicked a log at the edge of the fire before spitting onto the coals. Right from the start the lines had been clear. There were the settlers and freed convicts who had come over with Collins, who opened up the countryside, built the houses and farms only to have them taken from them and given to friends of the administration. And, for whatever petty crimes that were done back in Britain, it was transportation, the 10,000 miles to the end of the world that was to be their punishment.

He looked James in the eye. 'We weren't sent out to be slaves to rich pricks that just want to set up plantations, fill their pockets, and strip the place before returning to England, wealthy on the blood and toil of others.'

Geary swatted a sandfly from his face and, cursing under his breath, spat onto the forest floor. He had no argument with Howe. They shared a common view of their purported overlords. 'Hypocrites to the damned last! They're always quite happy to send some silver our way if we inflict damages upon their rivals. The rot goes right to the top. Even the esteemed Mr Lord has bushrangers on his payroll. Corrupt to the bleedin' last!'

'We've had our small victories, plundered the bastards' houses, and scared the shite out of them, but in the end, we can't win this war. You and I need a way out, before we meet worse fates than poor old Whitehead. I want to get a letter to the enemy. We have to try and negotiate the terms of a surrender.'

'And what makes you think this new governor, Sorell, will accept these terms, Michael?'

'Have to move quickly before the taint gets to him too. For a start I'm more than happy to offer him up the names of those scoundrels playing both sides. Let's tell him who the real vipers be!'

James pondered over this for a while. 'As long as you do what you can to let me and my more trustworthy lieutenants run free, I am willing to help. I've a friend, a former comrade from the 73rd Regiment, who has the governor's ear. We'll have to make it seem that he was an unwilling party though, keep him nice and clean, otherwise he will never agree to it.'

Howe began to feel a glimmer of hope and for the first time in months he smiled at his friend. 'Let's set this up so that it looks like a raid. Instead, though, we will make it my farewell Hoorah for the boys.'

The Lascelle Farm, Iron Creek, Pittwater

The farm sat on a broad plain of long golden grass, the area having been cleared of trees by convict labour almost a decade earlier. Alexander Laing was in an outer barn, tending to the horses while the farrier from the nearby town changed their shoes and hammered adjustments into the curved blue iron. Laing kept the charcoal fires hot so that the new shoes could be heated, before being bent into the correct size for the horses' hoofs. Even given the crash of hammer on anvil it was a credit to the stealth of Howe's entourage that Laing had not heard them ride up to the property. He did note, however, that there was some laughter, and the sounds of carriages stopping, and he remembered that Lascelles and family had been planning to entertain guests from nearby farms and steads that day.

When Alexander had finished stable duties, he returned inside to find his master in the parlour, standing amidst a large group of guests, joking and making introductions. It took him only a short while to guess that the men present, rough and somewhat unwashed-looking, were bushrangers. He also surmised that their presence was deliberately contrived to give the impression that a raid had happened just as guests were arriving. There were, however, no signs that the outlaws had forced their way onto the property, nor that they posed any threat. He noticed that the man who had been addressed as Commander Howe seemed to be well in control of the less savoury-looking characters in the gang. Howe's men were taking tea, and coffee, while refraining from the wine, brandy and rum served to the other guests present. Howe himself had gone to the kitchen to fetch the tea and coffee. When he returned he asked Lascelles, 'Who in your household plays the fiddle, Ensign? I noticed one in a green bag in the kitchen.'

In reply Lascelles simply pointed to Alexander. 'It's young Sandy here! A very masterful fiddler he is at that.'

Howe turned to his offsider. 'What do you say, Geary, shall we have a tune for the better entertainment of all the good visitors and the servants?'

Geary replied, smiling wryly. 'Yes, Mickey, by all means let us have a little frolic once in a way, it's not every day we meet a fiddler in our line of work.'

Turning to Laing, Geary asked for his name. Then, introducing himself as a fellow musician of sorts, he informed

Alexander that he had been a military drummer, before he deserted the 73rd Highlanders to roam the bush.

Howe retrieved Laing's fiddle from the kitchen and set up a stool on which he could play, away from any dancing, or nonsense that might follow.

Meanwhile Laing had deduced that Geary and Lascelles had been comrades in the 73rd, and that they had remained in touch, even after Geary had taken up a life ranging the bush, outside of the law and civil society. Geary and Howe, Laing had heard, believed themselves to be fighting in a war of liberation, even though they were perceived by the establishment to be common criminals. It also appeared to Laing that his master, Lascelles, was sympathetic to their cause, even though he was a direct beneficiary of the status quo.

Howe offered Alexander a glass of wine, but Alexander had decided that, given the situation, he might be better off staying sober. Howe suggested that Alexander's refusal to drink was because, him being a Scotsman, perhaps only a single-malt whisky would suffice. Laing feigned a laugh and nodded, deeming that it served him best to humour Howe who, as suspected, let the matter go.

Laing performed bawdy songs, humorous ditties that some of the assigned servants and the bushrangers sang along to. Next he played 'Neptune on the Seas', 'The Bird on the Branch', and then a set of rollicking hornpipes. The indentured servants and the guests from neighbouring farms danced along, clapped, or simply ignored the music while immersing themselves in frenetic small talk. Most were showing signs of being quite tipsy by the time the table was set for dinner.

While the assorted assembly seated themselves at the table to eat, Laing fiddled out some slow airs, delicate minuets, and other genteel tunes, hoping to restrain the mood and to keep the atmosphere as calm as possible. He noticed then that his master and Howe had stepped into the study for a bit. After a while he heard an outer door close and the sound of boots upon the cobbles and so assumed that they had taken to the garden for a walk. Neither man would return for two hours.

When they finally did return, Howe addressed the assembled crowd. The guests, farmers, tradesmen, free settlers, convicts and bushrangers alike listened intently as Howe gave an earnest and detailed account of the various injustices and mistreatments he and his men had suffered. He railed against tyranny and cruelty then praised Lascelles, and those masters like him, who treated their assigned convict workers with kindness and respect, rather than with the casual brutality so many others dished out.

When the hour of seven o'clock drew near, Michael Howe called to Alexander to play up 'Jack Tar' for a last dance before his men took their leave. One of Howe's men, however, had danced himself into a frenzy and was reluctant to go. When Geary grabbed him, he drew out a pistol as if to threaten the second-in-command. Howe responded like lightning, taking the tiny pistol while slapping the man briskly. Unfortunately, the altercation caused the pistol to fire. Laing's left arm jolted as the violin flew to the ground. His heart skipped a beat, but he quickly contained his shock, taking a slow controlled breath while wiping the new beads of sweat from his brow.

The shot, it seemed, had recoiled from the stone hearth where it had struck, before knocking Laing's fiddle onto the floor on the rebound. Geary quickly dragged the offender outside to be disciplined for tainting what had, for the most part, been a sober and civil day of entertainments. Meanwhile, Howe picked up Laing's fiddle from the floor, apologising for what had happened. 'Is it all intact, my good man?' he asked.

Laing was grateful to find that it seemed unbroken, though now completely out of tune. He re-tuned, and, at Howe's request, resumed playing. It was then he felt it. Two-thirds of the way down the neck, a tiny ball of lead had embedded itself into the wood and left an annoying indentation to catch on the flesh between thumb and fore-finger and so trip up the fingers.

Lascelles noticed him examining the now pitted neck and reassured Laing. 'I have an acquaintance who is a fine cabinet maker. I will have him fill that indentation and smooth the neck out for you this coming week. Sorry that such a fine day's sport ended this way. On behalf of all gathered here I thank you, earnestly, Sandy, for entertaining us all during this raid. You certainly lifted our spirits.'

'Thank you, sir,' replied Laing, feigning both gratitude and innocence, as he knew full well that this had not been a raid.

Having served his period of assignment, Laing was granted his full emancipation. His military background was taken into account when the officials decided how he might be of most use to the colony. Soon he was offered the position of constable. In this role he would spend his career stationed for a few years, here and there, in one town after another. Laing was determined to redeem his reputation and remove the 'convict stain' from his name.

Alexander made good use of his skill as a violinist, playing for the gentry in each settlement. He gained great favour by composing tunes in dedication to the prominent folk of the colony. Tunes would be crafted in honour of this magistrate or another, or for the various lieutenant governors that came and went, or for some officer's wife, or some doctor's daughter. If he had no inspiration to compose a new tune for a commission, he would simply rename a less-known folk melody, or a tune by one of the great Scottish fiddlers, all the time hoping that no one would notice his lapses into plagiarism.

When he had saved sufficient funds he paid for his good Cremona-made violin to be shipped out from Scotland. He came to use the beastly McBride fiddle only when an investigation required that he travel long distances on horseback.

It was on one such visit, this time to the penal colony of Port Arthur on the Tasman Peninsula, that he came to stay with William Champ, commandant of that prison station.

Port Arthur Penal Colony, 1847

Laing was genuinely fond of Champ, who otherwise seemed to be despised by most of the colony's powerbrokers. He was more impressed with Champ's wife, however. She was a generous soul, dedicated to gardening and entertaining guests and was always happy to accommodate Laing during his occasional visits. Laing even composed two tunes in her honour. The Champs were unduly flattered by Laing's offerings, and begged him to return. The couple shared a great love of Scottish fiddle music. Consequently, William begged Laing to present yet another performance. 'Please come again, dear Sandy. You know I am starved for music on this dread peninsula. Among these lost souls, each languishing in their lonely cells, good music is needed more than ever.'

Laing thought to himself that he would be happy enough to revisit, as long as Commandant Champ didn't insist on playing his little Spanish guitar and singing so badly.

To demonstrate to the Champs that he intended to return sometime, he handed William his fiddle. 'I will return when I get a break from my duties, sir. Meanwhile, may I leave this with you? My other violin, a prized family heirloom, has finally arrived from Scotland, and is waiting for me at home. If you keep this here, it will be available for me to play whenever I am called back down here. Meanwhile, if another fiddler finds their way to Port Arthur, please offer it to them so they may perform for you.'

And so it was that in the Champs' house, set amid Mrs Champ's splendid rose garden, there at Port Arthur – that much-cursed penal station for serial re-offenders, lost street-children, and the criminally insane – the *secondi* Testore found lodging.

Laing never did return to the Champs' house. The following year, however, the culture-deprived Champs began to organise structured entertainment for themselves, their guests and a few prisoners who had earned special privileges.

William Champ had heard word of a fine fiddler and instrument-maker who was doing time at the Saltwater River Probation Station. Consequently, he put in a request that the said internee be allowed to be relocated to Port

Arthur. Once there, he would be commissioned to organise a string ensemble for the moral and cultural betterment of those convicts who were so disposed. Neil Gow Foggo was a descendant of the acclaimed Scottish fiddle composer, Niel Gow, after whom he was named.

Chapter 11

Dover, Tasmania, 2023

Autumn was drawing near, bringing cooler evenings. Normally this would mean that Jesse slept more deeply, and more peacefully, than on the warm restless nights of summer. This Sunday, however, Jesse roused abruptly from a disturbing dream and found herself wide awake at the hour when the chorus of the birds sings in the dawn, loudly over the gardens, the hills, and the bay. Knowing that her mother would not arise for an hour or more, she took a moment to reflect upon the night's dreaming.

In her dream she had been out in the dinghy with her dad. He had taken her fishing in the bay, as he so often had throughout her childhood years. They placed the baits upon the hooks before dropping their lines into the crystal-clear brine. Her father pulled up a flathead, then a mackerel, then an Atlantic salmon which must have escaped from the farm pens beyond the bay. She had been getting no bites at all, until she noticed a strong tug on her line, one that got even stronger as she tried to pull her catch in. She saw a flash of blue as the creature tried to escape.

She asked her father's assistance in pulling it onboard. Together they reeled it in, only to find that it was not a fish but a blue violin, one having grown to the size of a small cello. She was in shock, not knowing whether to be proud of her catch or disgusted. She turned to her dad for guidance but saw that he was gone. Her mother, Diane, had somehow taken his place in the boat. Jesse could not move, feeling as if she was gripped by a paralysis. Diane unhooked the wild catch from Jesse's line and in her grip it shrank, transforming into a sleek, silver-blue whiting. Jesse watched her mother release the tiny fish back into the water. In the dream Diane spoke, then, in an attempt to console her. 'Sometimes, Jess, you just have to let one go.'

When she had shaken the sleep from her mind, Jesse dressed and went straight to the water's edge, as if to see if any traces of her dream remained upon the sheen of the sea.

As the morning sun rose from behind the hill, the scene over Dover Bay gained light, colour, and a clarity of outline. Looking towards the point, Jesse could make out a lone figure gathering mussels and oysters from the rocks. She squinted, trying to better focus. *That looks like Tyson*, she thought.

As younger children she and Ty had been best friends. They had played upon the beach together, collecting drift-wood, shells, dried out seahorses and a thousand other treasures. In the forested hills beyond their houses, they had built forts and teepees where they played out the unashamed imaginings of childhood. Jesse could not recall exactly when that had all ended. She had begun, at some point, to feel her body change. The simple pleasures of childhood faded, as she found herself, more and more, in the company of other girls. There she discovered a new type of friendship, but also a competition among her peers, where each tried to demonstrate their mastery of more categorically feminine pursuits. From her point of view, the world of boys had become something quite other, an alien land of body odours, farts, testosterone, and sport. As the years progressed, however, she could tell that her friends and the boys had begun to stare back across the gender abyss with mutual fascination and with the unpredictable disquiet of longing.

Jesse never felt as if she had deliberately tried to get into the clique of girls that others referred to as the 'cool circle'. Before age twelve, she had gained the general admiration of her age group because of her brilliance in the music classes. When she gave away violin, and soon after, fell into a spiral of anger, self-harm and grief after her father's sudden death, none among her peers thought the worse of her.

From the outside, sadness and anger often manifest in the illusion of a rebelliousness of spirit. The more wilful and restless among her classmates started to see her as a fellow traveller, on a road where having a challenging attitude was a badge of honour. When Jesse was being more honest with herself, she would admit that she never felt really at home in the company of the harder and more precocious girls. But having been accepted by them she felt some protection in being identified as one of the 'cool sheilas'.

She had maintained ties with just one older friend from her days playing in the string ensemble. Anthea had stuck with violin and with the ensemble, and Jesse respected her for that. For Anthea, learning the violin had not come easily, but she played the long game, stuck at it, and managed not to get distracted by drinking, smoking, boys and truancy. Jesse herself, also, rarely engaged in such things. She did avoid school on those dark days when she was too weighed down by the black dog to face the place. Mostly, she never thought too long and hard about the blokes at school either.

Looking at Tyson, bare-chested, out on the point, she had a flash of a near-forgotten memory. They were only little kids, back on that day, when he had placed a shell necklace that he had made, around her neck. In return she had kissed him. For a moment they had just stared at each other, before both bursting into a fit of giggling.

Jesse walked back over the road to her place, to her mother and to breakfast, all the time wondering about something indefinable that she had lost upon the way.

Larsen's Workshop, Hobart

Looking down from his kitchen window high above Hobart, Aaron studied the play of light upon the river. Between patches of water, ruffled into dark blue velvets by the breeze, there were areas of silver sheen, untouched by the winds. He was reminded of the Testore violin with its patchy layers of damage and repair, each imposed on the original finish, and each marking a story in its mysterious life.

He had messaged his old mate, Roberto from Cremona, telling him about it, sending photos of his work so far, and asking for any constructive advice he might offer. Roberto had replied the next day.

This is certainly an interesting item! Did you know that because so few reject, or secondi, violins survived, some collectors now will pay good money for one, simply to keep as a display item. At the Academia Cremonensis, there is a verified 'reject' Stradivarius that somehow was never culled by the master. The lecturers there use it to show which failures in construction, or finish, counted as lapses in excellence for Stradivarius. It provides, how do you say? Lessons in 'what not to do' for the aspiring master luthier.

Aaron's photos had conveyed to Roberto the care he had taken to remove the messy outer layer of varnish. Seeing the cracks in the belly plate, Roberto had added, *You know that you will have to remove the neck and top plate completely to glue and reset the wood?*

Aaron already knew as much, and was prepared to completely disassemble the violin. He also knew that instruments of this vintage must be worked on carefully, one delicate step at a time.

Soon after returning to the workshop, and to his project, Aaron managed to coax his finest knife under the ebony fingerboard, to slide it upwards, and so lift the fingerboard carefully from the neck. The dark wood revealed small pits where fingers had pressed down in the most used regions of the fingerboard. There were also fine nicks left by ungroomed fingernails. All this was to be expected, but the fact that there was not even more wear and tear on such an old and much played instrument indicated that this fingerboard was itself a replacement for the original. Aaron dated the replacement fingerboard as mid nineteenth century, halfway into the Testore's three-hundred-year life.

Turning the removed fingerboard, he noticed that the bottom surface had been shaved in a way that was presumably meant to compensate for the asymmetry of the neck itself.

As he was examining this, he saw there, faintly scratched into the ebony, three very small letters: N.G.F. 'And what might you mean?' he asked them, knowing that he had no idea what the letters might signify. He perused his library but was left no wiser. He came across one similar set of letterings found on an eighteenth-century Scottish violin, this time on the inside back plate simply marked N.G., possibly indicating an owner rather than a maker. Aaron dismissed this as being unlikely to be connected to the marks on the fingerboard that he had just removed from the Testore.

Still, each little discovery tantalised in its own way. He wished he had someone with whom he could share the joys of such tiny mysteries. For a moment he considered ringing Haley McGribben and mentioning what he had found. Then, judging it to be too trivial a matter for her consideration, he thought the better of it. He found himself, however, thinking of her smiling eyes and of the little row of freckles beneath her glasses, and somehow this made his workshop seem an even more empty place. 'Such is the lot of the long-distance craftsman,' he thought out loud, before turning in for the day.

Outside his window, the sky had darkened, and over the Derwent a squall was coming in from the south.

Chapter 12

Van Diemen's Land, 1848-1870

Time and again, Neil Gow Foggo was reminded of the terrible weight that his esteemed family name carried. He was reminded every time that he was requested to play a composition by Niel Gow, or Nathaniel Gow – the acclaimed Scottish fiddle composer after whom he was named. In keeping with the family tradition, his parents had him well schooled both as a violinist and as a luthier. His future was, he was often reminded, already laid out for him.

There are those though, who through will, luck, or misadventure, can break away from their allocated path. For such a divergence there is often a price to pay, along with all the burdens of regret about what might have been. For Neil the price would be paid many times over before he found a peace, of sorts.

Even before being transported to Van Diemen's Land for theft, he had, in a simple attempt to reinvent himself, fled his home town and abandoned a lucrative career as an instrument-maker. He had learnt to sail, and later learnt to row a whaling boat and to trail and harpoon the great sea-beasts. There he had exchanged the majestic strathspeys of his family's repertoire for sprightly hornpipes and jigs, just as he had exchanged the genteel company of cultured men for the mateship of men so rough and ready that they grew barnacles on their skin like the bows of ships.

When he was sent to the Antipodes for stealing, he constantly reoffended, doing a stint as a second offender at Port Arthur. After being granted freedom he joined an American whaler, the *Hudson*, working from Van Diemen's Land to Perth in the West. The freedom of the seas was cut short, however, for back on land he soon reoffended yet again. This time, Foggo's skill as a violinist came to the attention of William Champ, who managed to get him brought to Port Arthur.

Champ had never truly forgiven the fiddling constable, Laing, for failing to return as promised and again entertain them at the penal station. In Champ's plans, Foggo was to take Laing's place, and more. He would entertain the Champs, the children, the visitors, and even those prisoners furthest on the path to reform. Finally, he would be charged to teach the most gifted amongst the guards how to play the violin, viola, and cello, and form a string quartet for the betterment of the convicts. He would then conduct the ensemble, and would arrange and compose music for them, in keeping with their progress as musicians.

At the request of the Champs, Foggo took possession of the violin left there by Laing. Noticing immediately the warping of the neck, he borrowed the Champ family Bible and attempted to harness its weight to straighten the line.

After a week of being weighed down by both God and by gravity, only the slightest improvement to the beast's playability was noticeable. *Better than nothing*, thought Foggo, but he guessed that given that weird grain and the ever-present humidity at Port Arthur, it would probably return to its contrarian angle over time. Still, it would suffice for now. Ah, but if only he had the tools with which he had plied his trade back in Scotland!

When William Champ had finished his time as commandant at Port Arthur, his fate took an interesting turn. Van Diemen's Land had been renamed Tasmania and had been granted self-government. The election of Tasmania's first parliament had led to a stalemate between two parties. Their elected members, somewhat perversely, chose Champ as premier because both sides disliked him with equal intensity. He was to hold that role for only one year, but in this time, he had the opportunity to advocate for Foggo, who had served him so well during his time in the penal station. Port Arthur was becoming a shipbuilding centre, where convicts and former convicts were trained in carpentry and boatbuilding. Around the district small farms flourished, while fishing fleets and whalers left from nearby docks.

Champ offered Foggo the opportunity to open a small shop and workshop in Hobart, resuming the trade of his youth, making and fixing instruments. Neil, however, told his former overseer that he would rather stay in Port Arthur. His mates were there, his string quartet was there, and it was there, inspired by Champ's confidence in his talents, that after so many failures, he had finally turned his life around. Champ understood Gow's appeal, so he agreed instead to present Neil with a workshop at Port Arthur, complete with the timbers and tools to make instruments and do repairs from there.

The workshop did well. Orders and jobs were to come from Hobart Town, and from anywhere across the island where a musician needed an instrument to be made or repaired. Gow was particularly proud of the carved violin fingerboards that he made from imported ebony. On the underside of each he left his insignia, N.G.F. In that time, he made himself a new violin, far superior to the one that Laing had left with the Champs. When an order came from the north of the colony for a cheap, second or third-hand violin, suitable for a country fiddler, Gow had no hesitation in sending off that old beast of a fiddle that Champ had passed on to him all those years ago.

The fiddle was delivered by coach courier to one Liam Donohue, Golden Valley, care of the Post Office, Deloraine, Tasmania. Donohue, a free settler from County Kerry, Ireland, received the fiddle in 1867.

Three years later, in 1870, Neil Gow Foggo passed away in his cottage at Port Arthur, a free man, much loved for his music, but ever a rogue. Just over a decade later Port Arthur was renamed Carnarvon, in an attempt to erase the stain of cruel reputation that haunted the penal station.

Chapter 13

Dover, Tasmania, 2023

'String ensemble is dumb, why don't you quit and just hang with me after school instead?' said Kirra.

'That's a bit harsh, Kiz,' Cheryl replied. 'Miss McGribben is really nice, and I enjoy playing my cello, even if the music is, well kind of boring sometimes. Ya know, the group needs me too, I reck. The school wants to send the group to some Eistedfodd thing. Two of the violin players have already dropped out. Turns out it's good that the new hippy-girl, Wattle, just joined, otherwise we wouldn't have the numbers.'

Kirra curled her top lip and sneered. 'Wattle's such a stupid name. I bet her parents are greenies or something. Don't see how you could like playing with her.'

'Well, she has only started. Has a bit of catching up to do to be able to properly play the music Miss McGribben has given us, but she's very musical you know, she'll get there alright.'

Kirra dropped the subject and let Cheryl head off to the music room without further comment. *The more I hear people talk about this Wattle*, she thought, *the more I despise her. She's not like us; doesn't fit and don't belong here.*

Kirra had pretentions of being one of the alpha girls in her year. She played women's AFL, took the hard knocks on the Saturday, then came to class on the Monday, showing off her bruises as badges of honour. She had played recorder up until year seven, but she gave up after her mother's boyfriend broke it, saying that the 'racket' she made messed with his nerves. The following year she dropped the music option and instead took the outdoor-recreation leadership course. When Jesse, who had been the top in her year in music, had also dropped out of music class, Kirra had felt redeemed. She then worked at building a friendship with Jesse, who she had previously considered to be up herself and too self-contained to be interesting.

For a couple of years Jesse had refused to go to school from time to time. After a few weeks she would return, looking gaunt and thin, and sometimes with new scars visible on her forearms. When she was back in class, she could go from moments of dark brooding to sudden outbursts aimed at other students, or even teaching staff. Kirra mistook this behaviour for toughness and self-assurance, and so had wrongly assumed Jesse to be a kindred soul.

Towards the end of school that day, Jesse, bag over her shoulder, found herself walking down the corridor towards the exit. Passing the music room, she heard the string ensemble rehearsing some new material. She grunted, annoyed that part of her really wanted to listen in. *Why the crap do I even care?* Hearing the group tuning up, she couldn't help but recall her humiliation at the string camp when she was just twelve. It was like feeling an old wound opening up and wrenching in her gut. Vacillating between contrary emotions brought out her anger. *Well, what the fuck anyway?* In the end, however, curiosity got the better of her, and she peeped inside the open door.

Haley had been struggling for weeks to find music that would keep the teenagers sufficiently engaged. A few years back a friend had given her string ensemble arrangements of music from the movies *The Pirates of the Caribbean* and *Frozen*. Haley understood, however, that popular culture is absurdly ephemeral, and what was considered cool for a year or two could soon lose the capacity to excite interest.

Consequently, she had worked on her own string ensemble arrangements of a few pop songs including 'Flowers' by Miley Cyrus and 'Unholy' by Kim Petras. The cellos would have the bass parts, violas would cover some of the notes from the guitar chords, and the violins would follow the melody that the artist was singing. Haley had put a lot of time into these transcriptions and arrangements, and they seemed to work. When the group had played them through, she scanned each face. Anthea simply said, 'Yeah!' Cheryl was smiling, the viola boys nodded, and Wattle commented, 'I get how this all fits together now.'

That moment, though, was short-lived. Haley and her group were suddenly taken aback when Jesse burst into the room, declaring with an unexpected intensity and eloquence, 'That's not real violin music! It's like the worst of both worlds. It will never sound as kick-ass as the original recordings. Strings are all wrong for those songs. Worse still, it cheapens the violin to be playing that sort of music, when there's so much beautiful classical, folk and even jazz music composed specifically for it. A violin is not a cheap substitute for a guitar, it's its own thing.'

Haley was almost struck dumb, unable to find a response to Jesse that would not sound either defensive or dismissive. Luckily, Jesse simply turned around and left, having surprised herself that she had even cared enough to have made such a scathing judgement. *After all,* she thought, already regretting the outburst, *Anthea is still a good friend and Cheryl is kind of a friend too. And Miss McGribben's only trying to do her best with what she's got. I get that. I'll apologise to her next time I see her. I'm not really like this – or am I?*

For her part, Haley was thinking that the point of Jesse's criticism was mostly legitimate. Nevertheless, she was furious at Jesse and thought, *What craps me off the most is that if Jesse wanted so much to lift the standard, then undermining my best efforts was not the way to go about it, and she should know that.*

Whatever her opinion about Jesse's judgement with regards to the music, Haley knew that Jesse had probably damaged that sense of a worthwhile shared project that she had only just built between herself and the kids in the ensemble.

Before Haley drifted further into despair, however, Wattle came up to Haley and spoke directly to her. 'I think we can make these tunes really kick, Miss McGribben. Not everyone is going to like them, but I do.'

A collective 'Yeah!' went around the group. Haley's composure was soon restored and they got on with things, sorting out the issues in timing and emphasis.

Gotta remember that one needs a thick skin when working with this age-group, Haley reminded herself.

Anthea and Cheryl had both noted Wattle's contribution in restoring the balance, and both gained a new-found respect for her.

After the ensemble members had left, Haley stayed back and tidied up the practice room. She could not deny that Jesse's uninvited intervention had set her nerves jangling, but she determined to do her best to distract herself. She had yet to pack away her own violin. As playing a bit could sometimes be a balm to the soul, she decided to run through some pieces. Avoiding the pieces that the kids had been working on, she warmed up with a few sprightly and well-known session tunes, the 'High Reel' and 'Drowsy Maggie'. Remembering that the next day was Friday, when she would be teaching private students from home, she played through some of the material that she would be teaching them. Then, finding the sheets of music that she had copied from her adult student, Lucy, she launched into the *Barn Dance Set.*

When she had finished the three Huon Valley schottisches, she was surprised to hear applause. She looked up from the music to see the smiling pink face of the school caretaker. Kev Burgess had been doing the rounds, locking up for the night.

'Don't hear them tunes very often these days,' he remarked loudly. 'My old dad used to play 'em on the windjammer, you know? What mainlanders call melodeons.'

'Windjammers, what a delightful name for an accordion,' Haley responded.

Kev grinned. 'I know that first one. Some say that was made up by a bloke from up Mountain River way called Sid Machem, but he was long before my time, or even Dad's.

Anyhow, lovely to hear them! Childhood memories for me.'

'I'm amazed that you'd heard these ones. And I'm so glad you felt I was doing them justice.'

'You play so beautifully, could listen to you play all night! But I best lock up now. Will you be okay to go now?' he said, rattling his keys.

Haley checked the wall clock and was shocked at the hour. Sometimes playing violin induced the wonderful illusion of timelessness. Time had certainly flown by when she was lost there in her own musical pocket-universe. Ah, let it be. 'Might see you next week, Kevin,' she said as she left the building.

Driving home, it occurred to her that her mother had not yet replied to the letter that she had sent to her some weeks earlier. *Time flies. It'll be May in three weeks. The days are getting shorter, and the nights have that foggy chill to them; a touch of real autumn after such a long-drawn-out summer.* She drove home along the main road rather than the coastal route this time. Coming down the bends, deep into emerald-green Glendevie, and then beyond towards Waterloo, she saw not one, but two brown falcons, the fastest fliers of all the Tasmanian raptors. Noting the abrupt turning of the seasons, and the dimming of the long bright days, Haley felt a sudden urgency to tie up the loose ends that she had left hanging.

As soon as she was home, Haley rang Aaron Larsen to see if he was making progress with the restoration. He sounded genuinely pleased to hear from her.

'Oh, hello Haley! I was going to call you tomorrow. It's going well, but slowly. I'm trying to remove the back plate at the moment. There are some wide cracks in the wood that were filled with what seems to be marine varnish. I've removed all the varnish, so removing the back plate risks letting these cracks become full-on splits. To make things worse, some tough old furniture glue has been used to reglue the belly and back plate to the sides. It's absurdly strong, but whoever did it made a mess of it. My guess is that at some point the whole violin started coming apart, and this was a rescue job, by someone who'd never fixed an instrument before and was working with whatever was at hand. It's likely to be the same person that smothered the beast in that heavy varnish I just removed.'

Haley hesitated before commenting, 'Well, that sounds challenging, but also interesting. What say you about me dropping by early Saturday evening and having a look? I've never seen a major restoration. Perhaps you could show me the steps up to this point and beyond.'

Haley had not considered that she might be sounding a little too eager to see Aaron again. The thought hadn't occurred to her until now. When he quickly replied that he was looking forward to seeing her, however, she began to worry that she might be sending the wrong signals. Then she wondered, *Or, am I?*

Chapter 14

Golden Valley, Northern Tasmania, 1867

They sat next to each other on the cart that was the family's main form of transport when the distance was too far for easy walking, and which served as a hay cart in summer. The sun in the sky, the gold of the fields, the spontaneous good cheer, and the random songs that his father exuded at all times and without a thought, guaranteed a pleasant day's journey.

Fergie was always amused by the way his father would sing when working on the farm, when out walking, and particularly when driving the family carriage. His dad, Liam Donohue, referred to it as 'lilting with the mouth'. It was a way, he informed Fergus, by which a singer could render a fiddle tune or a flute tune with all the intricacies and ornamentation of the original instrumental version. 'Doing so, Fergie, keeps all the tunes fresh in the memory.

In the absence of an instrument to play upon, they would otherwise walk out the door, never to return to me.'

Fergie's friends in the valley had fathers of the kind often referred to as 'the strong silent types' by the local women. The other boys smiled whenever Liam was nearby, lilting his way through farm tasks or casual engagements alike. Music poured out of his mouth, day and night, while his legs and hands would be tapping little rhythms on chairs, tables, railings, and saddle leather. *Tippy-dee-tapp-apper-dee.*

Though Fergie thought it funny to hear such sounds constantly flowing from his father's mouth, he was used to it and he liked it. It had been part of his father's way of being, something essential to his presence, from before Fergus could even remember. Today, dressed in a good jacket, taking the rocky road from Golden Valley to Deloraine, the nearest large town, Fergus noticed that Liam's singing was stronger and more animated than ever.

'You seem happy today, Dad,' he remarked.

'I told you what our main business is today didn't I? I mean apart from buying feed and selling a wee bit of butter and the like? Bruce down the road told me yesterday that a parcel was waiting for me in the postal office in Deloraine, and I t'inks I know, for sure, what it must be. Some time back I ordered, from a restorer of instruments in the south, a good second-hand fiddle, one that wasn't going to send us all broke in the buying. If my guess is right it has arrived and's just waiting patiently for my gentle touch.'

Fergie had never heard his father play an actual instrument, but he had heard the stories. His mother had told him that before they left Ireland, they had to sell everything they owned, just to cover the fare out to Australia for the whole of the young family. Liam's much-loved fiddle was one of those precious possessions sacrificed to the cause. Now, after just three years here, the Donohues found themselves becoming prosperous enough to acquire a humble replacement.

Liam had been prompted in this direction when, a few times, he had travelled to Westbury, Deloraine, and Latrobe for dances in sheds and halls. At one such event, a Swedish immigrant called Orm Lindberg had been playing fiddle with his band. When Orm stopped for a break, someone suggested that Liam have a try at it. Borrowing the Swede's fiddle, he got up and sawed out a few sets of tunes that he found to be still under his fingers. Orm was clearly impressed and, after, had shaken Liam's hand. 'Some fine playing there my friend. If ever you get your own fiddle, I can find plenty of work for you around the way, playing in shearing shed dances and the like.'

'I've heard your playing, Orm, and I am more than impressed. I can't see why your band would be needing another fiddler.'

'Here's the long and short of it,' replied Orm. 'I'm good for the polkas, the waltzes, the varsoviennas, the barn dances and the mazurkas. You seem to have handfuls of jigs, reels and the like. I'll teach you my tunes, and you can teach me your Irish fiddle tunes. Then we'll have a band for all kinds of tastes and all kinds of dancing. What say you?'

'I will be most keen to take you up on your kind offer, sir. One more good harvest and I should be able to afford a modest instrument. When I do, I'll be in touch. Don't you live in the Fingal, at Swedish Town?'

'Not anymore mate, have moved into Westbury. A little closer to here, I believe.'

And so it was that Liam had determined that it was time once more to take possession of a fiddle, and to replace lilting with the mouth for the real thing.

As they came closer to Deloraine, Fergus again interrupted his father's musical meditations. 'Why did we leave County Kerry, Dad?'

'Well, in the twenty years after the great famine, those that hadn't died were leaving or thinking about it. Mostly they went across the Atlantic to Canada or America. The heart of the place had almost stopped pulsing. There was little work, and no market left for any crop you might succeed in growing. An English lord was buying up the abandoned properties all around ours. He gave me a good enough offer on my family's farm, and so your mother and I agreed on trying our luck down here.'

'So do you ever miss it?' Fergus asked.

'Well, yes and no! I miss the neighbours I grew up with, the stories peculiar to the place, the particular curving of the roads from the hills down to the sea. But I never miss the poverty, nor the weather, where it blows and rains more days than not. The soil here in Golden Valley is richer and deeper, the rainfall is just about perfect most years, and here towns and villages are growing and thriving, not shrinking. Here you, and all the others, will have better prospects as you each make your own way into the world.'

'Do you think that you could teach me fiddling one day, Dad?'

'I already intend that eventually you, and any children of mine, will have their own fiddles, or whatever instrument they fancy. We will just have to wait to see if the fields, the dairy, and the potatoes keep on bringing us in good money. And I am pretty sure they will!'

Once Liam had taken possession of the old fiddle that Mr Foggo had sent him, he rarely put it down. Even in the dairy he would play to the cows. The thousand Irish tunes that he had lilted for years still came to him at will. But soon he had also absorbed all the schottisches, barn dances, mazurkas, waltzes and varsoviennas that the folk around his area liked to dance to. Together, he and Orm set one summer dance after another alight with the mastery of their duet playing, in all styles. When he could afford a new fiddle, one made to order from a Sydney luthier, he passed the dear old beast to Fergus, who had also taken up the penny whistle and then the melodeon. Fergus and his father invented a new way of setting up the melodeon, with straps, to facilitate fancy playing. For generations Donohue musicians would use this set-up.

After the death of his first wife, Liam remarried and had a second brood of children. By that time Fergus and his siblings already had their own families. In a few generations the area around Golden Valley, Jackies Marsh and Deloraine was home to tribes of Donohue cousins, part cousins, aunts, and uncles.

When Fergus could no longer play the old Foggo violin, he passed it down to his own youngest son, Denny Donohue. Denny, who had become a wizard on the button accordion, as well as the fiddle, formed a duet with his cousin Dan. Together, they went on to become a popular duet in the central north, playing all the old tunes, but adding music hall favourites, cakewalks, and rags to the hornpipes, jigs, reels, mazurkas and waltzes and other forms that their fathers and grandfather had played. This was around the time that Tasmania became a state within the newly federated

Commonwealth of Australia. Denny and Dan were masters at the hybrid shed-dance music that had grown in Tasmania from English, Scottish, Irish, German, Polish, Swedish and American roots. They still played one Scandinavian waltz that Orm had taught their grandfather, 'The Onboard Waltz', which by the mid-twentieth century was known to every Tasmanian bush musician, while remaining virtually unknown in other states.

For all their brilliance as musicians, both Denny and Dan were in awe of their cousin Gundy. Gundy focused mostly on the melodeon, and could play more tunes with more variations, faster and more confidently than any other traditional musician they knew. Gundy had also begun to compose some ripper tunes, set dances and waltzes in a uniquely Tasmanian style. As a playful tribute to their gifted cousin, they would always play some of Gundy's compositions in their sets; a waltz, a set dance, a hornpipe, and a schottische, all named after their author.

By about the mid-1920s the Tasmanian economy had already begun to falter, bringing about a decline in demand for both farm labourers and country dance musicians. Despite the banks still being happy to lend out money to investors, down at the grassroots level people were suffering. The word around was that things would only get worse. Consequently, Dan and Denny decided to try their luck playing in Melbourne. They made the journey over Bass Strait, on the cheap, paying their way by playing for the crew on the merchant schooner, the *Alma Doepel*.

They were on the deck of the square-rigger, having a little practice, when Denny put the old beast down on the portside railing, while he reached down to pick up his melodeon from the deck.

It had come without warning, a sudden trough of swell lines, and a slight change in the wind, hardly worth mentioning – but enough to send the old violin off the narrow railing and into the brine, never to be touched again by Donohue hands.

It was never the best of fiddles, and he knew he could find another, but still Denny's heart choked in his throat. 'Ghosts of my forebears, please forgive me,' he whispered under his breath. He felt that he had betrayed his family by losing his grandfather's violin, the same one that had played so many tunes and set so many feet a-dancing.

Badger Island, Furneaux Group, 1925

Affie Saltmarsh went over to Badger Island a few times every year. His ancestors had lived there, whaling, sealing, running some cattle, and harvesting the yolla, the bird that the white fellows called mutton birds because they thought the taste, and the fat, were a bit like those of lamb. He always had a laugh at that. By his day, however, only a few people still resided on the island.

He came over to maintain the huts in readiness for the mutton-birding season, to scope the rocks for seals, or to shoot a wallaby or two.

Last night's gale had come up from the west without warning. He had heard a little singing in the she-oak and marram grass as the wind shifted direction. The swell on the rocks had seemed to pick up a little too, and continued to do so until he could hear a more definite crashing of waves on the shore. Then, during the night, the wind gods and the storm gods came out to play. For a while he had feared the roof was going to be lifted from his hut. *Pity any poor buggers out in their boats in this*, he thought. By the morning, however, the wind had died off, and while a solemn greyness hung over both ocean and coast, the water had become still, other than a remnant swell beating out a regular drum roll on the stones.

After storms like this one, Affie liked to gather kelp, which he would wash before feeding it to the island's cattle. He would also look around for any interesting flotsam and jetsam, a pastime appropriate on an island of old and recent shipwrecks. He discovered that there were a few nets and buoys washed up, a craypot that would come in handy, and the neck and top plate of a violin.

This last discovery was a strange and rare find. Curious, he scoured every nook and cranny along the stony western shore. His search bore fruit. He found a badly damaged violin bow, then the whole back plate, cracked but intact, about half a mile from where he had found the rest of the violin. He retraced his steps along the shore on the way back towards the hut, and noticed some light wood tangled up in the kelp they call Neptune's necklace.

Ah, the bridge. Pretty sure I can fix this, Affie assured himself. Clearly other parts were missing, but he could whittle these up from driftwood, and glue them back in. He'd pick up some carpentry glue and marine varnish back on Flinders, and then he'd see if any of those fiddling boys over on Cape Barren had any old or spare strings they might give him or trade him.

So it was that Paolo Testore's '*bestia arrabbiata*' came to the Bass Strait Islands to be reborn once more.

147

Chapter 15

The Glen, Huon Valley, 2023

Haley felt some relief. After the drama of Thursday's string ensemble, teaching in her home studio seemed like a breeze this Friday. Even the terrible twins, Cable and Seth, appeared to be trying to concentrate. The highlight, to that point, had been Anthea, who was finally starting to play with a looser and more relaxed bowing arm.

During the lesson Anthea apologised to Haley on behalf of her childhood friend Jesse. 'Miss McGribben—'

'For goodness' sake Anthea, please call me Haley when I'm not teaching at school!'

'Well, Haley, I hope you weren't too upset about Jesse's outburst yesterday. I've known her since we were in kinder together. I love her dearly, but she has got so messed up since her dad passed away. I've seen her cut herself with a pocketknife just to show that she doesn't give a damn about things. Sometimes she doesn't eat for days. Deep down though, she's nice. Honestly, she can be lovely. Just give her time. It was rude of her to burst in on our practice like that. My feeling is she already regrets that she did it.'

'Well, she certainly revealed that she still has strong opinions about the violin and music. Just quietly though; her mum and I are hoping to get her playing again. But we both know that this is something we can't rush. I have no hard feelings about her little outburst. What say we leave it and just get on with things?'

Anthea played through the arrangements that Haley had written for the ensemble. She sounded as if she had practised all night. Her renditions were quite strong and confident, and Haley let her know how well she was doing.

'That's so great,' she said to Anthea, while silently adding the corollary, *Now all that remains is to get some groove into it.*

Before Anthea packed up, she noticed a pile of music on the desk. These were the tunes that Haley's later student, Lucy, had asked to go through with Haley. She picked one up. '"Down Longford Way" ... What's that piece like, Miss Haley?'

Haley had to admit that she had not had a chance to look over or play that one yet. Before she could say as much Anthea went on. 'My gran was from Longford!'

Haley felt inspired by Anthea's sudden show of interest to have a closer look at the photocopied score. There was a melody with guitar chords above, and two harmony parts for second and third violins below.

'Do you think your dad would mind if we run a little overtime tonight? Lucy will be here any minute and we can all play this together. Which part would you like to try?'

'Can I play the main tune first time around, and then maybe we can swap. I'm a bit shy about playing with new people, so can we run through this now, before Lucy arrives?'

By the time Anthea had a good handle on two out of the three parts, Lucy had arrived. Being a little shy at first, she was nervous about playing with the teenage girl who had more experience than she herself did. Haley, though, had always had that gift of getting students to take a calm and playful approach to playing, and so she worked her magic. In no time at all, 'Down Longford Way', by the late Kitty Parker, sang out through the little cottage in the Glen in beautiful three-part harmony. Anthea's dad, who had been waiting a while in the next room, came in and listened intently.

'What was that tune?' he asked, barely holding back the welling tears. 'I remember my mother used to play that on piano. She told me her old piano teacher had composed it.'

After Anthea and her father had left, and after Lucy's lesson was finished, Haley put on some food and while waiting for it to cook, sat down with a cool glass of Riesling. The sound of that tune, played in three parts, was still running through her mind. She contemplated taking it along to the Saturday Irish session but understood that there, sheet music was taboo. Maybe she could find another student at Dover who could play it with her and Anthea, she thought as she went to check on the trout baking in the oven.

The Doolans' Home, Dover

Kirra had come around to visit Jesse. Her mother let the girls be, doing whatever it was they got up to in there, behind the locked door of Jesse's room. *Glad she has a few friends who drop in still*, thought Diane, feeling that even this was progress of a sort.

Kirra opened Spotify on her phone. 'Can I plug your speaker system into this, Jess?'

'No worries! What have you got for me to listen to?'

Kirra was not a fan of female pop divas singing torch ballads. She went, instead, for hard, angry or brutal music, in all of its forms. Together, they listened to one track after another, fem-punk, neo-goth bands, a bit of electronica – which both girls decided was not for them – some nostalgia rock from their parents' generation such as Suzie and the Banshees, and some post-hip-hop. They eventually settled on a Japanese band that placed heavy metal riffs over a punk-style wall of distortion, and over-layered the whole thing with cutesie-pie, girl-pop vocals.

'What the bleedin' hell is this, Kirra?' Jesse shouted out above the racket.

'Well, the style is Yami-Kawaii, well kind of, some Japanese shit. The band though is called "Babymetal", and they kick everyone's ass!'

'This is fucking unreal,' remarked Jesse. 'Sounds like death metal, speed metal, punk, goth and cutie-pop, all at the same time!'

Together they listened to a whole album by the Japanese girl band. Jesse did her best to focus on each track but could not ignore Kirra's frequent interruptions where she would slag off about school, the teachers, about Cheryl being gutless, and about how she felt about the new girl, Wattle.

Risking Kirra's wrath, Jesse interrupted. 'Maybe we should give Wattle a chance, Kirra. What do we really know about her?'

Kirra promptly filled Jesse in with the few things she had heard around town.

Jesse soon got the impression that Kirra was obsessed

about finding some dirt on the new girl. What Kirra had dug up, however, turned out to be pretty innocuous.

'Well, her mum stood as a Greens candidate for council once, so they already have a few enemies in the log-trucking families down here.'

'Well why did they move down here?'

'Word is that her parents moved from Cygnet. They bought a larger farm outside Dover, where they're planning to rebuild some old dairy.'

'What to do? Milk cows?'

'I heard they make what they call boutique cheeses; what shit is that, ay?'

Jesse shrugged as Kirra continued. 'Wattle apparently went to some hippy school called Peregrine, then was doing high school at Tarremah, another hippy-bullshit school. She moved to Dover District because it was close.'

'Where did you learn all that, Kirra?' asked Jesse.

'I was told this from Xavier and Tyson who seem to have gone out of their way to get to know her. Maybe they want to shag the bitch?'

'Kirra, honestly! I think you might be a bit obsessed. It's not healthy you know. Wattle's not done anything, that I have noticed, to make me think that she's a bitch.'

'Well, she doesn't seem to care about which girls are at the top of the pile here, and I think that she needs to know?'

'Oh, for fuck's sake Kirra, just let it rest, will you?'

By saying this Jesse had just revealed that she wasn't playing the 'game of thrones' that any high school kid should acknowledge as the realpolitik of the campus. Jesse could see that Kirra was clearly shocked by her reaction. She appeared to be taking it as a personal insult.

Jesse immediately sought to break the circuit before a

fuse blew. 'Kirra, we're friends, and I hope we always will be. If I tell you you're speaking crap, it's because I respect you enough to think that either you'll take it on board, or if not, brush it off like the water from a wood-duck's back.'

'Whatever!' replied Kirra in the lingua franca of every teenager who finds that they are outmatched in eloquence and logic. 'Anyway, I've gotta go. Women's footy is on later this arvo. You should come and watch us play, Jess!'

'I won't be able to watch you play this time, too many chores to do to here,' she lied. 'Thanks for coming around, Kirra. I loved having your company. That Babymetal band is the GOAT, made my day! Good luck with the game, give my best wishes to the other girls.'

As soon as Kirra had left, Jesse opened the window and let the breeze off the bay cool her room. Then, at last, she could listen to her own playlist. She collapsed onto the bed and shut her eyes. The square timber house by the beach rang out with the music of Emily Sheppard playing violin, then some Jenny M Thomas and Bush Gothic, some Irish fiddle tunes by Martin Hayes and the Gloaming, and finally, the third movement of the Sibelius violin concerto played by Hilary Hahn. When the playlist had been completely exhausted, she rose from her bed, satisfied that Kirra's bogan bullshit had been cleared from her room and from her mind.

Larsen's Workshop, Hobart

The Testore reject now had its fingerboard removed. It had also been completely stripped of the crude marine deck gloss that had covered over the original finish and the various cracks and blemishes alike. Aaron had then given the surface a careful light rubbing with the finest grade of sandpaper that he could find.

He had entertained the notion that he would leave off removing the back plate until Haley arrived, so that she might see the care and accuracy with which he could slice through the glued surfaces without damaging the wood above and below.

Aaron had tremendous pride in the delicacy of his touch and in the perfection of his line, when separating the parts of the instruments that he worked on. In his days back in Copenhagen Aksel, his mentor, had insisted that he practise on cheapo, hundred-dollar Chinese student violins, the cheaper the better. He had spent weeks slicing through the connective tissue of each instrument and sanding or chis-elling them until each plate was properly tuned to a clear musical tone, before regluing each part then touching up the finish. His mentor had insisted that before he could work on valuable instruments, he must be able to deconstruct, improve and reassemble the cheaper instruments in such a way that no one could identify that the violin had ever been worked upon. *Thank you Master Aksel*, he thought, reflecting on his time in the workshop. A torrent of nostalgia followed.

He recalled how, on those crisp Copenhagen mornings, he would stir Roberto into wakefulness by tapping on his door in the old nineteenth-century Christiania building in which they both lived. They would take off on their push bikes and cruise over the Freestate's cobbles, through the square, past the graffiti laden walls, and the sculptures of trolls and the like, past the creatively constructed own-er-builder houses. They would call out '*God morgen*' to the more eager groups of Freestate citizens already up and doing their tai chi or their hatha yoga. After they left the gates that separated 'Freestate Christiania' from Copenhagen, they would breakfast at either the Union Kitchen or the Packhouse Café or, alternatively, grab some pastries from Lagkagehuset on days when they were running late.

Pondering over these recollections, Aaron decided that tonight he would ride his bike down to town for his dinner date with Haley. She had her own car after all, and if he left a few minutes early he'd arrive back at the workshop not long after she did. He needed the exercise after standing and sitting at the workbench all day.

Aaron remained curious as to exactly what taking the back plate off might reveal. The more he thought about this stage, the more his desire to show off the virtuosity of his bladework to Haley faded.

She isn't concerned about seeing my technique, he reminded himself. *It's only whether or not the restoration will be successful that she's interested in.* Despite having pride in his work, in the acuity of his line, and in the steadiness of his hand, Aaron had always despised those master craftsmen who needed to show off. He despised it in others, and he now felt ashamed that it was a sin he had almost fallen into. The final result was everything; the capacity to produce a well-finished and playable instrument was all that mattered.

With this soliloquy encouraging him, he took up his blade, slid it under the back panel and peeled it off, as if he were removing the skin of an exotic fruit, slicing right through the rubbery glue that the previous, very amateur repairer had used. It came off so neatly that a part of him continued to wish he had an audience. Carefully, he laid down first the belly, still attached to the block and neck, and then the newly separated back plate. The heavy and sloppy glue that had bonded the plates after some previous separation was here and there over the inside, in blobs and in lumps. But three other things immediately struck Aaron. The same carpenter's or bootmaker's glue had been used to glue the soundpost in place. Soundposts were fitted, but never glued. However, having a soundpost glued tight to both the top belly and the bottom plate was, in this case, a blessing, being the only reason the beast held together after forty years hanging on a shed wall. Second, Aaron noticed that the soundpost was not a fine piece of dowel but a neatly cut-down carpenter's pencil. *That was innovative!* The previous repairer was obviously someone who had to make do with whatever was at hand. Rubber glue, marine varnish, and a pencil! Aaron couldn't help but admire the resourcefulness, if not the quality, of the job done.

Along with the make-do repairs by that mystery bush carpenter, another's handiwork suddenly became evident to Aaron. Dried out, in one corner of the top plate, was a lumpy line of red earth. 'What the Frigg is that?' Aaron remarked aloud. He noticed tiny holes on the clay and realised that he was looking at the remnant of a wasp's nest.

'Well, that's a first!' The Testore reject had been found in the Huon Valley. Aaron Larsen knew the area well, having done seasonal fruit picking there when he had first left school. He also knew that this red soil did not come from that southern valley. 'Yet another mystery, yet another story to tell.' He pried the remnant wasp nest off the edge of the plate, where it had apparently become a single strip of pitted terracotta. He put it aside. *Can't wait for Haley to see who once lived in her recently acquired fiddle!*

He got out his phone and took a close-up photo of the wasp's nest. He then captioned it before emailing it to Roberto, knowing that given the time zone difference, his friend would have just dragged himself from his bed. The thought prompted him to check the clock. Shit, it was later than he thought! Better get ready and go. Haley would be finishing up at the diddly-diddely session by now.

The New Sydney Hotel, Hobart

Haley had thrown herself into the session today with an unusual zest and confidence. She had begun to remember three-quarters of the most played tunes, and had worked out which double-stops and ornaments she could add while still supporting the group sound. In every session there are session leaders, those who will begin a tune-set with con-fidence, and enough projection, to allow those less familiar with the pieces to lock in and follow. Every afternoon's session will be punctuated, here and there, when all the usual session leaders are up at the bar, at the lavatory, or just stopping to talk with friends. In such times, the other players might doodle on their instruments, until a tune comes to the surface that the rest of the throng recognise and know well enough to join in on. If this doesn't happen, someone with a lesser-known tune that they have been working on has the opportunity to solo. Now one such opportunity had arisen. Haley had not really planned anything, but Kitty Parker's 'Down Longford Way' was going through her mind, as it had been all the previous night. She began to play the A part in a gentle, understated way, as she knew that the tune was unfamiliar to this session group. Consequently, she was surprised when a harp player joined in. The harpist smiled at Haley and said to those on either side, 'I know this one.'

Haley and the harpist took turns playing the main tune, then alternating to one of the harmony parts. Each time through, their rendition became stronger, and somehow more moving, until, as if determined by some telepathic cue, they both ended with a mournful diminuendo. When they had finished some in the session circle applauded, while others nodded from behind their pints. Haley was pleased to have introduced a new tune to the session. She noticed that there was a hush over the throng, as if their playing had brought a stillness to the rowdy bar. Then followed some questions about the tune. One or two noted that they had heard it played before. Others express surprise to learn that it was a Tasmanian piece. Then one of the session leaders returned from the bar, and before long, a set of familiar jigs had reanimated the assembled musicians and broken the spell.

After that day's music was over, Rose told Haley that she had really enjoyed listening to her play. 'You must be in good spirits, Hale! You're playing up a storm today, and that duet with the harpist on that slow tune was exquisite.'

'Thanks, Rosey!'

'Will you be joining Charlie and me for a counter meal?' asked Rose.

'Sorry, mate. I've got a reserved table upstairs. Aaron is meeting me for dinner. We're kind of talking business about violin restorations and stuff.'

Charlie Dempsey, who had been listening in, smiled before commenting. 'Ah, you're having a date night, Hale! Good on you and about time.'

Haley was about to say *well not really*, but she decided to play along, and so slyly winked at Rose and Charlie.

Nearly fifty minutes later Haley found herself sitting at a table for two in the loft area, but with no sign of Aaron. She couldn't help but listen to the incessant clinking of cutlery and the fragments of small talk around her. She had memories of nights back in Adelaide, in the last years of her relationship with Richard. She remembered, with bitterness, how he had become progressively preoccupied with his own projects, and often turned up late for dinner dates, leaving her waiting long after the appointed time, bored, lonely, and feeling that bit more devalued each time. One time Richard had left her waiting by the silver balls in Rundle Mall, for a full two hours in the Adelaide sun, without calling to explain. Good thing she'd learnt to be happy on her own. Still, she hadn't picked Aaron for someone that wasn't punctual, or wasn't thoughtful enough to ring if something had come up.

Rose had ordered, eaten, and paid before popping upstairs to say goodbye to her friend. Seeing Haley alone, with still no food in front of her, she immediately knew that something was amiss.

'You haven't been stood up by the inconsiderate bastard have you, dear?' And proceeded to give Haley a reassuring hug.

'No idea what's happened to him. I definitely had the right time. Now I'm hungry and maybe a little upset. I tried ringing Aaron, but I think his phone was off, or something. Yes, I'm disappointed. Think I'll just write tonight off and head home.'

By the time Rose had said goodbye, however, Haley's phone rang. It was Aaron, sounding a bit shaken. 'Haley, I am so sorry. I'm in the emergency ward at the Royal. My phone was off.'

Haley imagined the worst and felt had a sudden adrenaline rush. 'Are you okay? What happened?'

❧

Prior to that moment Aaron had been staring at a wall in Emergency, trying to piece together what had happened. They had triaged him, patched a few cuts, and given him a CT scan then a cognitive test, which he seemed to pass alright. Sitting waiting long enough for them to rule out concussion, he watched a passing parade of car accident victims, and drunks who had staggered and fallen and presented with broken arms or twisted ankles. He saw a woman who had clearly just had a stroke, then another person in the process of having a psychotic episode, and just earlier, a young man who seemed to have taken a drug overdose. Compared to those, he felt that he was fine, and wondered when he would be released to go home. He still held the two broken halves of his bike helmet. He had reached down, felt his phone there in the pocket of jeans that now had the arse ripped out of them, and suddenly he'd remembered Haley.

'I was on my pushbike. Heading down to meet you, and some clown turned the corner in front of me, on the wrong side of the road. He clipped my front wheel and I went flying off into the kerb. My bike helmet cracked on impact, my head and neck took a nasty jolt, and I lost skin on my knee and elbow. They've patched me up, but they asked me to stay for two hours' observation, in case I show delayed signs of concussion. I'll call a cab and should be home in forty-five minutes, if you're okay to wait at my place.'

'No! Wait there! I'll come and get you! Oh, you poor darling. Text me when they're ready to release you. I'll be in the lobby near the main entrance. We still need to get some dinner. Shall I pick up a takeaway? How is sushi?'

As it sometimes does, fate had intervened and thrown a spanner in the works. Nevertheless, they did get to eat together. Aaron proceeded to show Haley the progress that he had made in dismantling the rogue Testore. He showed her the sound plates, now free of the crude varnish that he had so carefully removed, showed her the heavy, rubbery glue that had been used previously, and showed her the improvised pencil-soundpost. Aaron wobbled on his feet, slightly, as he was pointing out the things he wanted Haley to see. He hadn't yet got around to showing her the dried-out, brick-red lump of the wasp nest that he had extracted from the beast.

Needless to say, Haley was too distracted by Aaron's condition, and so paid little notice to the carefully disassembled parts of the violin. Instead, she looked at his eye, before insisting that he go straight to bed. He relented, cleaned himself up, and agreed to let her nurse him. Then without thinking, Haley declared, 'I can't leave you alone. I think I should stay the night.'

Chapter 16

The Furneaux Islands, Bass Strait, 1925

The waters between the islands were tossed by contrary winds. Affie breathed in the salt air and buttoned his oilskin coat. *Nearly home,* he assured himself. *Not a lot to show for it all.* He had tacked his small boat in an erratic zigzag from Badgers Island to Flinders. He then followed the coast and rounded the point before rowing the remainder of the way to the jetty. There Affie docked his boat at the little hamlet of Lady Barron, on Flinders Island, where he lived. Back on Badger, he had set his craypots at a favourite reef and had checked them when returning home. *Just two this time, but a couple of real big 'uns.* He threw the rock lobsters into a bin of water to keep them from drowning in the open air. He had also killed, skinned, and butchered a fur seal, after having shot it from some distance away as it lay sunning itself upon the stony shore.

Then there was the violin, reduced to bits of broken

flotsam. *I reckon I can fix that thing, we'll see.* He contemplated what to do with it, once it was back in one piece and playable. For a while he considered selling it to one of his fiddle-playing cousins from Cape Barren Island, across the water. But no – he would keep it, and learn to play it properly. Back in his school days, his teacher had tried to teach him, and later old Willy Maynard had shown him a tune or two; but that had been as far as he had gotten. Maybe he wasn't too old to learn by himself, he considered. Then he could entertain with a set of two at a dance or something. Who knew? It would at least give him something to amuse himself with on the long lonely nights. Yes, he'd have a go.

The next day, Affie set off on the track to Whitemark. On arriving, he went into Blundstone's General Store. This was the main, all-purpose store on Flinders Island. Some of the older folk still called it 'Harleys' Store', after the previous owners, who had drowned at sea when a mutton-birding expedition went awry, some forty-five years back. Joh Blundstone was behind the counter. At this time his father, John, who owned the store along with other businesses and farms, was of a great age, and was rarely seen up and about these days. The Flinders Blundstone family were a branch of the Hobart Blundstones, who had made a good fortune from their boot and shoe factory. The Whitemark shop even stocked Blundstone boots. These were much loved by the island's farmers, but cost a pretty penny, putting them way out of Affie's reach.

When Affie entered the store a farmer's wife, as white-skinned as a lily, looked up from the fabrics she had been perusing. After one glance at his dark skin, she left without even a nod of acknowledgement. Joh, however, was, as always, amicable.

'Good day to you, Mr Saltmarsh,' he said, genuinely pleased to see Affie. 'What would you be after, my dear man?'

'G'day mate. How's your old dad doing?' Then, before Joh had time to reply, he continued, 'I'm after a good strong glue to fix a broken violin, and also some varnish, or shellac if you have some.'

'Doing a bit of fine craftwork are you, Aff?'

Affie just laughed, knowing full well that his reputation for rough and ready bush carpentry was notorious on the islands.

Joh thought for a while before saying to Affie, 'I'll get some bootmaker's glue ordered from the family factory in Hobart. My feeling is that it will be the best thing for fixing your instrument. It's strong, but it stays flexible and never gets brittle like some glues. I'll telegraph the order now, and it should be on the boat by next week. As for varnishes, all I've got is this new one that the merchant navy boats and the fishing boats are using for their decks.' He picked a can off a lower shelf and showed it to Affie. 'It's an extra thick marine varnish. It creates a very dense layer that waterproofs the decks, as well as filling the cracks and joins, so that water doesn't leak into the cabins or cargo holds every time a wave crashes over the boat. You can have the varnish now, you won't need the big can, so I'll decant some into a jar for you. That'll cost you ten shillings, and another twelve for the glue you've ordered.'

'How much if I give you a fresh crayfish, Joh? Pretty large ol' cray too.'

'Twelve shillings and one cray for the lot then, Mr Saltmarsh. Come back next Tuesday and the glue will be here for you.'

'You're a good bloke Joh. Thanks again, and I'll be back

in just over a week. Oo-roo.'

Joh Blundstone returned the compliment. 'Have a good day, Mr Saltmarsh, and enjoy that long walk home.'

Ten days later, Affie had what he needed to fix the broken instrument. A few days previously, he had made a quick journey across the wild water to Cape Barren Island. One of his cousins, Lester Smith, played fiddle, and had a lovely instrument that his grandfather had won in an impromptu fiddling competition.

Forty years previously, an American whaling ship had been forced to find a safe port at Cape Barren, during a week of wild storms. Among the bored sailors sitting out the stormy seas in 'the Corner', as the island's main settlement was called, was a fiddle player. The American player was a crack-a-jack at hornpipes, and at a kind of American quickstep that they called the breakdown. Hearing that some of the local boys played a bit, the American proposed a competition with any local fiddler who was up for it. The loser would have to promise to give his own fiddle to the winner. The Cape Barren boys thought the wager sounded like a prank, but Lester's grandfather had accepted the challenge anyway. A show of hands, by an equally numbered gathering of locals and crew members from the American ship, was to determine the winner. The American fiddler thought that this was going to be a breeze. He launched into 'Bonaparte Crossing the Rhine' then 'Sally is a Goodin', before finishing with a cheeky version of 'Turkey in the Straw'. The audience, both the natives and the visitors, applauded loudly and all were genuinely impressed by the performance. What the Americans had not understood was that fiddling had already been strong among the Palawa of the Bass Strait Islands for a century. Sealers, whalers, and traders from all around the world had docked there in transit; some had based themselves there. All had brought their music, be they from England, Scotland, Ireland, Holland, Norway, Canada, or the United States. Every new tune fell on fresh ears and was quickly absorbed into the local repertoire. A Cape Barren fiddler could bring tears to the eyes of a harpy, call a lost mutton bird back to its flock, or turn back the Roaring Forties with the sheer strength of his playing; or so it was said.

When the applause for the American's fiddling had eased off, Lester's grandfather picked up his own fiddle and tuned it. Knowing that he was born for this, he grinned a wry smile, then launched straight into a Cape Barren version of the very tune his rival had just ended on. His own version of 'Turkey in the Straw' lacked the humour and syncopation of his rival's. Instead it was played straight ahead, at twice the speed of the American's version, the volume of the piece boosted by the continuous use of double stops. It was neither better nor worse than the sailor's rendition, but it was just as good in its own way. He then slowed things down and played a beautiful schottische, ornamented with every trick within the realms of good taste, and characterised by impossibly complex runs of triplets. To finish, he launched into an island favourite, 'The Black Cat Piddled in the White Cat's Eye', as if to emphasise who was bound to be the inevitable winner. Needless to say, that day Lester's forebear received the greater show of hands, by some margin. However, before his American adversary could despair about losing his precious fiddle, the islander offered his own in exchange. Both men shook hands and embraced, and the day went down in folklore.

◦৵

Two generations later, and it was Lester who played that fiddle, and it was a beauty both in form and in sound.

Affie held Lester's violin up to the light, turning it over and over. He then asked Lester what the raised area at the join was.

'That's the purfling, mate.'

Then, looking through an f-hole, he noticed something else. 'What's that vertical post thing between the top plate and the bottom made from?'

'That's the soundpost. Keeps it from collapsing, usually a piece of maple dowel.'

Affie hadn't told Lester why he was asking these questions. He wanted to sail across again when his violin was properly repaired, and when he had learnt a tune or two that he could show his cousin. Noticing that Lester kept a handful of used strings in his violin case, Affie asked whether he might have them.

'What would you do with them, cuz? Garrotte a wallaby or two?'

'Ha ha mate! I was looking for some fine wires like this to repair a craypot I found washed up over on Badger the other week.'

'Okay, I always keep them. I've got some spare sets so you can take them ones if you really want?'

'Many thanks to you, Lester! I'll be back over in a few months. When's the next big dance over at the Corner?'

'We're always dancing down here, cuz. I'll see you when I see you.'

And so Affie bid farewell, and taking all that he had gleaned, sailed home to begin his project.

In the absence of a uniform piece of dowel, Affie Saltmarsh decided to saw his carpentry pencil in two. Then, filing both ends of one half flat, he created the soundpost for the instrument. A violin soundpost is held in place by upwards pressure from the back plate, by the downwards pressure from the belly plate, and by friction. Affie could not see how one might insert such a post once the violin was already reassembled, and opted instead to use the Blundstone's boot glue to fix the post in place – first securing the pencil to the bottom plate, then leaving a large blob of glue at the top end of his makeshift post to await the upper (belly) plate. He then put copious amounts of glue around the edges of both plates before jamming them together, with a towel around them to stop the vice from damaging the wood. Before doing this, he had filled in any cracks and splits, using a mixture of the marine varnish he had purchased at Whitemark and resin from a nearby radiata pine tree, which he had melted over the fire in an empty soup can. Blended together, these ingredients made a strong enough filler. This he applied where necessary, before drying the repaired plates near the fire for a few days and then adhering them to each other. One of the tuning pegs had been lost somewhere on the turbulent waters of the Strait, but Affie didn't worry, knowing that he had a handy collection of driftwood timbers that he had salvaged from shipwrecks and abandoned boats. Among these was a strip of dense black timber that looked similar enough to the ebony of the pegs. A night of gentle whittling and he had carved a new peg, so close to the others that it would take a trained eye to know that they were not all of a kind.

When the instrument was once again whole, he reset the bridge before stringing it with his cousin's second-hand strings. He wasn't sure how to find the correct pitch to tune them, so he walked three miles to the McGregor farm to ask if he could hit some of the keys on their old upright piano. From Affie's childhood days to the present, he had occasionally visited the McGregors' home to sell crays, fresh fish, or wallaby meat, but he had never been invited in beyond the corridor and the veranda. He had oft times heard the tinkling of the piano coming from the parlour, and sometimes had secretly stayed back, squatting outside the window to listen. Although he had known them for years, the McGregors seemed to exist in a world far apart from Affie's shanty, his little sailboat, and his life of fishing, hunting and beachcombing.

When he arrived, the lady of the house feigned distrust. Affie, not recognising that he was being teased, felt obliged to better explain the reason for his visit.

'I just want to hear an A, a D, a G, and an E, so that I can get this fiddle to true pitch! I won't be hanging around or anything, and I can take my boots off before coming in.'

The fact that he was virtually pleading amused Mrs McGregor, who relented and led him into their drawing room, with its vases of flowers, lace curtains and uphol-stered chairs. There she played the notes that he had asked for, while he turned the pegs, and so tuned the strings. Mrs McGregor then said, 'Well now you owe me, Mr Saltmarsh. I'll have you play me an air on that thing before you leave.'

'Oh, sorry Mrs McGregor, I can't play it yet, but when I've got some music coming from these fingers I'll come around and try not to scare you to Hades with the racket.'

She laughed in response, before commenting, 'That bow of yours looks like it is well on the way to being bald! Come into the stable with me and I'll clip a few hairs off the tail of the draught horse.' Affie was delighted with the offer. He had no idea how to restring a horse-hair bow, but he knew that, given a bit of trial and error, he would figure it out.

Through the long winter months, the wind-wild months, the house-bound months, when only a few days were safe for sailing, he set it in his mind to teach himself to play. He remembered the few lessons that he had way back, and so set his hand in first position. He worked out the scale for each of the open strings, singing, as if he was back in primary school; Doh, Ray, Me, Fa, Sol, La, Te, Doh. Then he tried playing a tune, but gave up in disgust at his poor efforts. He then had a go at singing and whistling every tune he could remember before trying to find them on the violin. At first he found a fragment here, and another there, but in a few weeks he had stitched together three tunes, from start to finish. He tested his pitch by singing along with each note, until he was satisfied that his fingers were matching his voice. His bowing hand was stiff, as if he was rowing his boat. He recalled watching his cousin, who seemed to bow just from the wrist. He tried this himself, and his bow floated more lightly on the strings.

He was amazed by the volume of this instrument. Louder than a flock of black cockatoos when a storm was on the way! Over the next several weeks he started remembering more tunes and began to really enjoy the mystery of trying to find them on the fiddle. All of this helped the long nights, spent alone, in a drafty shanty lit by kero lamps, pass more quickly.

As winter turned to spring, and then spring gave way to the first warm kiss of the summer, Affie decided to sail back over water to the Corner, on Cape Barren Island. He had it in mind to show his cousin Lester Smith what he had done with the salvaged violin, that he had first found in pieces. He also wanted to show off his progress on the instrument. To Affie, the brown-skinned cousins over on Cape Barren all seemed to have the music flowing through them – his own branch of the family, not so much. Nevertheless, Affie now felt like he had made up some ground, and was ready to show what he could play. Further, he imagined that if there was a dance on when he was there, he might be able to join in, and keep up with the local fiddlers for a set or two.

When Lester saw the violin, he seemed genuinely impressed. He picked it up, smiling a bit at the messy varnish job, but he considered that Affie's workmanship was, on the whole, pretty good considering this fiddle had been made up of salvaged parts. Lester began to play a tune on the beast then recoiled.

'Holy! She is a loud old girl. Good for the dances.' He tried playing some octaves and grimaced, but didn't mention to Affie that the intonation and action were all wrong. He was careful not to hurt Affie's feelings, and he did admire the repairs his cousin had done. He handed the fiddle back to Affie.

Affie, shyly at first, started playing a few tunes, an approximation of 'The Onboard Waltz', a version of the 'Jenny Lind Polka', 'The Old Clog Dance' and then 'The Wellerman'.

'Not bad, cuz! Not bad at all. You just learned yourself all that since I last saw you?'

Affie smiled back nodding. Lester pulled out his own fiddle, tuned the strings, then tightened his bow before rubbing it with some rosin.

'Let's run through the 'Onboard' again, mate.' Affie played through the waltz, starting pretty much as he had the first time, but this time, Lester stopped him here and there, to correct a note or two, perfect a cadence, or add some better phrasing. Before long the two violins had begun to blend into a single voice. When they had finished both men smiled. For Affie it was his first true taste of a musically satisfying experience. It wasn't just the sense of achievement, but the fact that, together, they had made something beautiful. For true music can erase all considerations other than the piece itself, and can take the players somewhere outside of the here and now, while still being firmly in the here and now. That is its paradox and its wonder.

As a dance was scheduled for that Friday night, Affie stayed on Cape Barren Island for a full week. Come Friday, the hall was lit up with electric lights and kero lamps. Fine powder was put on the floor to ensure that the surface allowed fast and smooth turns for the dancers. Greenery and flowers were hung here and there, and an array of scones and cakes was laid out on benches in the corner. There were several musicians with their fiddles, melodeons, whistles, and the like, all set to go. Lester asked them if his cousin might try joining them on a set or two and they seemed fine about it.

Affie was beside himself, both with nerves and with excitement. Since childhood he had dreamed of being a musician playing for a community dance. But his mother had once told him that he wasn't born with the music. What is more, until now, he had never owned his own instrument. He now so wished that his mother was alive to see him, but she was long gone, having died giving birth to a second, stillborn child when Affie was only ten. After that Affie had been raised solely by his father, a man who was not particularly liked by neighbours, either black, white, or brindle. 'Rough as guts', they would often say, and that was true enough.

However, old man Saltmarsh had his share of the pioneering virtues, and had taught Affie to sail, repair craypots, shoot, fish, hunt, do basic carpentry and grow a few vegies.

Unlike his father, no one who knew Affie disliked him, but some still kept their distance. Affie realised that he felt more at home at Lady Barron village on Flinders than at the Corner on Cape Barren Island and more at home in either place than in Whitemark, the biggest town on Flinders Island, where he was not allowed to drink in the bar at the Interstate Hotel, despite the fact that no one could determine if they should think of him as Aboriginal or Anglo.

Affie sat out the first set of tunes. These were two schottisches that he hadn't heard before. The second set was all polkas and he knew two out of the three of them. He was surprised how well he could hear his own violin above the other instruments, but that seemed to be a bit of a problem for the other players, as Affie was struggling to maintain the faster dance tempos, and his loud instrument sounded like it was pulling against the group sound. He sat out the next two dances, then joined in again for a nice slow waltz set. Lester positioned himself close to Affie, to help steady Affie's tempos, which he had sensed were not quite regular.

By the end of the night, Affie had gained a clearer sense of the shortcomings of his musicianship, but also a better idea as to how he might remedy these things.

Practising alone can obscure little mistakes, where one misses this, or fudges that. He sensed acutely that he would have to spend more time with Lester, learning how to emulate and to lock in to his cousin's sound. All in all, though, he was elated that he had made a start, and that he had stood shoulder to shoulder with the island's best fiddlers. *Another year or two, that's all I need to catch up*, he thought.

Sailing home on Sunday, Affie Saltmarsh had not counted on the capricious nature of the ocean swells when they came in, with equal ferocity, from both the west and north-east. It wasn't that the winds were exceptionally strong that day, rather it was just the swell lines meeting, then breaking across each other, on the reefs around Flinders and near the point, coming into the jetty at Lady Barron. He was virtually home, despite a near misadventure, where massive swells were breaking on a reef that he hadn't even known was sitting below the surface until that day. Despite the chaotic seas, he made it to the jetty, and was just about to tie up when a freakish wave threw his boat hard against the jetty pole, splitting two planks. As he alighted onto the jetty, he noticed that his boat had begun taking water. He removed his things first, then deducing what had to be done, he went on land to where a boat winch and cable were fixed. He hooked the cable to his craft, then hurried back to the winch and turned the wheel for dear life. Eventually, after sweat and blisters, the little boat came out awkwardly onto the stones and sand. She was gravely injured, but at least she hadn't sunk into the deep water at the end of the jetty.

For a hunter and gatherer such as Affie, to be without a boat jeopardised his whole way of life. It was essential that he pull out all stops to fix her. It was beyond his skills. There was, however, a wooden boatbuilder who had set up a work shed outside of Whitemark.

Affie had always prided himself on not asking favours from the neighbours, and especially not from the 'white as snow' farmers. But he remembered that he had promised Mrs McGregor that he would play some fiddle for her. At last, he knew that his playing was just about good enough to not send her into hysterics.

He went to the farm and played for Mrs McGregor and her husband. Both expressed genuine appreciation. 'You've come along very nicely with that fiddling, Mr Saltmarsh! To think it was only six months ago that you first fixed it up and started playing! Well done to you, sir! Come back and play for us anytime when you're free. There'll be scones and tea as payment, I can guarantee as much.'

'I'm so glad you liked my efforts. I'm still only just beginning, though I have the passion for it, you see. But there is a little favour I need to beg of you. Forgive me, but it's quite embarrassing to me to even ask. My boat needs repairs and I have to get it to Whitemark, to Wheeler's boatshed. She won't float at the moment. I was wondering if ever you are taking your cart or dray through, I might humbly request if you can lug her there for me.'

'Oh, you poor half-caste bugger,' said Mr McGregor, not realising that he was being more patronising than benevolent. 'I'm happy to help you. Can't have you down there all alone with no way to make a livelihood. How's Thursday? I'm going there to pick up some stock. I'll take the hay cart. I think that's big enough for the job. I'll get my son down to help us lift her in place.'

'When the boat's back in the water, I'll fix you up with fresh crayfish whenever you want one,' Affie replied in an oblique expression of gratitude.

A former Hobart shipwright, Anthony Wheeler was good at his job, and could work quickly if need be, but he had a reputation for over-charging Aboriginal customers. When he told Affie the cost of fixing his boat, it struck like a blow. Affie was distraught; he had only half of what was needed. He had so little to sell in order to get cash. Without his boat he was unable to bring in seal meat and skins, crayfish, wallabies, rabbits and mutton birds from outlying islands, or anything worth trading. Wheeler pointed to Affie's swag. 'What have you got in there, me mate?'

'All that I have with me now is some dry meat and bread, a billy and some tea, a coat, in case the wind picks up, and my violin.'

'Show us your fiddle then, Mr Saltmarsh!'

Affie slumped, struck by the terrible inevitability of it all. He knew in his heart that he had no option. Either way he was going to lose something essential to his being.

Wheeler appraised the fiddle. 'I don't know much about violins, but there is a bit of demand for these back in mainland Tasmania. I wager I could sell this for you, and get enough to cover the amount that you will be owing me once I fix your little boat up. How does that sound to you? Whatever cash you have, and the violin, and I'll get straight down to replanking your pretty little sea-lady today.'

Affie had never yet had a woman in his life, he had never even had a chance to court one, but that day he knew how heartbreak felt. He had raised the violin from the dead. Found her, like an empty silkie skin on the stony shore, and breathed life back into her. He had learnt to love her, and she learnt to move with him, and to sing back to him. Now, so soon, she would be taken from him, as so much had already been taken from him since his childhood. He accepted Wheeler's deal but first asked for one last play upon the violin. Wheeler handed it to him without a word.

I'm sorry, said Affie silently to the violin. *What shall we play together now, what song of parting?* He intended to play 'The Onboard Waltz' but the tune came out differently, and drifted into something else. He heard the wind in the marram grass, the song of the yolla returning, a whale mother calling to its calf; he felt his mother's touch, his father's fist, the waves against the reefs, and then he understood that the violin was playing him, opening him up, and letting everything pour out, and then some more. His improvisation sounded liked tears, then laughter, then there was a touch of an Italian tarantella, then something that sounded Irish and harp-like, a twist and he could hear a tune that tasted like Scotch and sounded like bagpipes, then he drifted into a Tasmanian mazurka that he was sure he could never have heard; without let-up the violin kept feeding him the music and he flowed with it. When the piece reached its final cadence, it came like the boat smashing into the jetty pole. It went from climax, to an abrupt rupture, that led to shock and then to bleak silence.

Wheeler stared at Affie, open-mouthed, before saying, 'Shit, mate, you are an abo Mozart. Well, I'm convinced that I'll get a very fine price for that violin. You never know, save up for a few years and you should be able to afford another.'

And so it came to be that the beast was sold to a shop in Launceston, for what turned out to be, for Wheeler, a disappointingly modest price. The proprietor had it from Wheeler that this was an amazing instrument. When he saw it, and then played it, however, he laughed in Wheeler's nonplussed face.

'This is one of the roughest restorations that I have ever seen. To make it worse it plays like a crippled mule. Can't see any orchestral player or classical teacher even looking at it. Maybe okay for a bush fiddler. Can't believe you promised a week's work repairing a boat just for this beast.'

Wheeler left humiliated, but despite his initial anger, he thought the better of blaming Affie, who he now considered had, through some act of conjuring, got the better deal. *I'll just have to stick with what I know, and not try to get too sneaky and too clever for myself. Good on Mr Saltmarsh for getting one up on me this time, ha ha!*

Chapter 17

Bathurst Street, Hobart, 2023

Aaron pulled a spare mattress onto the floor of his lounge room and threw a pile of sheets and blankets down for Haley. She insisted, however, that he not fuss over her, and that she could sort herself out easily enough.

In his own room, Aaron stripped naked and went straight to bed. Haley found a Panadol in her bag and brought it in to him with a glass of water. She couldn't help but notice that his eyes still lacked focus. With his consent she removed his wheat-coloured locks from their topknot, allowing his head to rest more comfortably upon the pillow.

'Thank you for tonight, Haley, I feel I owe you big-time now,' he said sincerely, before closing his eyes.

'Just rest, mate. Let's see how you shape up tomorrow. Sweet dreams.'

His complexion was still pallid, though a touch of colour was returning to his cheeks. Haley pulled up a chair next to his bed and sat watching over him as he slept. After a few hours she had begun to feel the cold night settle, and so lay down next to Aaron and pulled a blanket over herself. She took hold of the sleeping man's hand, and held it gently until dawn.

The next morning, when Aaron awoke, Haley was already up. Having no doubt given up trying to negotiate his kitchen, she had slipped out, returning with two coffees and some sandwiches from a nearby café. He smiled, noticing the aroma of the long blacks filling the house, harmonising with the constant sweet scent of wood shavings that drifted up from the workshop below. Looking in the mirror, he saw what Haley had already seen: the hint of two faint bruises forming beneath the eyes, indicative of mild head trauma.

After they had shared breakfast and conversation, Haley determined that it was safe to leave Aaron. She felt more assured after he promised not to do any work for the next twenty-four hours.

As she bid her goodbye, they embraced. Aaron held her close and whispered softly in her ear, 'Thank you so much, you beautiful person.'

In such circumstances, when a fond embrace is merely platonic, each person releases their grip by what seems like a pre-allotted time. But this morning neither person would be the first to end the hug. Both hung on slightly longer than the unspoken protocols of simple friendship ordained. He could smell her sweetness, so proximate. She smelt the musk of his sweat, amidst the sweet aroma of shaved pine, maple-wood sawdust, and resin.

Aaron surprised Haley, as much as he surprised himself,

offering her a shy kiss. Haley felt her skin being tickled by the ginger threads of Aaron's beard. It was not a passionate kiss, just soft and brief, a warm and respectful expression of his care for her. She reciprocated, just once, before pulling back, all the while still holding his hand. Finally, when they had both loosened their grips, she turned, and walked outside to her car. 'You, take it easy, sweetheart!' she called, only half aware of how he might interpret those words. He waved at her, then as she pulled away from the kerb, he blew her a kiss.

Dover Regional High, Monday

Jesse felt the need to test the waters with Kirra. She was concerned that Kirra had been hurt by the rebuke she had given her on Saturday morning. 'How did your footy game go, Kirra? Didya win?'

'Only just. Should have been there, Jess. It was an awesome game. The tall girl playing ruck for Kingston had a nasty fall after taking a mark. Mangled her ankle something terrible. They took her straight to hospital. I managed two goals and a behind, even though I was playing back near the centre most of the game. Cheryl took some nice marks too, but she got knocked around bad in one tackle. Toldya you should have been there. Xavier and his older brother were there cheering us on too! His older brother's a bit of a stud, I reckon!'

Jesse felt reassured by the banal ordinariness of Kirra's response. *Water off a wood-duck's back*, she thought to herself. *Thank goodness.*

There was a fine balance in schoolyard dynamics. One slight rupture and the membership of ingroups, and outgroups, could shift suddenly. Jesse did not really care whether she was in the cool group, or an exile. However, she was kind and sensitive enough to not want to hurt those who had offered her real friendship and support when she was going through her own dark times. It was just that she sometimes couldn't completely trust herself not to be brutally honest, even when it might come as a shock to others, whether they be friends, her mother, or members of the teaching staff.

While Cheryl and Kirra were showing off bruises, and flashing some leg at passing boys, Jesse noticed Wattle Darcy coming down the path, holding what looked to be a battered guitar case. She carried herself with such easy confidence, and there was a rhythm in her step as if she was moving to some lilting internal soundtrack. It was obvious to Jesse that this was so different from the guarded tension in the body language that Kirra and most of her group of friends had cultivated.

When Kirra noticed Wattle, her lip went immediately into a sneer. 'She's so up herself. Wonder what she plans to do with that guitar? Look at the walk on her!'

Jesse couldn't figure out where Kirra's animosity was coming from. It seemed to be something more than an attempt to communicate dominance.

Wattle could not help but hear Kirra and Cheryl mumbling about her. She turned in their direction, a head full of brown braids spiralling in the air as she focused her green eyes right on Kirra, who was given pause by the directness of Wattle's response. Reasserting her position in the exchange, Kirra looked at the new girl and said loudly, 'Up yours!'

Rather than being disconcerted, Wattle took this in her stride. She walked straight towards Kirra and, undaunted, made direct and unblinking eye contact. Jesse saw that Kirra, the toughest girl in their year, seemed frozen in place. It seemed that Cheryl had noticed too, as she looked back at Jesse, eyes wide, as if to share the surprise. *Must be that Medusa hair*, thought Jesse, amusing herself with the analogy she had made, while wondering if the others would have understood the reference.

Wattle took advantage of the paralysis that she had conjured and spoke first. 'You're Kirra aren't you? Attitude is your thing, right. I get it. Maybe you might like me if you bothered to get to know me though. You never know.'

Jesse expected Kirra to yell out *Fuck off hippy bitch* or something, but Kirra seemed to choke. Jesse caught Cheryl's eye. They shared expressions of incredulity. Cheryl leaned towards Jesse and quietly whispered, 'This is a first! I've never seen Kirra so lost for a comeback!'

Jesse had intended to nod agreement but, before everyone had registered exactly what was happening, Wattle simply turned and, still carrying her guitar, disappeared around the corner of the building.

After they had eaten their lunches no one spoke another word about Wattle, or weekend football. Instead, an earnest discussion ensued about whether the music of Ed Sheeran was still 'the dope', or whether it was old hat. Jesse, who had no opinion on such issues, slipped away after a while and went for a walk to stretch her legs.

Jesse wandered out along the hedgerow, thinking about the day. Earlier that morning she'd had a brief appointment with Dorothy, a psychologist who regularly visited the school. Dorothy had told Jesse how pleased she was with her progress.

'Your mother said that you're eating normally again, and

enjoying the taste of your food like you used to do. That's a very good sign.'

Jesse had never been very responsive in such sessions. This time, however, she found herself pouring out her feelings to Dorothy. This was not merely catharsis, rather it was an earnest attempt to express how she saw her progress out of the black hole that she had fallen into. She stared at the floor, reliving the awkwardness she had always felt in these sessions, but then took a deep breath, flicked her hair back and made solid eye contact with Dorothy.

'Yes, Dorothy, I feel like I've been living in a world of black and white since my dad was killed. Nothing was worth doing, nothing much made me happy. But lately, bit by bit, the colour's coming back into the world for me. Honestly, I don't think I'll ever be that happy little girl that I once was. But I might find something, someone, who I'm meant to be. I have noticed that I care a bit more about my friends. I've started to actually give a fuck about what others do, and how they're going. I can taste and feel a bit more. I've even started listening to music again, I mean really listening to it, not just turning up the volume to drown my thoughts out. Even school feels better.'

After the session with Dorothy, Jesse had returned to class and managed to get just a little enthused by the lesson in plant biology.

During the break Jesse was walking alone. Shadows from the straggly willow by the red-brick wall made complex patterns on the path. In her mind she re-ran the events of her session with Dorothy and the realisations that led to her outpouring. The flow of Jesse's thoughts broke suddenly when she heard, coming from just around the rear corner of the main building, the sound of a beautiful voice singing on the breeze, accompanied by sweet harp-like patterns, played skilfully on an acoustic guitar. Jesse gasped at what she was hearing. It was live music, pure and direct.

She stayed where she was and just listened. After the song was finished, she turned the corner to determine its source and its maker. The first thing she noticed was the two boys, Xavier and Tyson, sitting on the grass, staring with adoration at the singer. Jesse looked at Tyson, then at Wattle, and was shocked by what she felt. *So, this is jealousy. Me jealous? Shit, why am I feeling jealous?* she asked herself. *Wattle, it seems, is a wonderful musician, so it turns out. Anyone would want to sit and listen to her. I did, from round the corner. Why not the boys? Shit, I wonder how she learnt to play guitar like that? It must be a beautiful instrument.*

Then she looked directly at the guitar. It was an old guitar, unremarkable except that Wattle had painted it with bright colours. Primary colours, reds and greens and then that blue, the same blue as her old blue Chinese Valencia violin had been. Then a thought that she had not dared to entertain rushed into mind. Perhaps the colour was not relevant, but rather it was the soul of the instrument and the heart of the player that mattered?

The boys turned, noticing Jess was watching.

'Hi Jesse,' said Tyson. 'What did you think of Wattle's music? Did you hear it? Pretty wow, ay?'

Jesse hated the fact that she felt herself mirroring Kirra. For a moment she felt like saying *Bitch!* but then shelved the thought as the counsellor had taught her to. Instead, she turned to Wattle and said in all honesty, 'You are amazing.'

'Thanks Jess,' replied Wattle earnestly.

⌇

After school there was still enough light to be squeezed from the day for a walk on the beach. Anthea had messaged her mother to pick her up from Jesse's house, and the two young women went for a stroll by the shore in that last hour before the fog, the cold, and the gloaming set in. They spoke of school and of Kirra's little episode with Wattle. Anthea expressed her own impression of Wattle. 'She's a lovely girl. Just really easy, and light. So many of the kids at school that you try to get close to hitya with a wall of attitude, as if to challenge you to breach it, before they'll let you get near them.'

'I know what you mean,' said Jesse.

'Wattle's just the opposite,' Anthea continued. 'She just smiles, says g'day, and gets on with it. Makes her great in the string ensemble, Jess. She's improving so fast on violin that one day I'm going to be the one catching up to her! Like you used to be, you know.'

Jesse, not sure how she felt about Anthea's last comment, scuffed the sand with her feet while she gathered her thoughts. 'You know lately, with some of the crap easing off in my brain, I've been missing playing the violin. I still listen to string music whenever I need time out from everything. To be honest no other instrument touches me that way. I'm glad now that I refused the meds when the shit went down for me. I'm getting better slowly, but somehow, I don't see myself going back to it.'

Anthea looked frustrated. 'Then why?'

'Geez, I don't even own a violin anymore. Mum sold it, and gave me the cash, which has all been spent now, and I have sweet-F-all to show for it. My bad, I know, but life sucks sometimes and leads you to do sucky things, if you know what I mean.'

Anthea, responding without hesitation, placed an arm tenderly around her friend's shoulders.

'If you did start playing again, you would be fine at ensemble. Most of the players are only just getting to where you were before you quit. Seriously! Also, there've been a few drop-outs and Haley, I mean Miss McGribben, is desperate to get a full ensemble together. Even if Dover can't do the next Eistedfodd, it would be great to have a decent-sized group of players again.'

Jesse felt the touch of a cool breeze and shivered slightly. 'You never stop working on me do you, Anth? I love you for it, but I have been so fucked up and I really don't want to disappoint you and everyone else.'

Above them, the whole sky had come ablaze with colour, as if all the remaining light of the day was gathered for one last stunning show at sunset. In stark contrast with the reds and oranges in the stratosphere, a huge sea eagle swept down from a bare-limbed tree, gliding just above them on its great white wings.

'Wow, that's speccy!' said Anthea. 'You're lucky living right on the beach here, you know!'

Jesse didn't reply. Her attention was fixed on a tall figure dragging in a canoe about 300 metres down the beach.

Anthea had seen him too. 'Hey, there's Tyson. He's not wearing a shirt. Looks better that way than in the school kit don't you reckon?'

Jesse knew that Anthea was trying to be funny, but for her own part seeing Tyson half naked made her feel oddly uncomfortable. She felt a nervous shudder, and a little sadness pass through her body.

Jesse was saved from delving further, as they both saw

Anthea's mother's car pull up at Jesse's house in the distance. 'Best get back before it gets too dark to see the track up to the road.'

As Anthea left, the two friends both returned well practised renditions of 'See you at school tomorrow.'

⤸

Diane seemed in good spirits, and for Jesse it seemed like the right time to spend some quality time with her mother. They cooked, ate, then watched a Netflix show together and were still on the couch when Diane turned to Jesse.

'Can I ask for your honest feelings, Jess? How would you take it if I started seeing a man?'

'Who?' was all a startled Jesse could say.

'Oh, just a bloke from the café in Geeveston that I go to sometimes?' Diane replied.

'Mum, he's gay!'

'No, not the barista, I mean the owner and cook. I can assure you that he's not batting for the other side.'

A few months ago Jesse would have fallen into a state of hurt silence, before leaving the room with a slamming of doors. A large part of her still wanted to respond that way. The thought of her mother dating, and being with a man that was not her father, was something that she had dreaded. This time, she found herself just laughing along with her mother over that last comment.

'Mum, you've been alone with me, your misery-guts daughter, too long. I think it's time you had some fun, whatever comes of it.' When the words came out, Jesse could hardly believe she had said them. Diane looked visibly relieved. She reached over and put her arm around Jesse and they exchanged a small kiss.

Diane could not remember the last time Jesse had allowed herself to be kissed, much less proffering a kiss of her own.

She looked at the scars on Jesse's arm, remnants of an attempt at self-harm, reflecting silently. *They've healed well, and in a year or two, they should be almost invisible, provided you don't try it all again. Please my love, stay strong.* She slowly released her grip on Jesse's hand. Hope had been a rare thing and when it arose it had to be savoured.

Jesse retired to her room and lay in the dark. She had only just drifted off into the first stages of sleep, when a dream began to fall upon her. She was staring at a sunset so vivid that it seemed as if the sky was on fire. Then she felt that it was her, who was on fire. Looking up she saw Tyson with his open boyish smile and his wiry muscles. She woke suddenly, feeling hot and damp between her thighs. The feeling was strange to her – novel, and disconcerting, but somehow pleasant at the same time. She lay in bed staring at her ceiling that was barely lit by the rays of the new moon through her window. As she rested there, the feelings of pleasure were overlayed with a sense of gaping incompleteness, and a longing for something undefinable. Soon she drifted back into sleep, and into a new dream.

This time, she saw Wattle, dressed in torn jeans and a diaphanous blouse, playing fiddle, while leading a group of listeners down a path through a thick glade of ferns. Noticing Tyson among the followers, she called to him. He turned his head, just for a moment, but it was clear that she had become invisible and that no one could see her.

Chapter 18

Gunns Plains, Tasmania, 1929

In the midsummer sun, the Leven River moved like a silver snake. It flowed on its winding way, from the deep ancient canyon amidst towering mountains, to the broad and fertile farmlands, just twenty miles south of Ulverstone, in Tasmania's fecund north-west. There, dark alluvial soils built up, alongside rich red volcanic soils. Gunns Plains offered premium land for dairy farming and vegetable growing, but for a family with seven children even that was not enough to make ends meet and keep food on the table. When the dawn chorus sang, Eileen's father was up and out of the house by five every morning and on his way to the gravel pit. Each day he would hammer and crush the blue metal used for road building. It was torturous work, but for six months or more each year, it was the only way to supplement their meagre income. As soon as the kids were old enough, they worked the dairy, brought in the cows, and did the milking and a score of other jobs. In season, they would harvest the potatoes, digging them with spade and fork from the rich red clay.

The family didn't really observe the Sabbath. On Sundays, like any other day, there were jobs to be done around the farm; milking, hay baling in summer, collecting eggs, plucking chooks, pruning in winter, turning the soil, feeding the pigs, making sure the horses had enough feed, harvesting the potatoes, or swedes, or carrots, or greens, depending on the seasons. Indoors, there was washing, cleaning, cooking dinner, baking bread, churning butter, and a hundred other smaller tasks. One day, when her father was out, and a sudden heavy rain kept them confined indoors, Eileen and her sisters went into the boys' room. Out of a curiosity born of boredom they worked open a rusty latch and lifted the lid on the old tin trunk kept there. They were searching for anything that might serve as a toy, a costume, or a prop, to aid in their imagined journeys.

Eileen found, wrapped up in a blanket, her father's fiddle. Though her father played only a few tunes, he came from a long line of fiddlers. The violin had been in the family for many generations, and looking inside one could still see the date, 1764. *That is really ancient!* She paused in astonishment. In an era when rural families had few personal possessions of real value, Eileen well understood the transgression.

When Eileen's mother noticed that she was handling the precious violin she scolded her and told her to put it down immediately, knowing that her husband would be angered seeing it removed from the safety of the old trunk.

Eileen had heard her father play, and her elder brother, who owned his own fiddle, would sometimes play for lounge room dances and shed dances. She was drawn to the instrument like a moth to a flame. Stubborn in her resolve, she appealed to her mother to just let her try. Her mum couldn't play, but knew how to tune the instrument by ear. She herded the younger girls out of the room and locked the door, then tuned up the violin and handed it back to Eileen. Eileen bowed the open strings and found that even those seemed to suggest tunes that she had heard. Her mother said to her, 'That's good, but now you have to find the other notes.' Hours later, Eileen had a rough and ready version of 'Annie Lawrie' under her little fingers. When her father arrived home her mother, pre-empting his inevitable protest, remarked: 'I want you to listen to what Eileen can do. She worked it out all by herself!'

Eileen scratched her way through that first tune, and her father was sincerely moved.

'Next time we go to town, I'll get you your own instrument if we can find one that we can afford.' Then he qualified his offer. 'But you'll have to show me that you can play another tune on it, or I'll take it back to the shop!'

When they did venture to Ulverstone in the family carriage, they failed to find an instrument for sale anywhere in the town. Eileen was clearly disappointed, so her father reassured her. 'Why don't you take the train to Launceston tomorrow. You're old enough to go by yourself now. I'll draw you up a street map, so you can find the shop that sells instruments and such things. You just have to remember which train to catch coming back, and I'll pick you up in the cart at the station. How does that sound? Here is six pounds, that's all I've got, see if that covers it Eileen.'

She kissed her father enthusiastically and said, smiling, 'Oh, I love you, Dad.'

Launceston

Finally! she thought. *I must have walked right past here already, but I've found it now.* Her father's map was accurate after all. Looking for the 'antiques and instruments' shop, she had already walked twice around every block in the commercial precinct of Launceston, or 'Lonny', as the locals called it. She opened the wood-framed glass door and walked right up to the main service counter.

The proprietor, a smug and somewhat rotund man, wearing an expensive looking vest over his starched shirt, took one look at her and smiled, saying, 'And what can I do for you, my little missy?'

Eileen wasn't sure that she liked being addressed this way. She was twelve, and already considered herself as a young woman, albeit one just stepping beyond the realm of childhood. *After all, hasn't Dad trusted me to catch the train and to purchase an instrument?*

'Good day, sir. I have come to buy a violin. I have five pounds to spend. Can you help me out? I like the look of those four on the stands there! May I try each of them?'

The proprietor laughed audibly at her. 'All of those instruments cost over a hundred pounds, and two of them cost several times that. I can't just let anyone pick them up and try to play them. They are reserved for special customers, orchestral players, and students from very wealthy families. I don't carry 'seconds' stock here, I'm sorry to say!'

Eileen blushed, fully aware that she was being patronised. Though she was a shy girl, she had her limits. 'Sir, that is very rude of you! Just because I'm a farm girl, it doesn't mean that your manners should go on holiday. I have come all the way from Gunns Plains, and my train home leaves in an hour! I need to find myself a fiddle today. Can you help me or not! If not, I will enquire elsewhere.'

The man behind the counter winked at her, genuinely impressed by her gumption. He paused to think for a while, and then remembered the rough-house violin he had got from the Flinders Island boatwright. It had hung on the wall, almost unnoticed for a few years, and none of his regular customers even bothered to tune it up and try it. He had eventually decided to use the space for other instruments. Consequently, he placed the beast in a spare case that was lying around, and relegated it to the storeroom out the back where it lay, forgotten until now.

'Well, my missy, I remember now that I have just the thing for you, packed away out the back. The bloke I bought it from told me it had belonged to a magical fiddler from Flinders Island called Affie. You can have it for five pounds and, because I came across as a bit brash earlier, I will throw in a bow and some rosin for free. How does that sound?'

'Can I try it first?' she asked prudently.

'You certainly can.' He retrieved the case, removed the violin, and tuned the instrument up, before passing her a third-hand bow and a block of rosin. She applied the rosin as she had seen her brother do. She then picked the fiddle up and scratched out some bits of tunes she could recall. She was very happy with the strong voice that sang from the old instrument and curious about the varnish and the blemishes that gave it its unique appearance.

'I have one concern, sir. I must be able to work out a new tune on this by tonight, or my father insists that I will have to return it. Do you take refunds?'

'If you decide to bring it back, I can only refund four pounds and not the full price. This is not a shop for short-term rentals. I must make some profit here! But yes, I would take it back. I hope, however, that it suits your needs, and that you learn to master it. I can tell you that this instrument has not been cherished for quite a while, but it should be perfect for your needs. Have we got a deal then?'

She nodded, handed over the cash, then smiled, less in gratitude to the seller, and more because she had proven to herself that she was capable of finalising a deal against an experienced haggler.

The train ride home passed wooded hills, crystal rivers, productive farms, and wild coastline, but however breath-taking the scenery, it was lost on Eileen that day. She found a carriage with no passengers, and there opened her new violin case, tuned her instrument, then worked over and over, one phrase at a time, stopping to correct the notes until she could play 'Two Little Girls in Blue'. A porter in a dark blue uniform was walking from carriage to carriage, checking which passengers would be disembarking at up-coming stations, and determining who might need assistance. He applauded when he heard Eileen's playing. 'Very good, young lady. I recognise that one. Might you know "My Father was a Dutchman", by any chance?'

'No, sir, but I will be learning it, so that next time we meet on the train I can perform it for you.'

'Is that a promise, lassie?'

She smiled and replied playfully, 'As sure as the soils of the north-west are red, it is!' They both laughed, as through the window they could see the red volcanic soil of the potato fields, one after the other, stretching out as far as the mountains in the distance.

By the time the winter had come, the days seemed clipped short for lack of light. The long nights, however, meant all the more hours to practise and to play. Eileen's oldest sister joined in on her slightly out-of-tune piano, and her elder brothers would often play along, one on melodeon, and the other on his fiddle. Sometimes a neighbour would come along and add in some harmonica and some random notes on the swanee whistle.

About once a fortnight they would put on an impromptu dance in their lounge room or in the shed. Their dad would teach them some of his tunes and dances. Sometimes a mazurka, sometimes a varsovienna, but most often little polka tunes that their mother would sing amusing words to.

By the next summer they felt that they were playing well enough to book the community hall and host dances, to which all the neighbours were invited.

Every two weeks it would be another dance. Once in a while they might get an invite to travel further afield, to another district, and to attend and play for the dances there.

One such occasion occurred in the following year when Fred, the man who purchased most of the milk from their dairy, had come by to talk business with their father. He lived way over past Deloraine, in a place called Golden Valley. He suggested that the kids might benefit from coming to one of the regular dances they held there, it being an opportunity to pick up new dances, tunes and tricks of stagecraft. Eileen's father replied, 'We'd have to stay over. That's way too far to drive the cart all the way back home in the middle of the night!'

'Not a problem, old mate. We have four guest rooms in the manor at Deloraine. It'll be nice to see some new faces there, and to show you and your lot around. No cost, no pressure.'

The shed at Golden Valley was really a vast barn. It had

been emptied of its workbenches and hay for the recreational activities that occupied the warm months.

'Look at the size of those roofing beams,' said Eileen's eldest brother. 'Each one must have been a massive tree!'

Eileen was more impressed with the efforts made to prepare the dance space. Flowers hung from the walls, and large tables with floral tablecloths were covered with an impressive spread of foods for supper. She noted the egg sandwiches, slices of ham, new potatoes in butter, fresh bread and cheese, scones, lamingtons, and fairy bread. The floor had been greased with beeswax to facilitate quick turns and agile footwork. She had heard of this practice, but had never seen it before.

At one end of the hall there was a makeshift stage built of wooden pallets. Several chairs were set aside for the musicians. As the locals began to trickle in, each dressed in their best for the night, Eileen began to vacillate between excitement and nervousness. Her nerves soon eased though, as she found that she could lose herself unnoticed in the crowd that had filled the shed. There were a few girls her age. They were dressed in lovely florals, and one even wore stockings. Now, at fourteen, Eileen had started to compare herself with other young ladies, and more importantly, she had started noticing boys in a different way.

There was a man, with a megaphone voice, who was acting as master of ceremonies. He asked that those gentlemen who wished to dance assemble on the dance floor, while the ladies who wished to dance were directed to the chairs set in a row, on the right side of the hall. There the ladies would sit, awaiting invitations from the men to join them on the floor. As the numbers were close to being equal, most would end up with a partner for each dance.

The man with the loud voice then introduced the band. He called on everyone to give a round of applause to welcome Golden Valley Gundy and the Deloraine Tigers. The leader of the band, Gundy Donohue, received a massive round of personal applause. Eileen guessed, correctly, that this 'Gundy' was probably related to half of the patrons at the dance. The MC called the first dance, 'The Esk Rivers Quadrille'. Eileen had played a few of the quadrilles and square dance sets. She had a tune set for the 'Lancers' and another for the 'Prince Albert's Quadrille', but she had never heard of this one. Perhaps it was just a locally known dance. She wondered what types of tunes would accompany the sets. A very tall and muscular man, called Dan, yelled out 'One, Two, Three, Four', while playing a double-stop introduction on his fiddle, and so the Tigers set to. Eileen's jaw dropped as she heard the group play three hornpipes, back-to-back, for the first figure of the dance set. An awkward-looking young man, wearing a fuchsia flower in his lapel, asked her to dance. Politely, she refused him but said, 'Thanks but I don't know this dance. Please consider me for a polka, or a mazurka, those I can do without tripping us both up.' They shared a laugh, and he replied that he would be back later.

The truth was that Eileen's full attention was focused on the band. The tempo was so fast, and they played with such authority, that it scared her, and humbled her. Dan was a terrific fiddler, far ahead of her brother, her father or herself. She was thinking she should ask him for a lesson, but then she saw Gundy Donohue step forward. He was playing his windjammer, the local name for the melodeon. She listened in awe, as he effortlessly played melody, ornamentations, harmonies and basses all in one piece. She couldn't believe that one instrument could pour out so much music. She

had never heard a box player like him. He stood up to perform, and as he did, he danced a percussive clog dance as
he played, while the rest of the band held down the backing
rhythm. Never had she seen such energy. Then Dan called
'Next figure!' and the second box player kept the music
going while Gundy put down his melodeon, and picked up
a fiddle from its stand on the floor. The dance had become
a progressive waltz, the local dancers showing that they
could execute the change seamlessly.

Oh, that's so beautiful! thought Eileen. And then Gundy
started leading as they went into a second waltz tune. 'The
"Ortaba Waltz", boys!' he called to the rest of the band. She
was entranced by the majesty of his musicianship. Her senses
were fully awakened as she took in everything that Gundy
was doing. He would execute a lovely vibrato, jump octaves,
then from time to time he would make strange whistle-like
notes sing out above the melody. She listened as the tune
switched to 'The Beautiful Tamar Waltz', another piece she
had to ask about, as she was, it seemed, totally unfamiliar
with the Deloraine repertoire.

Listening to these slower tunes, Eileen was struck by
contrary feelings. She imagined that she was in some stately
great ballroom and, even while seated, she could feel the
gentle swoop of the waltz lifting her weightless body. Yet,
at the same time, sorrow and yearning fell upon her when
she heard the violinist add a quivering vibrato to this note
or to that.

Then as abrupt as thunder, Dan stepped forward, yelling,
'Quickstep and Polka'. He counted a fast four, and led the
band into a set that started with 'One Dozen Roses', then
transitioned into a three-part polka, before ending with a
blistering rendition of 'The Soldier's Joy', one tune she did

recognise. The way they played these fast tunes made her skin tingle, and set her nerves ablaze with a kind of mad excitement that she hadn't previously experienced.

After the set, the boy who had invited her to dance returned and asked her if she enjoyed watching the quadrille. All she could think of, though, was the music.

'This band are stupendous. I never dreamt that people could play like this. And that Gundy, he must be ten years older than me, he's like an angel or a devil, how did he get so good?'

'Gundy's my second cousin. Our extended family runs to about sixty of us hereabouts, and mostly we're descendants of Great-Grandfather Liam Donohue, who came out from Ireland and settled here way back. He was a master musician. Most of us play a bit, but Gundy lives and breathes it. Mind you, Tassie Hills and Dan there, are not far behind.

Eileen joined in for several dances that night, mostly with the same young man, and found herself enjoying the night very much. At the supper break she mustered the courage to approach Gundy. When she was about to speak, however, her nerves got the better of her and she made a strange choking sound. Gundy looked at her and grinned, saying, 'Don't try eating the lamingtons in one mouthful, dear!'

Eileen almost fainted with embarrassment but then remembered to breathe.

'Hello. My name is Eileen. My family are visiting from Gunns Plains. I'm a fiddler, of sorts. I know some lovely varsoviennas. I'm wondering if you do that dance around here too?'

'We sure do. We finish the night with the varsos. Would you like to start the set off with the ones you know, and we'll just follow. Then you can try to pick up ours, for the second part of the set.'

A wave of terror broke over Eileen. *What just happened?* She couldn't lead in a dance like this! How could she play along with their varsoviennas if she had never heard them? Somehow, though, Gundy's aura of indefatigable energy and enthusiasm touched her, and she threw all caution to the wind.

'Let's try it then! Thanks so much. It's been an honour to meet you, Mr Donohue. See you on stage.'

Through some magic of the moment, Eileen managed to keep up with the band. With their backing, her own tunes were made to sound richer and more lovely. When they ventured into their own pieces, she played quietly, featuring just the more important notes, here and there, once the melodies had consolidated in her memory. Somehow it worked out. She was congratulated by all, although her younger sister sneered just a little and said, 'It's always Eileen!' That night Eileen could hardly sleep. Lying in bed, all the evening's tunes played over and over in her mind on an endless loop.

The journey home was long, taking all the morning hours and continuing into the early afternoon. Their route wove through a maze of gravel roads and tracks, of villages and vales, hills, dales and always the trees, the bush, the hedgerows and the farms. Eileen was relegated to the rear of the cart, as she insisted on practising on her loud violin all the way home. Her sister, by way of teasing, kept asking her to stop the noise, but Eileen was determined to recall, piece together, and work out every tune that she had heard played at the dance. Having heard Dan and Gundy play their fiddles, she determined that one day she would play as well, or even better than they did. *I'm going to pick up every tune I hear, and every trick of the bow and the fingers I see, as if I'm an old chook scratching for seeds and insects all over the place.*

By the time they had arrived back at their Gunns Plains farm, Eileen's sister had clearly had enough of the noise, and so concocted a plan. The next day, just before they went off to the one-room shed that served as the only school for twenty miles, her sister waited till Eileen was getting ready. Taking Eileen's fiddle outside, she poked as much red clay into the f-holes as she could. She then cleaned the now heavy instrument, so that at first glance her elder sister would not notice. *This will quieten the thing down,* she thought.

Picking up her instrument to do some practice after school, Eileen sensed the crime right away. She screamed for her little sister, who had reacted strategically, retreating outside to hide in the shed. Eileen was furious. She teared up, but her mother calmed her.

'What a sneaky trick. Oh well, it was probably only meant in fun. Let's get the dirt out of it now. I'll get a knitting needle, and a bit of bent fence wire, and we should be able to dislodge it all. Don't worry dear.'

And so, they got down to the task by first removing the strings and unlooping the tail piece. Eileen's mum then used a needle end to mark where the bridge should go, once it was ready to be put back in place. Then, they took turns shaking, digging, scraping, until it seemed that there was no more of the red dirt to come out.

Eileen was still unhappy. 'The clay has made it all wet

inside! That will kill its voice.'

Her mother tried to console her. 'No problem, dear, I'll sit it on a chair in the kitchen, not far from the wood stove, but not too close. It'll be dry in no time. Then we can restring it.'

By dinner time that night, the instrument was dried, cleaned, and restrung, with the bridge back in its proper place. Eileen played on it. It sounded good to her, but she felt that something in the tone had changed a little. She chose to forgive her little sister, but not to forget. That night when her sister tried to get into bed, she found that Eileen had short-sheeted it.

For another few years Eileen played for regular dances. By this time, she had acquired hundreds of tunes. However, as fate had it, she was to marry young. Raising her four children was to leave her no time for music, and so the beast lay unplayed in its case.

Years later, after that marriage had fallen apart, she began to play again, but a great shyness had come upon her, as if the fire within her had been dampened down by all that life had presented.

It happened one day that a neighbour introduced her to a young man who had dropped in for a visit.

'Eileen, come over and meet my good mate Athol, his folks were from round Gowrie Park, there under the mountain. Since I last seen him he's been making a bit of a name for himself, singing the country and western songs all round the outback.'

Eileen felt oddly shy around the young man with his cowboy shirt and snappy banter. Thinking of how boring her own life seemed, she mostly listened, quietly and coyly. The singer and guitarist Athol McCoy had been bemoaning the fact that Peter Mollerson, his crack fiddler from Canada, couldn't join him for his next tour of outback towns on the mainland.

'Well, Eileen here plays the fiddle, Athol. You oughta try playing together.'

Athol beamed and looked at Eileen. 'I'll drive you home and you can get your fiddle!'

'No need,' she replied. 'I only live across the road. Just wait here!'

And so, in 1964, Eileen began the long journey back into the world of music, and into the arms of Athol McCoy, whom she soon married. By this time her father had passed away, and she inherited the family's violin. A beautiful old instrument, with a nuanced voice and a rich provenance.

She kept her first violin up until 1968, but being constantly on tour, she and her new husband recognised the need to lighten up their hoard of possessions. Thus it was that she bid farewell to her first instrument, selling it to a bloke from the south of the island called Tommy McGuire.

Tommy was what they used to call a bit of a ratbag. He was a very ordinary musician, and rode around on the coattails of his cousin, the pianist Tops McGuire. Topsy tolerated her cousin, his drinking, his gambling, and his scheming, and his out-of-tune fiddling, for one good reason. Tommy owned the truck that they used to transport Tops's piano from one country hall to another, one shed dance to another, and one pub to another, and so, despite his lack of virtues, he stayed on.

Chapter 19

The Huon Valley, 2023

It was a fog-bound Monday morning. Mist rolling, ever seaward from far upriver where the Huon forms in the west, fed by sparkling mountain streams, before being joined by other rivers and tributaries, the Anne, the Cracroft, the Picton, the Weld, the Arve, the Russell and the Little Denison. Each of these rivers, running through ancient forests, remote wilderness and craggy highlands, seemingly pulls the clouds from the sky to weave the great white dragon of fog. Loved and hated by the residents of the Huon Valley, it is a fog that settles in for a morning, or a day, or even a week, if no wind comes to cast it off.

At the Glen, Haley had recovered from the dramas of the weekend. She felt ready to meet the new week with both optimism and that enchanting lightness that comes when one has had just a taste of romance, after years of being alone. Haley had in-school private students over at Cygnet

Primary School that afternoon, but her morning was her own. She put on her ugg boots and a coat and walked the fifty metres or so to the letterbox to check the mail. A heavy dew covered the ground. *Two months' time, and it will be a frost, rather than dew, covering everything,* she mused.

At the letter box, which shared the corner post with boxes belonging to several neighbours, she found three pieces of mail awaiting: a catalogue from Bunnings, which she considered perusing before throwing it away, a water bill, and finally a letter from her mother. *At last, Mum! You certainly make me wait to hear back from you.* Haley took her mail and turned back towards the cottage. As she turned, she saw, on the ground, a long brown feather. She picked it up and turned it in her fingers. *A wedge-tailed eagle's feather. That's something you rarely find on the ground. Must have been from a giant creature.* When she was back inside, she placed the huge feather in a jar containing other feathers that she had collected over the past year or so. She then set about reading her mother's letter while drinking her first coffee for the day.

Dearest Haley

Sorry that I haven't written. I didn't want to ring and tell you bad news, but Jack had a scare a month back now. He had a minor stroke, and is now on blood thinners and a stronger blood-pressure tablet. He had trouble walking; a balance thing, but has been going to the physio in Port Elliot and is pretty much back to normal now. Needless to say, it was scary for both of us. I depend on him so much, and now he is equally dependent on me. Still, I am so glad that we have each other. I truly hope that you will find someone one day too. You know that I would love to have some grandchildren.

Regarding your question about Artie's family dairy; in truth all I can say is that the track there was somewhere off the right-hand side of Daleys Rd, if you were heading south. It wasn't marked, apart from a sign nailed to a tree saying 'McGribben's Dairy', that had an arrow pointing up the track. I remember, that once we were on that track, we headed west for about five or more miles. When the track rises into the hills it splits in two, one track goes even further into the hills, the other descends back down to flat pasture. Take the latter.

I can't help you with the problem of how to find the initial turn-off to the track, if the sign and the tree are gone. It was so long ago and I only ever went there twice. My memory of that whole area is a bit foggy. I am surprised I could even remember that the track split in two, further up.

Sorry if that is all a bit vague. Most things are a bit vague for me these days. I hope your business is doing well. We miss seeing you. Maybe next summer you can come over for a visit?

Your Loving Mum,

Liza.

Compared with her previously obsessive curiosity, Haley's desire to find the old McGribben dairy had already diminished somewhat. She now had more immediate concerns. There was her ever-growing batch of violin and cello students, her new enthusiasm for folk and community music, her friendship with Aaron Larsen, which seemed to be morphing into something else, not to mention the Dover District High String Ensemble, the problem of Jesse Doolan, and finally the enigma of the Testore. Finding her father's childhood home now seemed the least of her concerns, even an indulgence. Nevertheless, she was glad to get mail from her mother, whose letters were becoming as rare as hen's teeth of late. Haley sighed. If only her mother would get a smart phone, or email – but she knew full well that it was too late for her mother to enter the digital age.

Aaron Larsen's Home and Workshop

Aaron's headache had finally begun to ease. He had spent most of Sunday in bed. He had a lot to ponder upon. By Monday morning he had found a new lease of life. He drove down to the city and bought a new wheel for his pushbike, to replace the one mangled in the crash. Then, returning home, he suddenly felt how empty the place seemed.

Haley had stayed just one night, but somehow her presence had filled his house with something that he hadn't even recognised as missing up until that point. He recalled their last embrace, the shy but intimate kiss, and that feeling of not wanting it to end. Thinking of Haley, though, reminded him of the beast in all its fragile pieces, waiting for his gentle care, there on the workshop bench.

Over a coffee, he sat taking stock of his motivations. Now he had more reasons than ever to knuckle down to work. However tricky the job was, he needed to get it done now, for at least three good reasons. First, he had to have it done in time for his assessment for the Cremona scholarship entry – he didn't have long. Second, if that Dover girl was going to have it by her birthday it had to be finished soon. Finally, he really wanted Haley to see that he could come good on his promises. And if that Jess girl didn't want it, Haley would have a restored antique instrument that she could play herself or sell on.

With the most tender touch, Aaron began scraping out the varnish and resin that had filled cracks in the plates, and in some places kept them from falling apart. He could neither identify nor match the strange European pine from which the plates were cut. He experimented with various timbers that he had lying in the wood bin in the workshop, but found that none of the local or imported timbers in his collection matched.

After a break for lunch, he tried to distract himself, from what seemed an intractable problem, by contemplating giving his beard a trim. He had been asking himself whether he should attend more to his appearance. He hoped that Haley liked him as he was. Looking in the mirror, he was about to give up the idea of trimming his whiskers when he noticed something out of left field. The edge of the mirror was made of celery-top pine, a golden Tasmanian timber that had become more valuable as it became ever more scarce. The mirror and frame had been a gift from his father, who had made the frame himself. Consequently, it had some sentimental value for Aaron. He realised it was exactly the same colour as the timber used on the Testore and, further, the grain was not too dissimilar. He unhooked the mirror and took it back down to the workshop. It was as close a match as he was likely to find, short of visiting Italy and going looking there. He needed about four strips to fill those cracks. He turned the mirror over, and made a judgement that he could shave the inside edge off each side of the frame. In this way he would not visibly damage his father's work.

In a short time, he had the perfect filler for the cracks on the Testore. He shaped the shavings into delicate splinters, matched by eye to the size of the cracks they were to fill. He used a gum and hoof glue, mixed in accord with an Italian recipe from the Baroque era. He squeezed the splinters into their places, wiped off excess glue and then left them to dry.

In a day or two he would sand them back, so that no flaw in the curvature of each plate would be visible.

By the Wednesday he had two perfectly sanded plates. The plates, however, could not be re-joined yet. He needed to check their pitch, as Aksel Frederiksen had taught him back in Copenhagen. More challenging though, was the problem of the neck.

It had been made, so it seemed, with green timber, an offcut from the pruned branch of an apple tree. It had an eccentric grain that had twisted, despite the efforts of at least one earlier restorer to straighten it. Aaron considered his choices. He could buy some suitable maple, or other hardwood, and make an entirely new neck, but that would be untrue to the project of restoring a 300-year-old violin with fidelity to its original timbers and components. Alternatively, he could try to get this recalcitrant neck to do something that it had never done, and somehow force it to follow a true line. Perhaps he should text Roberto, or even Aksel, and see if they had any advice. He had straightened a guitar neck that was just as badly warped, but with this ridiculous violin neck, he had so little wood to work with. What to do next?

Dover

Diane and Shelley were sharing stories about the challenges of raising teenage girls.

'Anthea has the usual issues but seems easy-peasy compared to your poor little Jess,' said Shelley.

'Jesse was no trouble at all for years though, Shell. When she suddenly stopped playing her violin it was bad enough, but since Alf died, she has never been the same. Recently she seems to be getting a little steadier in herself. Less tantrums, and she's now eating regular meals again. The therapist suggested that in her age group anorexia's sometimes an expression of a desire to remain in childhood, and might be part of an anxiety and sadness about the big changes we've had to go through.'

Shelley nodded and placed her hand softly upon Diane's. 'Anthea told me how much Jess misses her dad.'

'She still has dreams where he appears, but thankfully she doesn't claim to actually see him now, like she said she did for a while there. You know, Shell, she was such a Daddy's girl. It's hard for her to give up all that.'

'Well, Anthea can get moody too sometimes, but I put that down to period pain. Think she would be used to it after two years.'

'Does one ever get used to it?' asked Diane jokingly. 'I was worried that Jesse was never going to get her periods again. They had only just started a few years back before they stopped. Refusing food for so long seemed to have kept her body from maturing. Now that she is back to eating properly, her monthlies have finally started again. Mood swings and grumbles or not, I take that as a sign of normality!'

They both laughed.

Dover District High

Jesse was noticing the changes in her body more than anyone else was. She had started looking at boys differently, and a few would respond looking back at her, as if to evaluate their chances. She guessed that she must face the inevitable, sooner or later. Cheryl had once asked her why she hadn't had a boyfriend.

'Don't see the point, don't feel the need. Perhaps I'm just a late developer,' she had remarked, trying to pass off an honest self-appraisal as an expression of wilful individuality. Either way, Cheryl had seemed to accept that answer at that time.

Now, though, things for Jesse were different.

When she was in science class, she chose the desk next to Tyson. While the teacher was busy writing on the board she leaned over and whispered, 'Hey Ty, saw you out in the canoe just before dark the other day. How was that sunset?'

'I'm trying to get out on the water at least four times each week. If I wake up early enough, I sometimes go for a paddle before school even,' he replied.

'That's so cool!'

Seeing the teacher had turned around, they ended the conversation and got down to pretending to write study notes. Tyson wrote something and slipped it to Jesse. *Would you like to come out in the canoe next weekend? It has two seats and I've got a spare lifejacket and an extra paddle.* She merely nodded. She'd reply more fully during the lunch break, when they were not drawing the attention of the science teacher.

When lunch came, however, she stopped and ate with Kirra and Cheryl before going off looking for Tyson. As they sat on the lawn Wattle came past with her guitar, slim and upright, with a mass of dark braids bouncing along with her confident gait. She flashed her green eyes and nodded towards them in acknowledgment before heading off in the direction of the music room.

'Smart bitch,' mumbled Kirra. But the others chose not to respond or chip in.

After she had eaten, Jesse went looking for Tyson. She couldn't locate him anywhere around the grounds. She tried the sports hall. Still no luck. In the corridor, she heard voices coming from the music room. Looking in the door she saw Tyson holding one of the school guitars, while Wattle seemed to be showing him a chord and a picking pattern. They were both focused intently on whatever it was they were doing, and neither had seen her. Though she felt like barging in on them, a voice in her mind told her to save face and just walk away unnoticed. For a second time she had felt the red blush of jealousy rising within her. She hated the feeling, and even more despised that her own vulnerability had been revealed to her. *Seems like Kirra was right about that green-eyed opportunist. I guess she'll be saying 'I told you so!'* she thought.

When she again found Kirra and Cheryl, they had just come back from the oval, where they had been kicking a football with some year ten boys. Kirra was beaming as if she was in her element, which of course she was. When she had cooled down, Jesse decided to confide in her. 'Kirra, I want to share my feelings with you. I have to tell someone, it's driving me mad.'

Kirra made a face as if she was not sure what to make of this, but responded nevertheless. 'Let it rip, love. I'm all ears.'

When Jesse had confided in Kirra, both about her recent feelings for Tyson and how it seemed that Tyson and Wattle had hitched up, Kirra was quick to reply. 'Jesse, you have just got to go up to Tyson, and tell 'im that you like him. And, yeah, you might feel silly doing it, but he's not going to read your bloody mind for you. But, first things first, just tell Wattle to piss off and leave our Dover boys alone.'

Jesse was no stranger to anger, but despite the occasional outbursts at her mother or teachers, most of that vitriol, and the harm that followed from it, had been directed against herself and at the hand that fate seemed determined to deal her. She never felt comfortable with Kirra's quickness to anger towards her peers and rivals. Kirra's anger seemed always one brimming with the implied threat of physical violence. *That's not me, but maybe I have to become more like Kirra and the other hard nuts around here.* She thought it over to herself, uncomfortable with the idea, but feeling the potent inevitability of it all.

Chapter 20

The Huon Valley, 1968

It breaks its banks every seven to ten years. A week of torrential rain, incessant and unrelenting, fills a hundred mountain streams, which, in turn, swell the Huon River until it spills over into the flatlands and paddocks, from Judbury to Huonville. Even when the wide green fields have become duck-ponds and lakes, the floodwaters do not relent, instead they gather and grow until they spill across the bridge and down the Main Road. Sometimes sand-bagging saves the shops and other businesses from real damage, but sometimes not. This Friday the swollen river was up to the bridge, but had not yet spilled down the road. Yet the unrelenting torrent of tannin, mud, dead cattle, spoilt fruit and uprooted trees threatened. The locals were all on tenterhooks, listening closely to the radio for a weather update.

Coming down from the dry plains of the Coal River Valley, Tommy McGuire hadn't bothered to check the weather further south, in the Huon area, even though that was where he had to be before dark. His job was to drive his cousin, Tops McGuire, to this gig or that, whether it be travelling as far south as Franklin, or as far north as Oatlands. Most weeks he would haul her iron upright piano onto the truck; rolling it up the incline on boards that he kept in the tray. He would tie the piano with ropes, to ensure that it was secure, then cover it with old woollen blankets and a canvas to protect it from the weather.

Topsy would be there waiting for him, all made up, in her long yellow dress and with her golden hair in its perfectly trained beehive. He would pick her, and her piano up, and they would drive to whichever village hall, or orchard shed, or pub, was hosting a country dance or old-time sing-a-long. This Friday, they would be heading up to Fern Tree, around the old Huon Highway, then down from Vinces Saddle into the Huon Valley.

An orchardist from Franklin, in the Huon, had rung Tops asking if she could come down and play for a shed dance, in New Road. He had assured her that she would not have to play for the whole dance, as there were a host of local melodeon players who would cover the dance sets whenever she needed a break. He also mentioned that those local musicians had heard of her, and would enjoy a chance to play along with her if she wanted that. Tops was always up for these sorts of gigs. Playing for dances and parties was her life.

As a child, Violet Topsy McGuire had taken formal piano lessons, but after she reached her mid-teens, her parents, strapped for cash, pulled the rug on her lessons. She had stopped playing for a few years. Throughout that time, she attended all the country dances she could, from Bagdad to Kempton, from Brighton to Richmond. As she danced, she would listen to all the old fiddlers and melodeon players who played for these events, and soak up the melodies she heard. There was hardly a mazurka, polka, waltz, hornpipe, or schottische, and the like, played in Southern Tasmania, that she couldn't whistle from memory.

Eventually, she tried finding these tunes on the piano. The melodies were easy enough to grasp, provided they were in the common keys of C, G, D, or F. However, she was not satisfied just playing the simple tunes, as alone they lacked the impetus to propel a dance.

Her real reintroduction to piano came after a visit to Hobart. From the street, she had heard someone playing piano in a city music store and went in to listen. The man playing seemed to be in his mid-forties, sporting a head of curly hair. He paused playing to say hello to her, introducing himself as Ian Pearce. Watching Ian play, she figured out that he was using his left hand to play a bass note, followed by a chord in the middle voice. With his right hand, he was playing melodies and tricky fills, sometimes rocking them a bit off from the beat established by the left hand. He informed her that this way of playing was called 'stride'. While his approach was, to her ears, very jazzy, she understood right away that the technique could be adapted for country dance music.

After only a few weeks spent playing around with bass and chord patterns, then getting them to fit the traditional dance rhythms, she had figured out her own style. Thus it was that she left Chopin behind, as she mastered her country–stride hybrid.

This approach turned out to be perfect for rendering the set tunes used in the Tasmanian country dances. All she needed to do was to hum through a traditional folk melody, and she could play it, adding a lively stride accompaniment that few dancers could resist. Hers was a rare skill among piano players.

Topsy was addicted to the music, yet she was smart enough to know that her performances would not bring in enough cash to pay the bills. One year she embarked on a short apprenticeship, training under a piano tuner. This skill proved a valuable supplement to performing. She could be booked to tune pianos in the regional towns, on the same weekends that she was visiting them to perform.

As she didn't have a truck, Tommy would pick up her piano and take it, and her, to wherever she was asked to play. He demanded only petrol money, drinking money, and the right to jam along on his rough-house fiddle. Tops acquiesced to this arrangement, but made certain that her own robust piano work drowned out Tommy's badly out-of-tune violin playing. She had tried to tell Tommy that he should get a few lessons, or at least practise, but he didn't feel such a need. Tom's ear for music was so far from perfect that he was unable to notice his own shortcomings as a musician. Thankfully for Tops, Tommy usually only played a few tunes, just to be seen on stage, then proceeded to the bar, or any equivalent, where he could drink or play cards with the locals.

It was up to Tommy to be abreast of the road conditions and the like. This time, however, he had not bothered to listen to the radio and the regional weather alerts.

The road through the hills snaked its way from Fern Tree, across Mount Wellington, towards the Huon. The Huon was a valley of small towns, small farms and neat apple and pear orchards. In the next five years a loss of export markets would gut the industry and mostly end the traditional way of life in the valley. However, in 1968, the year when Tops and Tommy rattled their way through the mountain bends, the growers still enjoyed good times.

As they approached the valley, they drove into a curtain of rain that took most of the light and colour from the late afternoon.

'Don't worry, Topsy! The tarp's waterproof. The piano will stay dry as a bone.'

'I'm not worried about that, Tom. I know they get more rain down here than round our way, but this is ridiculous. I've never seen such a downpour. I guess it's too late to swap your truck for a submarine though.'

He laughed at her ability to make any situation humorous. Tilting his head towards her as he drove he said, only half-joking, 'If you weren't my cousin, I'd ask you to marry me.'

She punched his arm. 'Pigs'll bloody fly!'

Such jokes were generally considered to be bad taste in rural Tasmania, being in some cases a little too close to the bone. What's more, Tops enjoyed being single. Nevertheless, she had what seemed to be an endless run of suitors. They took her to dinner, out on picnics, and off to dances, but before anyone could get too intimate, she would politely end that relationship, so making room for the next. It was itself a kind of dance; there was a rhythm to it and she relished the control.

By the time they reached Huonville, the largest town in the valley, they noticed water sitting over the road and it became clear that these were extreme conditions. 'Only five miles to Franklin, and we'll be there high and dry,' said Tommy, trying to reassure Tops.

While there had been a road sign, warning of hazardous driving conditions ahead, it had been washed away when the river broke its banks. Approaching the bridge that linked Huonville to Franklin, Tommy could see that water was flowing right over the bridge. Despite this, he was sure that the water level wouldn't be a problem for his beloved Bedford truck. He hadn't counted on his truck's battery dying just as they hit the halfway mark on the bridge. Tops looked out seeing logs, and drowned sheep, and rubbish flowing downstream and getting stuck on the bridge's railing. 'Geeez!' she said. 'We're well and truly bloody stuck!' She then punched Tommy's leg as hard as she could, yelling, 'Look where you have stranded us you thickhead! We could drown here if it gets any higher!'

Though it was not yet dark, clouds and rain had brought on an early twilight. No other cars were on the road. The locals, it seemed, were canny enough to stay closer to home in such conditions.

'I assume the shed dance has been cancelled,' said Tops, who was beginning to feel genuinely frightened about their predicament.

Tommy seemed paralysed by the situation. He considered getting out and wading back to Huonville, to use a pay phone or go to the local police station, but he was reluctant to leave his precious Bedford to such a capricious torrent. But as they both started to think that all was lost, another vehicle, having got a good run-up, started ploughing its way through the water on the bridge. After making it safely to the far side, the driver then got out of his car and waded knee-deep back towards them.

'Not a good place to choose to break down today! But I s'pose you've figured that out by now,' he said laconically.

Tops was going to beg him to do something, but the stranger was already onto it. 'I was just coming back from work. I've got the keys to the Town Council's machine garage. You just stay put and I'll run down and fetch a tractor and towing cable. You should be okay. Just don't get out, this current is ridiculous, nearly knocking me over at the moment.'

They both understood that their fate was completely in the stranger's hands, so they simply nodded and said meekly, 'Thank you, mate.'

The stranger returned in less than fifteen minutes, driving a large tractor. He stopped it ahead of Tom's truck, jumped off, and then hitched a cable to the truck's towbar.

'Put her in neutral now matey,' he yelled to Tommy, before revving up the tractor and tugging the Bedford onto the dry southern bank.

'You two were pretty lucky to get out of that. Good thing I'd stayed back at work a bit longer than normal.'

'Thanks so much, you're our saviour, Mr... what is your name by the way?' asked Topsy.

'Malcolm Johnstone, but just Mal to you, miss. Where are you heading?'

'I'm Tops, and this is my cousin Tom. We were off to play at an apple shed dance at New Road, Franklin.'

'Don't see that going ahead now. But you should be able to pick up some accommodation in the Old Pub. I tell you what! Why don't I continue towing you down there? I'll be late for dinner, but when I get you to Franklin I'll ring me missus from the pub, and she'll understand. Are you right for fuel mate?'

Tommy was quick to answer. 'Got three quarters of a tank still, but my battery's dead as a doornail. I hadn't checked the charge for a while, stupid bastard that I am.'

Tops nodded in silent agreement.

'Okay, I'll get my friend Marek to sort you out a new battery when we get you there. You can work out some way of paying him when you meet him. He should be in the pub. Spends a lot of his time there, after working in the garage, loves his eight ball you know.'

'Good thing you know this Eric bloke, Mal.'

'No! It's Marek not Eric! He was born in Poland. Came here after the war. Wanted to get as far from Europe as possible, so he ended up in Franklin. He's a bloody good mechanic I can tell you that. He says he did his training with Polski Fiat, the Polish branch of Fiat. That was until he went off to fight with the partisans against the Nazis. His wife was Jewish. She died in the camps and he never remarried. He still likes the girls though. Just warning you, Tops.'

Tops just laughed, and prepared herself for a slow five miles, sitting in a truck, which was being towed ponderously by a tractor.

When they arrived at the pub, they booked into the only two rooms available. Tops unloaded, then went downstairs and borrowed the phone to call the orchardist who had booked her for the shed dance.

'Yes love, we had to cancel it. No one was going out in this weather. I rang your home number but by then you'd already left.'

'Don't suppose you can still pay me?' asked Tops hopefully.

'Nope, I always pay the musicians who ask for pay by passing the hat round during the supper at the dance. No dance, no hat, no money. Again, very sorry but there's no accounting for the weather.'

Tops left it at that. 'Another lost cause,' she mumbled to herself, with stoic acceptance. Meanwhile, Tommy had been introduced to Marek, who had told him that he was happy to supply a new battery for a fair price.

Malcolm, who foresaw a long period of haggling, was more than ready to leave them to it. He tracked down Tops McGuire, who thanked him again before pecking his cheek with a goodbye kiss. 'Thanks again, you wonderful man. You better wipe my lipstick off your cheek before you get home though.'

He rubbed his face and laughed. 'Did I get it all?'

She merely nodded. Malcolm then turned and, without ceremony, slipped out of the pub before Tommy even had a chance to say goodbye.

Securing their rooms for the overnight stay had taken all their cash. It really hit home for Topsy when Tommy informed her that they would have to come up with even more money for a new battery in order to get home, assuming the river level fell back below the bridge the next day. She pondered for a while, before putting a proposal to the publican. The publican would allow them to play there. He would get on the phone and make sure the local box players knew about it. They could play as long as they wanted, but he would lock the doors to new drinkers at midnight.

By 6 p.m., the torrential rain had stopped abruptly, and a forlorn display of sunlight broke through the clouds before the sun disappeared behind the high hill west of the town. The break in the weather did bring out the local drinkers though.

The publican had told Tops that she could pass the hat around for donations when they played in the bar. Several of the blokes put down their beers, and in a series of pivots and grunts, they helped Tommy get the piano inside.

Tops started playing it before stopping, opening the lid, and doing a quick but adequate retune. In half an hour she was ready to start.

One of the locals who had recently come to the bar was a nervous-sounding bloke called Midge. He asked Tops if he could record her playing. No one had ever asked this of her before. She wasn't even sure how it could be done. But giving him her best Tammy Wynette smile, she just said, 'Sure you can!'

Midge dashed home, and was back in twenty-five minutes with a microphone, a mic-stand, and an eight track reel-to-reel recorder, which, in 1968, was state of the art equipment. It turned out that Midge had worked for the ABC as a sound technician before being replaced by a young whizz-kid from the Sydney branch.

Tops then went back up to her room. She changed into another yellow dress, then dried and brushed her hair before fixing it back into its neat beehive.

When she went back downstairs, she was surprised by the size of the crowd that had quickly packed into the bar. The publican had certainly been effective at engaging the bush telegraph, and people wanting something to do, given that their usual Friday events had mostly been cancelled, relished the idea of some live music.

The other pub in Franklin had begun to bring rock bands down. Bands with names like Midnight Revival, The Thunderbirds, or The Paul Shirley Show Band were in demand, but usually didn't need to play these remote rural venues. Tops, however, was not pop, country and western, or rock and roll. What she was giving them was her version of their own music, the old music that they had heard as children, music that they danced to in the apple shed dances, and the impromptu lounge-room dances. Music, in fact, that their parents and grandparents, and their parents before them, had danced to, and courted to. The drinkers knew that this music was not fashionable, but they also knew deep down that it was theirs.

Looking around, Tops could see at least three men holding bags, which she surmised contained instruments. Call them boxes, melodeons or windjammers, the button accordions had taken over from the fiddle as Tasmania's favourite folkloric instrument. Further, the blokes who carried them all looked at her with a special adoration, as if she was a long-lost sister, come home for the first time. One by one, they came up and introduced themselves. Lyall Mansfield, dressed in his best second-hand suit, was a mild-mannered country gentleman, with a head full of old tunes. His mate, Norm Burgess, had come from Geeveston, further south, a town without a pub. Though Geeveston was an avowedly Methodist town, Norm had been raised in a Salvation Army family; consequently, he would throw in Salvation Army hymns and gospel tunes here and there among his traditional dance-tune sets.

Over a blue flannelette shirt, the third man wore an old dinner jacket that looked like a leftover from many decades earlier. On his legs he wore a pair of baggy dungarees held up by braces. He had sparkling blue eyes, a square jaw, and shaggy hair already showing strands of grey, and had a pipe permanently fixed to his lips. Topsy noticed that the four fingers of his right hand were all missing their top joints, a clear indication of a sawmilling accident or the like. Nevertheless, he carried two boxes with him. One box, it turned out, was in the key of G, the other in C. His beaming countenance indicated that, missing phalanges or not, he was very keen to play some music with her. Tommy looked at this last fellow with a smile of recognition. They had worked side by side, harvesting hops, in the upper Derwent Valley two years earlier. He went straightway up towards him and gave him a brotherly pat on the back.

'Paddy Dawson! Been a while. I should have expected you to be here, it's your home town after all!'

'Hello there, Tommy. Keeping out of trouble old mate?'

'Doing my best, Paddy. You keeping as close to sober as is feasible?'

'Well, I still have a blow-out once a week or so. When I do, my sisters lock me out of the house and throw some blankets in the woodshed. They lock me out of the house till the grog's left me system. I s'pose it keeps me out of trouble.'

Tommy laughed, but knew Paddy well enough to know that the story was true.

'Did you do the hop-picking this year, mate?'

'Nope. There was a longer apple season than normal down 'ere, and I went and picked for Clarke's orchard. Picked 'em right through to the first weeks of April we did! A very good year for the growers.'

'Good on you! I'd like to introduce you to my cousin, Tops McGuire, the piano player.'

And so it was that on that cold, wet night in Franklin in 1968, local musicians Lyall, Norm, and Paddy met the travelling bush pianist, Topsy McGuire.

The box players let Tops start the night solo. She played a blistering polka set, with a rocking stride accompaniment. The local boys didn't know these tunes but listened carefully, each intending to piece the tunes together from memory over the next day or so. She then played and sang 'The Valley Where the Bluebird Sings', which Paddy knew well, but could not join in with as Tops's version was in an unfamiliar key. When she started playing, 'A Starry Night for a Ramble', however, all three box players joined in, and the roof nearly lifted off the old Victorian-era pub. The drinking crowd stirred, and the floorboards creaked with their dancing.

After a few more tunes, Topsy stopped playing and introduced herself to the crowd. She explained how they had been booked to play for a dance, but it had been cancelled at the last minute. She told the drinkers about the flat battery, and being saved from the flood by Mal Johnstone. Finally, she threw in a request for any donations towards the replacement battery, before returning to playing.

She played an elegant version of the 'Sunbeam Schottische' that the box players couldn't really follow. Paddy Dawson then started up a set of his own family's schottisches, starting with the 'Mountain River Schottische'. Tops had no trouble picking up these tunes, needing to hear each just once through to work them out. In no time she had added a swinging accompaniment, and her own frills and ornaments. The box players all smiled with that smile of recognition that is common to all musicians who understand that they are sharing a sublime moment.

Topsy then played 'The Onboard Waltz' and 'The Old Sleepy Town', and Paddy, who also knew these, played along. Tops and all three box players continued with a lightning-fast set that included 'My Old Woman', 'Goodbye Mick' and 'McGinty's Breakdown'. After the frenetic pace of that set, Paddy decided to play something restful. He guided Tops through his melancholy version of 'The Slave's Dream'; as usual, she picked it up quickly. It was tunes like this that reminded her of the value of all the Chopin études she had practised as a child, as they held the secret of ornamenting a piece without overriding its unique melodic content.

It was during this tune that Tommy decided to start playing along on his untuned fiddle, striking loud, and seemingly random, notes here and there. Tommy noticed everyone staring at him and, mistaking these glances for appreciation, began playing even louder. Just as he was pulling back the bow, he felt a powerful tug upon his arm. Marek gripped him and stared at him with Slavic intensity. 'For fuckas sake man. You are ruining a beautiful composition! Give that to me.' Tommy was aware that Marek was a bigger and stronger man, and so meekly conceded the point, relinquishing the instrument to him.

Marek was getting close to fifty. He had played violin in village dances back in Poland before the war, but had not touched an instrument since the Nazis ransacked his house and took his wife away. From then onwards, it was surviving, fighting, and running. He ran, in the end, all the way to the Antipodes, where he plied his trade, but never once felt the muse rise within him – until now. He took the violin into the next room, and tuned it properly before returning. He caught the melody in his mind, and played very softly, using his fingers to pluck the strings, rather than using the bow. Only when his fingers had familiarised themselves with the sequence did he begin bowing. His playing was tentative at first, but he found that his work-hardened hands could still remember how to do the gypsy vibrato. His playing locked into Paddy's melodeon and Tops's piano so well that the crowd was stunned. No one had known, until then, that the garage hand was a musician of any sort.

Tommy's jaw dropped as he heard what the Pole was coaxing out of the old beast. In that moment, Tommy realised something that had evaded him until then. This was how to play violin. This was something he could not do, had only ever pretended to do, something he would never be able to do. With this knowledge, his heart broke a little, and so he resorted to a typical bush remedy for such an ailment, by ordering a stronger drink.

The gathered musicians then played a version of 'The Prince of Wales Schottische', which the locals called 'Kick the Cow', followed by a varsovienna and then a brisk mazurka set. Tops thanked them all for their contributions before finishing off the evening's fun with a long solo bracket, singing old songs, while the men with the melodeons broke off, and went to the bar.

Lyall and Paddy confronted Marek out in the back bar, asking him how it was that he could play all the polkas, mazurkas and varsoviennas so well.

'Where do you think they originate, those dances ahh?' Marek replied. 'I was brought up playing tunes much like these, for dances back in Poland. The melodies and rhythms are a bit different down here, but the basic tune forms are much the same. I guess I am not the first Polack musician to come to these valleys ay mates!'

'Well, you're doing a bloody good job, Marek! You've surprised us all. All this time we thought you were just a grease monkey.'

After the night's entertainment had finished, Tommy once again passed the hat around, as Topsy and the box players all got a second round of applause and said their goodbyes.

Tommy counted the money, and soon realised that they were still a few dollars short of paying for the new truck battery. He was about to give Tops the bad news when Marek came up to him. Tommy went a little pale and was preparing himself to haggle, but Marek spoke first. 'Don't worry about the money. This violin is a piece of old junk, but I would really like to keep it. I'm not sure how it happened, but I think that it has called the music back to me. Let me have it, and you keep the battery. How does that sound?'

Tommy did not even hesitate. 'Marek mate, that violin sings for you, like it never did for me. I reckon you are meant to have it.'

Thus it was, that the beast changed hands once again.

Marek took the violin home, where each night after work, he would practise: Polish folk tunes, gypsy melodies, Klezmer tunes and then the many Huon Valley tunes that he learnt from Paddy Dawson when they got together to drink and play. He fancied Paddy's younger sister for a while, but she never showed any interest at all, so he stopped visiting the Dawsons before too long.

In his sixties, Marek hungered, more and more, for female company. He began visiting the girls who resided at the top end of Teetotallers Lane. There were rumours around the village that those women plied the oldest trade, but rumours are just that, and no one knows to this day if those stories had any substance. Marek, anyway, was never driven by some insatiable sexual appetite. Rather, he just enjoyed the company, and real friendship, of the girls there. He would help them with repairs around the house, and often, when other male visitors had all departed, he would play his violin for them.

It was in 1974, when Marek was spending the night with one of his favourite girls, that he suffered a massive heart attack. After regaining consciousness for a while, he looked up from the bed, seeing the women around him as angels, and spoke his last words to each. Less than an hour later, just before the ambulance and the paramedics arrived, he breathed his final breath. The girls were distraught that their strong, gentle friend had died, but were glad that he had been among them and had the chance to bid each a last goodbye.

After Marek's funeral they found a box for his fiddle, and locked it in the cupboard of the last room in which he had slept. There it remained for the next two years. In that time the property they leased changed hands. For the girls, though, life went on much as it always had until a few years later. There came a time when the new owners took the house off the rental market and were eager to move in. The women left for other lodgings in another town, leaving Marek's violin behind when they went.

Years later, long after the Federal Hotel had been renamed the Franklin Tavern, someone who recalled that magical night informed collectors of Tasmanian folklore and folk music that a recording had been made of the evening's music. Attempts to track down the recording proved unsuccessful, however. Unfortunately, where it might be – or if the recording even survived – remains unknown.

Chapter 21

Aaron Larsen's Workshop, 2023

It was the third place he had tried. It was easy to come to the conclusion that time and luck seemed to be running out for Aaron. His own steaming and bending unit had overheated and died, and as he hadn't needed it urgently before now, he hadn't bothered replacing it. One luthier had what he needed but was reluctant to allow a rival to use it, claiming, perhaps dishonestly, that he was using it all week.

One last chance, he thought. He remembered a boatbuilder that he had met at Harry's place at Franklin once. It was a longshot. This was going to be out of left field.

'Hello! Wooden Boat Centre here. How can we help you?'

'Hello there. My name's Aaron Larsen. I'm a friend of Tim's, well an acquaintance at least. I'm ringing to enquire if I could book in to use your steam box and gear, to bend a single, very short piece of wood.'

'You're lucky. No one's using it Wednesday and Thursday

this week. Does that suit you, mate?'

'Wednesday is perfect, but if I don't get exactly the right line the first time, I might need both days.'

'It will cost you $25.00 per hour. That's one hour, at least, for every 2.5 centimetres. How big is the piece exactly?'

'It's only around 14 centimetres long, but it's a brittle, delicate little piece that needs to be eased into shape.'

'Well, you'll have to factor some extra time in. I'd say that you'll be up for between $190 and $200. Does that sound fair enough?'

Aaron figured that he had little choice but agree to that fee. 'All good,' he replied.

'It'll be up to you to soak the item for a day or two before you bring it in. If you're driving down from Hobart, keep it humidified in the car so that it doesn't start drying out. Ask for Sarah when you get here, and she'll guide you through the process. Our machine might be different than the ones you're used to. Do you mind if I ask what the item is?'

'A violin neck. Three hundred years old and more.'

'Well, that's a first. We're mostly bending long boat timbers here. It might be worth watching to see how you go. It might need a bit more soaking first though.'

That was one problem solved. Aaron decided that he would immerse the neck straight away and give it three full days to hydrate, just to make sure that it would bend with precision.

Now to have a closer look at that top belly plate. The fine slivers of pine that he had inserted into the cracks in the top plate looked nearly perfect. All they needed was a bit more sanding back, and some oil, and French polishing, to match what was left of the original finish. In fact, he knew that he would have to take a lot of care, matching and restoring the original light stain, and the shellac, over the whole instrument. This did not overly concern Aaron, as that was one part of the process that he had done many times before.

Holding the belly plate lightly, he tapped it in various places. He knew that the violin had been exceptionally loud and bright. He did not want it to lose those qualities, but he was interested to see if he could find a way to make the bottom end of the sound spectrum a bit stronger and richer. Looking at the position of the bass-bar, the strip that runs under the belly plate, he determined that it was too close to the centre-line, and perhaps a little shorter than it should be. He made the hard decision to take it off and reset it from scratch. First, he removed it. He then found a piece of timber that had a similar density and glued this on to the end, and when the pieces had bonded, he sanded them into a single smooth piece. Between each phase, he took photos of the process, and progress, using his phone's camera.

In the next phase of the project, Aaron decided not to use a tuning fork to tune the plate as Aksel Frederiksen had taught him. Instead, he purchased a stethoscope from a medical supply store. He also used an electronic chromatic tuner attached to a dot-microphone. With the aid of these things, he could tap the plates in different places, and determine exactly which was the principal pitch of each part of the timber. He could also detect, by ear, the overtones or secondary pitches hidden within the stronger note. Through the stethoscope he noticed that some of these overtones seemed to be working against the principal pitch rather than helping reinforce it. This led him to experiment with sanding and even scraping the belly plate, making some areas thinner than they had been originally. He kept going back and listening, using the mic and chromatic tuner, then writing down the exact pitch of each part. On paper he kept a record of any changes that his sanding and chiselling had made.

It was ridiculously slow, precise, and time-consuming work. Aaron knew full well that if he sanded too hard, or cut too deep, he could damage the ancient instrument. He persevered though, and within a day he could detect a perfect harmonic series ringing out whenever, and wherever, the timber was tapped. He had never taken so much care in fine-tuning the pitch of the timber plate, or sound-board, of any instrument. This time, however, he was sure that his effort had paid off. The next day he went through the same process with the back plate, placing the stethoscope on every inch of the timber, reading the tuner, cutting a little, sanding a little, until the pitches he could hear across the back plate were in perfect accord with those he had heard and recorded on the top plate.

Then came the time to reapply the bass-bar. He again experimented with pitch. He asked himself what it would sound like if the bar was move further to one side, by a millimetre here, or a millimetre there. After an hour, he decided that he had found the sweet spot for the bass-bar. In this spot it would still support the curved belly plate and would also funnel the sound through the violin in a way that helped it sing.

Aaron was so excited by what he had done that he wanted Haley to come to Hobart after school to witness his sonic miracle. Haley, though, was going to be too busy with her private students, after school, to make the drive.

Instead, he asked an acquaintance, Anise, who was known for having perfect pitch, to come around and don the stethoscope. Anise confirmed that all the sounds the plates made, when tapped in different places, were in accord; so much so, that whatever section was tapped the hardest, set off what she termed a 'rainbow of harmonics' throughout the wood. Aaron was delighted and relieved. Now it was just the damn neck that needed care before he could reassemble the beast.

Roaring Beach, Dover

Diane had no work on this day. She took advantage of this, and of the fact that Jesse was at school, to drive around to Roaring Beach and go for a walk. Early white settlers were not always lacking for colourful names to designate places. However, Tasmania has at least five beaches with the unoriginal name 'Roaring Beach'. Some of these names fit better than others. The beautiful Roaring Beach, just out of Dover, would more appropriately have been named Crashing Beach. What swell there was was not generally large; rather, it was a remnant swell squeezed in between Bruny Island in the east and Southport in the west. Approaching the white sands of the long beach, waves rose to about waist height, then crashed directly down upon the shore like an axe. The water had a clear green tint to it. On the rocky, eastern point of the beach, sea eagles often made seasonal nests. Looking out further in the bay, one could make out the clusters of salmon pens, arrayed like tiny islands. The sands of the beach and dunes were bone white, and the air was cleansed fresh with salt-spray.

For Diane, walking alone here was a balm that helped calm the mind. The rhythmic crash of the waves, followed by the whispered susurrations as they withdrew from the shore through the coarse grains of granite sand, brought peace to her mind and order to her thoughts.

She was thinking about her recent dinner date. It had been nice. Having the attention of a man had been almost novel after the last few years of grieving and lonely nights. She knew that she might have come across as a little awkward at first. When the nervousness subsided, though, they had a good time making relaxed and congenial conversation, before planning an outing together in the near future.

Diane felt more concerned when her thoughts turned to Jesse. Jesse had been so much better lately, eating well and a lot less angry, but it seemed that she was running with a rough crowd. Diane knew from her own school days that this usually meant trouble down the track. Jesse had, until now, mostly turned her anger on herself. The anorexia and the episodes of self-harm seemed to have subsided, but Diane was concerned that they were being replaced by a general anger at others, and at the world.

Diane had been challenged by what life threw at her: the death of Alf, Jesse's stuff, and money worries. Nevertheless, in her heart, she remained an optimist. For her, the world was beautiful, life was to be valued, strong friendships were to be enjoyed and nurtured. Despite all that she had endured, she remained a light soul. Consequently, she was all the more disturbed by the unfamiliar darkness that Jesse carried with her each day. Diane knew, though, that Jesse needed an outlet for all of this, something to feed off the angst and to transform it. Music, and art in general, needed both dark and light in order to issue in something rich and profound. Likewise, Diane understood that Jesse needed music, to channel her pain, her passion, and her fear into something beautiful and life-affirming. *I still have to help her to stop damming up that part of herself*, thought Diane.

Diane sensed though, as a mother sometimes can, that Jesse's inner war had of late been overwritten by a more common pain. Jesse was experiencing a longing for something, or someone. As yet, it was unrequited. At her age there were so many rivals and so many disappointments. Diane sighed. *I just hope that whoever she chooses to love, treats her kindly.* She scuffed her shoes against a tuffet of marram grass to remove the sand before returning to her car.

Dover District High

Another day at school. This time in their English class, Jesse once more made sure that she was seated near Tyson. The English teacher, Ms Heaney, was very engaging, and was one of the few teachers that Jesse really liked. The class had been studying a poem by someone called James Macauley. The poem was titled 'Because'. It described a family where expressions of love had been repressed, and replaced by mere routine. It proceeded, though, to a claim that children can never know why their parents are as they are; and that, rather than judge them harshly, parents should be remembered with gratitude for the steadfast care they have provided. The poem ended with a reflection on the writer's own coming mortality and the question about how he himself would be judged. Ms Heaney asked the class what they thought of the poem.

'It's a bit bleak, Ms Heaney!' said Tyson.

Then Gary pitched in, 'It reminds me of how my father describes his own father. I never met him though; he passed away just after I came along.'

'What do you think, Kirra?' Ms Heaney asked.

'Not sure, Ms Heaney. My stepfather treats me like a piece of rubbish and can blow up at any time. I would be happy if he showed less emotion and was just a bit more into caring towards us.'

Jesse reached out to the next desk and took Kirra's hand and held it tightly.

Ms Heaney noticed Jesse's act of support and looked over to the next girl instead. 'What are your impressions, Jill?'

'Sorry Ms Heaney, I wasn't paying attention!' I'm busting, can I go to the toilet please?' This at least made Kirra giggle, and Jesse released her hand.

The teacher turned back towards Jesse. Jesse didn't really feel up to contributing but, motivated by something deeper, she poured it out anyway. 'My dad was loving, kind and funny. He was nothing like the stiff, repressed old fart in the poem. But then he died. I am not angry at him for leaving us, but I'm angry at the world or fate or whatever, for taking him away. I can understand what James McCauley is trying to say about being apprehensive about his own looming "Judgement Day". But he believed in heaven and hell, and I think that's crap. Sorry if I have offended anyone by that statement. But in the end we're going to leave our mark on the world for better or worse. I know, because I've made a cluster-fuck of things so far. I've done the closing-up thing myself. You end up making life hard for those you care about, but even worse for yourself.' At that point Jesse shocked the class, and surprised herself, by raising her wrists to show the scars from self-inflicted wounds. 'If you don't pull down your guard and show people that you love them, then what's the point of anything?

239

At that moment, Tyson looked over at Jesse with such a tender gaze that her heart melted. When the teacher had turned to another student he whispered to her, 'Still want to come canoeing some time?'

Jesse went looking for Tyson during the lunch hour, but couldn't find him. As she approached the corner of the building, she could hear someone playing guitar. Jesse could not bear the thought of seeing Tyson there, hanging out again with Wattle, so she turned around and went back into the building.

Going directly to the girls' toilets, Jesse found a booth, slammed the door and locked herself in. Then she dropped her head in her hands and began to whimper uncontrollably. She knew this feeling of old. The tendrils of hurt and anger tugging her down into their pit.

Just as she thought that despair might totally envelop her, she felt a very small but persistent voice in her mind whispering, *You don't want to go there Jess.* Taking a sudden deep breath and, feeling her abdomen start to unknot, she felt a moment of reprieve and consequent clarity. She went over what she had said in class and questioned herself. *Maybe that was all just bullshit. I feel like making myself throw up. But fuck, I hate feeling like this. Hurting myself didn't help before; it won't help now.*

Slowly her equilibrium began to return. She dried her eyes and looking in the mirror, straightened up her hair and clothes.

Seeking to avoid the yard and Wattle, and Kirra and Tyson and all the triggers of her panic, she headed down the corridor past the music room towards the hall. Passing down the corridor she couldn't help but hear the sound of two violins playing a tune. She listened intently, noticing that each player alternated between melody and harmony parts, taking turns. *Must be Miss McGribben and Anthea*, she thought. Anthea was playing so well now. They shouldn't mind if she listened and just stayed quiet.

However, when Jesse opened the door, things were not quite as she expected. When she saw the players the grabbing feeling returned to her gut. The duet, it turned out, was being played by Anthea and Wattle, who had clearly improved very quickly since she began lessons again.

Try not to show that you're jealous, Jesse told herself. This advice didn't help as it gradually dawned on her that Wattle had endeared herself, first to Tyson, and now to her best friend. Jesse remained silent, holding back until they had finished the tune. She went up to the girls, and each said hello. Jesse then turned directly to Wattle. 'I was surprised to find you in here. I thought I heard you playing guitar in the yard.'

'Ha! That would have been Tyson. He's been learning online for a while. I showed him some of my picking patterns that's all. He can do very well without me being there.'

Wattle's answer was not quite what she expected. Jesse felt unable to know how to respond. She really didn't want to come across as either hopeful, or jealous, or to show any feeling one way or another, if she could help it. She remembered a trick her therapist, Dot, had taught her. *First breathe and then distract yourself by thinking of a calming song or tune.* She thought for a while, then tried to bring to mind the sound of her former violin teacher's playing. There was a tune she had sometimes fiddled, a slow meditation in 3/4 time called 'The Druid's Prayer'. This was a starkly beautiful, old Tasmanian piece. It had apparently evolved from a nineteenth-century English composition but had morphed into something quite different than the source tune. Jesse had sensed that it had an otherworldly quality, one capable of slowing down time itself.

Her tension dissipated as the remembered melody replaced the gaggle of her thoughts.

Between moments, Jesse mustered the presence to ask something that she had been afraid to ask. At first she just looked at Wattle while trying to better organise her thoughts and feelings.

Wattle's intense green eyes met her and held her in her gaze as if to will Jesse to get it out, and say whatever it was that was bothering her.

'Wattle. Do you have a thing for Tyson? I mean, are you his girlfriend? I hope not, I've known him all my life, he's a sweety, and I really like him.'

That Jesse's last words amounted to an understatement was clear, both to Wattle and to Anthea. Wattle stared for a second, wrinkled her brow, then threw her head back and laughed. 'Ty's a friend, he's very nice, but I thought you might have figured out by now that I prefer girls.'

Wattle's unashamed admission froze Jesse in her tracks, not knowing what to say.

Wattle continued, 'I do have the hots for your friend Kirra though. I like those strong football-playing types. If I'm right about her, she'll eventually admit to herself that she likes me too. Denial can stir up a lot of anger you know. Obviously she hasn't come out yet, but I can pick 'em. Takes one to know one I guess.'

Anthea and Jesse just stood there in stunned silence. Wattle's words, just as her presence at the school had done, somehow shifted the ground beneath their feet. Everything was different now. They both understood that Wattle was right, Kirra was gay, she had been all along, and Kirra despised Wattle because she found her so darned attractive and couldn't bring herself to admit it. The truth had hit like a bolt out of the blue, before leaving an empty moment in its wake; an empty moment that was soon filled with the sound of three young women, first giggling then laughing together, almost to the point of tears.

The Glen, Tuesday night

Aaron had made a habit of emailing Haley the day-by-day photos of his progress. She would look over them, impressed, but not always sure if she was grasping all the technical details of the work. After she had reviewed his pictures, she rang him. They talked initially about the project, his work and her ideas about violin playing, but spoke more generally about their lives. They would ask questions of each other, prompting answers that led to still further questions. When Aaron told Haley that he was coming down to the Huon, early Wednesday, to steam the neck of the Testore, adding that the job might run into Thursday as well, she asked him if he wanted to stay over at her cottage.

'That's a very kind offer, Haley. I don't want to be a nuisance to you though,' he replied, trying to underplay his enthusiasm. 'Shall I bring wine, bread, and cheeses down? Or is there anything else you would prefer?'

'Well!' Haley paused a moment. 'You could bring me down some craft beer, a Shambles, or a Hobart Brewing Company IPA, preferably, or maybe a Moo Brew dark ale. I save my wine drinking for the weekends, when I don't have to work the next day. Beer's not as strong, and one or two is always enough for me!'

'I didn't know you were a craft-beer snob! Well, there are a few on your list I haven't tried yet. I'm looking forward to it. I'll bring enough for both of us!'

'Sounds good!' she said. 'See you tomorrow at my place, after work. I'll text you the directions. Bye, Aaron.'

Before Haley went off-line she noticed that there were new items in her spam box. She mostly did a blanket delete of whatever ended up there, but recently she had become a bit more careful after emails from the parents of her private students had ended up in spam and were deleted rather than read.

In the spam box she found the usual advertising and other rubbish, but then she saw an email from Richard. She was surprised to hear from her former partner and a bit perplexed by his tone. *Dear Haley, why have you neglected to answer my emails? Can we talk please?*

After she left Adelaide, she had tried her best to leave any thoughts of Richard behind. She did not give him her new mobile phone number, deeming that he didn't have to know. However, given that they had spent their formative years together, right through from school days to university graduation, they had too many shared memories for such to be erased by a simple act of will. She had loved him, but their love had become more routine than romance, and it had died a slow and drawn-out death.

Haley looked down the list in the spam box. Where were these earlier emails from Richard that she hadn't answered? She eventually found them. The first and earliest email was brief. It simply asked for her phone number and postal address, saying that he needed to talk to her then adding,

Sorry that I treated you so casually and took you for
granted. I was wrong. I have come to realise, too late, that
I still love you. Please get in touch.
Love Richard.

Haley felt physically ill. The mail from Richard was totally unexpected. It was something she didn't want to deal with. She found old feelings flooding back. The memories from her teen years, the comfort of familiar companionship, the love, the times, the resentment of being let down time and time again, the anger at herself for putting up with his routine neglect. It felt like too much to process just now. Haley went and made herself a cup of tea. As she poured the milk, she noticed that her hand was shaking. *Bloody Richard! How dare you spring this on me now just as I'm making a new life for myself. Fuck you!*

Despite her anger at Richard, and at this disturbance to her peace of mind, she could not help herself from being curious about the second, yet unopened email.

She despised Richard for thinking that he could just reach out to her, in the new life she had made, and expect things to be as they were. 'Fuck,' she said out loud. 'I hate that I still have even enough feeling for him to believe that I should at least read what he has to say.'

The second email was longer.

Dearest Haley
I understand that you might not want to hear from me again.
I admit that I took you for granted for too long, and that in
the end I was unfaithful. Because we had been together since
our early teen years, I was for a while restless, and desperate
to get an idea of what I might have missed out on. All that
time taught me though, is that I already had walked away

from what I really needed. In the year after we broke up there was a Haley-shaped hole in my world, and no one or nothing could fill it.

Every night I am haunted by dreams of your smiling eyes, your ginger curls and your lips. It took me a while, but I know now that without you, my life is not worth living. Lately I have been looking for positions in Hobart, in order to be closer to you. I would love to come and stay with you, and just be with you for a while. If you will have me, you could show me around Tasmania. I would love to be part of your new life.

One employer in Hobart has said that he is keen to have me on board. I don't mean to pressure you though. If you really don't want me back, I won't come over. My future is entirely in your hands.

Your love, forever,
Richard.

'You pathetic bastard!' yelled Haley. 'Why are you laying this on me now, it's been years for fuck's sake?' Despite the force of these sentiments, she started to find herself feeling sorry for him, and then sorry for herself, as their old love, and the loss of that love, broke back through the barrier of the walls she had built.

I won't write back. No, I won't. I need time to calm down and come to grips with all of this before I respond. Maybe I do miss having a constant partner. Maybe I do miss Richard even. I just don't know, and I am way too tired to make any decisions, and tomorrow I have to teach over at Cygnet, then take some students here, and then Aaron is coming around. Shit, it's too bloody hard. Damn you, Richard!

That night, despite the tug and turmoil of contrary feelings, Haley, paradoxically, slept deeply and peacefully.

Chapter 22

Braeside Road, Franklin, 1973

His feet crackled the frosty grass. *She's a cold one. Not too cold for you girls to lay though, I reckon!* Joe Flakemore slipped bony fingers out of his gloves just long enough to search through the straw nests in the chook pen. He gathered up a good half a dozen fresh eggs and placed them in an old pot before being distracted by something he saw out the corner of his eye.

Looked like someone over at Terry's place next door was setting up a tripod in the paddock where the orchard had been grubbed out a month before. *A surveyor. I know what that means. Poor old Tezza, guess he had no other choice. Well, he's just one of many. I'll pop over and chew the fat with him when I've milked Polly and 'ad some breaky.*

After eating, Joe noticed that the hoarfrost had only just begun to melt. In the distance the valley was still lost beneath the white river-fog, the taller hills jutting through like islands in the sky. The surveyor had been and gone before 10 a.m.

Terry had seen his old mate coming down the road and waved him over to the gate. Joe could not but notice the *For Sale* sign that Terry had just hammered into the winter ground. He read the signs of shame and defeat on his neighbour's face but knew Terry well enough to know that he would be met with stoic resolve and good humour.

'You selling up Tez?'

'Yes, mate. No bloody choice. S'not easy.'

'So the state government gave you a bit of money to grub your apple trees out. Wasn't ever going to be enough ay?'

'Joe, I had to weigh it up. I always imagined the young bloke taking over the orchard, keeping it in the family like it has been for over a hundred bloody years. But after he stepped on that mine in Nam he won't be doing any farm work, ever. I can't hold on myself. Should have mixed it up like you did and not just relied on one type of crop... but that was where the money was, until now.'

Joe hung his head slightly, quietly counting his blessings. He knew that this all-too-common predicament didn't really apply to him. 'Well, I never reaped big money from my little orchard, lived mostly on the poultry, the vegies, the cows and a bit of seasonal work. Things won't change so much for me, I'll have to sell a bit more firewood, that's all. But the valley as we know it won't ever be the same. Not after the last couple of years. Going to be sad to see you leave. We've been mates since school days!'

Terry smiled a sad half-smile and tried not to tear up.

'Well I won't be going far old mate. My daughter's husband is gunna let me and the missus live in the granny flat out the back of their place in Huonville.'

'That's good I s'pose. Well, I guess you've got to know when too much is too much.'

'Yep! We growers got hit by two big death blows, one after the other, that's about all we can cope with. Those damn hail storms last year, fucked the harvest for everyone. Now the Poms have joined the bloody Common Market and tell us they don't want Tasmanian fruit any more. T'was going to be a good crop too ... but no bastard wants to buy it and the Premier's offered cash if we grub it all out. It was either go with that or declare bankruptcy!'

Joe kicked a fence post in response. 'Yes, those Brits! How many boys from down here died fighting in the bloody Pommy wars? All those names on the honour boards in the Palais! Grandfathers, fathers, uncles, sons, good Huon blokes! Generations gutted and what do we get for it? They sign up to buying apples from the Krauts and the Frogs and leave us buggered, with our fruit rotting on the trees and nowhere to go!' Joe hadn't needed to replay this. Terry, too distraught to respond, averted his gaze to the distance and the fog that was beginning to break up on the far side of the valley.

Joe scanned the new pegs on the paddocks. 'I see you've subdivided into three acreages mate. S'pose we'll be havin' a bunch of new neighbours round here.'

'Yep. But I'll be gone.' Terry nodded in the direction of the grey timber barn. 'Already had a young bloke down looking at the old apple shed there. Strewth, you should have seen him! All long hair and shaggy beard. Didn't look like a bloke who'd done a day of farm work in his life. He checked out the shed. Said he planned to fix the foundations at the downhill end and set up a pottery in there. Doing ceramics or something! Good on him if he can get something going. Who knows what sort of townie weirdos will buy the other blocks?'

Joe saw his opportunity to introduce some much-needed levity into the conversation. 'Well it's a good thing that he'll see to those foundations, they've been dodgy for years. You never did get round to it didya Gunner? Still, I'm guessing there won't ever be dance nights in that apple shed again?'

'No, them days were grand old days, but they's over now, and I can't see 'em ever coming back. Remember how we'd host the dance one weekend, then the next weekend we'd take the bush tracks to Jacksons Road, or even New Road or up the Swamp Road, for the dances there. Every orchardist family trying to outdo the others with the hospitality, the music, the flowers, the spread of tucker. It was what we did, and what our grandparents before us did.'

Joe, feeling that nostalgia was taking a turn towards melancholy, redirected the conversation back towards Terry's shed. 'Yep, Tez! I well remember how your shed floor would shake, and dip, when the dancers went down the dodgy end. You'd always say you were gunna fix it before the next event!'

Terry and Joe laughed the familiar laughter of old friends reviewing cherished memories.

'Do ya remember that night when Paddy Dawson was playing his box for the dance there in that corner, Joe? One tune after the other, like a demon, but pissed out of his head, then still playing he just rolled off his chair and onto the floor and went out like a light. He was still there in the same position holding his blooming windjammer when he woke up there next morning!'

Joe smiled, relieved that their memories had brought some levity back to the situation at hand. 'Remember it as if it was yesterday! T'wasn't long after that that his sisters and big brother gave him the ultimatum. Stay away from the booze, and the pub, or sleep in the woodshed for the rest of your life.'

'Ha, it seemed to work. Mostly! But word is that Paddy still hits the grog every now and then. Doesn't dare go home until he's dry again. Edie, his younger sister, insists that he gets himself scrubbed up and sober for church by Sunday.'

'Well, Joe, it was always Edie what wore the trousers in that family, ay!'

Whatever fortune was to come their way, both Joe and Terry were the kind of men that would meet it with good humour, and stoic perseverance, more or less. The two old mates continued to relive the glory years for the rest of the morning. Later though, Joe returned home melancholy with the knowledge that he was losing a dear neighbour, with the knowledge that a way of life that had flourished since the 1870s was now over. Some larger orchard enterprises would likely survive, but the age of the small family orchards that bustled with the autumn harvests, and which rang with the joyous sounds of apple shed dances on the long summer nights, had passed forever.

Mick Flanagan, Hobart, 1975

Right away Mick had felt at home. Straight off the ship from Ireland and a friend had picked him up and driven him directly to a Sydney pub session. There, amid choruses of Irish songs, bush ballads, and Australian unionist broadsides, he had the first taste of life in his new country. Now, on his first trip to Hobart, Tasmania, there was something vaguely familiar about it all. He took in the old Georgian sandstone architecture, the harbour, the river, the tall ships, and the fishing boats in the docks as he walked on his way to check out the venue where he would be performing in a few hours.

The Sittin-in Folk Club at 63 Salamanca Place, Hobart, was known to Mick. Among folkies who had travelled to Hobart it had a sound reputation and he was very keen to play there. Though it was quieter during Hobart's chill winter months, he had heard to expect big crowds during these long summer nights.

Entering the old colonial building, he came first into a café and then was directed through a door at the rear of the café to the performance space. A central aisle separated two banks of seats, possibly enough for an audience of 200. Around the perimeter was an array of workshops for leather-workers, potters and glassblowers, as well as shops, boutiques and small galleries and the like. He was not alone. Hearing some happy strains of music, Mick raised an eyebrow.

From behind the stage area he could hear a lone fiddler practising. He smiled. *I know that piece!*

He wandered back there and saw a young blonde woman playing. She was facing the other direction and, being fully engaged in the music, neither saw him nor heard him come in.

Lovely tone, he thought, noting that she had the technique of a classically trained player. It was clear though that she was trying to adapt to more of a folk style with its lighter bowing and minimal vibrato.

Mick caught sight of the book on the chair beside her. He recognised it from the cover, *Chief O'Neill's Book of 1001 Irish Tunes*, a well-known tome from the early twentieth century. She was, however, playing a piece composed a tad more recently.

He stood by, listening silently and being careful not to startle the fiddler. When she finished the tune, he clapped softly.

His elfin smile beamed from behind his salt-and-pepper beard. She froze in surprise for a moment, then spoke. 'Oh hello! I didn't know anyone was listening.'

'I heard the fiddling and thought I'd see where it was coming from. Very nice rendition by the way!'

She tilted her head so that her fair hair fell across one shoulder. 'Do you know of "Cooley's Reel" then?'

'That I do. Not only that, but I was in the room back in Galway when my uncles Joe and Seamus Cooley stitched it together!'

'What! Really! That's such a coincidence given that I was just learning it. Oh, I'm Phillipa by the way. I'm pencilled in for a short bracket on stage tonight and I was just trying out a few tunes for my set.'

'Pleased to meet you. I'm Mick. Mick Flanagan. I'm singing some ballads here tonight myself.'

'New in town?'

'Just arrived today. Been outback mining. Before then I was in Sydney for a time.'

'How are you finding it so far?'

'Hobart seems a very pretty place. I could do worse than relocate here, but not sure what I'd do for work.'

'So you're from Galway originally?'

'Sure am. Raised in the Cooley household. My four uncles were all immersed in the music, one way or another.'

'It wasn't just Joe and Seamus then? They're two whose names I've heard talked about in Celtic music circles.'

'Oh yes. Then there was Jack. Played what we Galway Irish called the tambourine, but which is better known these days as the bodhran. He was in the Tulla Ceili band, along with Joe and Seamus.'

'I met another Irish musician who mentioned the Tulla Ceili band. Said they were important in keeping the music and the dances going.'

'They were at that. But Joe also travelled all over, reviving, teaching and collecting the old tunes.'

'Who was your other uncle then, Mick?'

'Oh, that was Uncle Tommy Cooley, a great unaccompanied singer. I also sing unaccompanied, like Tommy did, or at least I'd like to think so. Still, I have started tinkering on the button accordion and some guitar too. Could help with the busking, I hope.'

Mick noticed Phillipa opening a page of Chief O'Neill's tune book. 'What is the next tune you'll be practising then? Don't read the notes myself, but I must say that book is known as a treasure by those that do. Did you know that Frank O'Neill was the Chief of Police in Chicago in the early 1900s?'

Phillipa looked puzzled. 'Really? I'd always assumed that the Chief part referred to an Irish Clan leader. You know the band the Chieftains, well like that.'

'Ha! Lots of people think that. No, Francis O'Neill did a great thing. He collected every tune the Chicago Irish had brought from every corner of Erin that they had come from. I grant that this collection here saved Irish music back then when people were leaving in droves.

'When Uncle Joe got there in the 1960s though, the music had all but gone. The grandchildren of the migrants from O'Neill's era still held the Ceili dances, but they danced to recorded music. Joe saw to that. Ran workshops of traditional music and playing and in no time, Chicago had a vibrant Irish music scene again.'

Phillipa's bright smile indicated that she was enthralled by Mick's stories. Nevertheless, he decided to let her get back to practising.

Popping back into the café, he sat and perused the cards he kept in his pockets. On these he had written the lyrics of numerous songs ready for a pre-performance prompt.

The Folk Club café slowly filled with those there for the music; a few artist types, some hippies, and a few random drunks who had wandered in by mistake. As the crowd gathered and dusk came a fog gathered on the bay. Not too far away a ship was cutting through smooth waters. SS *Lake Illawarra* headed towards the mouth of the river Derwent and Sullivan's Cove.

On that same balmy night on 5 January 1975, the *Lake Illawarra* smashed into one of the great pylons of the kilometre-long Tasman bridge, bringing down a section, taking lives and cars, and splitting the city of Hobart in two. It was a night that Mick Flanagan would never forget.

He was already on stage, performing a set, at the Folk Club in Salamanca. A large crowd had come out for the music. On each side of the aisle the seats were full. Mick was new to Tasmania and its folk scene, but things seemed to be going well enough. From the stage his smile, tenor voice, and hoard of ballads held the gathered throng spellbound.

Suddenly, and without warning, the performance was interrupted mid-set. A young, long-haired man in white jeans, black motorcycle boots and an embroidered Afghani shirt abruptly threw open the doors from the café area and rushed up the aisle yelling loudly. 'Everyone, this is serious! Please pay attention! The Tasman bridge has collapsed. Honestly, the bridge has come down.'

Fully engaged with the night's entertainment, members of the audience responded dismissively, with shouts of 'Shut up!' 'Get out!' or 'Fuck off!' Clearly the majority of the crowd did not believe what they had just heard. Most imagined that, rather than giving earnest warning, the young man was most likely to be tripping on mushrooms or some other psychoactive substance.

Mick had yet to establish his credentials within the folk scene. For him this seemed like a strange and truncated beginning to things. He would soon be touched by another calamity that was to befall Hobart. Within weeks of the bridge collapse and the consequent severing of Hobart, the Folk Club at 63 Salamanca Place was gutted by fire. Attempts to relocate it to new venues happened but with indifferent results. The glory days of the Salamanca folk scene were over.

These events came at a time when the sudden availability of cheap land in the Huon Valley attracted artists, musicians, organic gardeners, and alternative life-stylers to the area. Ironically, the valley which had largely lost its own folk culture less than a decade earlier became the new centre of gravity for the folk music revivalists.

Franklin, The Huon Valley

Months after that tragic night, Mick's partner, Helen, joined him in Tasmania. Before long they established themselves as regular performers in folk music clubs and as buskers in the city mall. Ah year and a half later, they moved into a Federation-style cottage that Mick had already purchased in Teetotallers Lane, Franklin, taking advantage of the cheap prices for property in the wake of the collapse of the apple and pear industry. It was a quaint cottage on a steeply sloping block. A south-east-facing veranda commanded a spectacular view of the river and village below. They moved into the cottage having very little knowledge of its history, nor of its previous tenants other than a few stories and rumours. Consequently, they were much surprised to find, in a musty wooden cupboard left by the former tenants, an old, weathered violin.

'I wonder who this once belonged to,' Helen remarked. Mick shrugged then said, 'Let's string it up with new strings and keep it for when we have visitors who play the fiddle.'

Not long after they set up house in Franklin, Mick and Helen coordinated with other new arrivals to the area to launch the first official Franklin Folk Club. In this enterprise they were joined by fellow Irishman Frank Byrne, Manx man Ian Crelin and his wife Liz, blues and folk revival musician Chris Cruise and a handful of others. When Kon Reitler, a German immigrant who had made his money as an abalone diver, bought the Old Pub and renamed it the Franklin Tavern, he was happy to open his bar to the Flanagans and the other folkies. Once more, tunes and songs rang out as the ale flowed. Kon relished both the energy and the trade that the newcomers brought to the tavern.

The music the recent arrivals played grew out of the growing interest in traditional British, Irish and American roots music. This new generation of enthusiasts brought their music into the Huon Valley, while all the time remaining mostly unaware that only a generation earlier, the valley, like other parts of Tasmania, had its own deeply traditional music and dance forms. A seemingly archaic music that had flourished back in the decades before the local councils passed laws to prohibit unsolicited dances, before better radio reception had brought American pop and country music into homes and bars, and before the younger folks of the valley had begun to find their grandparents' music a source of embarrassment.

By the time the folk revivalists moved into the valley, the older local musicians rarely played other than for family and friends. Consequently the newcomers to the Huon Valley, for all their interest in traditional music, knew almost nothing of the local folk music which had evolved there over a century and a half.

One night in '79 Mick was running the club, and he noticed a roughly dressed older man standing and staring towards his table. Mick asked the older local if he knew someone at the table or in the folk club. Paddy Dawson smiled and replied whimsically, pointing to the melodeons sitting on the table. 'No, I don't know any of yous, but I do know those things!'

Mick and Paddy exchanged polite introductions. When Mick had determined that Paddy played the box, he asked him if he would like to perform a tune for the gathering. Without further prompting, Paddy pulled out his own windjammer from its hessian bag. It had been over ten years now since the night that Tops McGuire had come down to Franklin to play. Paddy's box-playing mates, Lyall and Norm, didn't get out much anymore and Paddy had few chances to play for people and fewer to play with people.

Paddy lacked teeth, and consequently his mumbled introduction, in his sing-song local brogue, came out sounding like a foreign language to most of the new settlers. 'I'll play yous all some tunes from the old apple shed dance days, tunes what my dad learned us.'

He launched into a set of quaint waltzes, some polkas, and rickety mazurkas that none of the folk club attendees recognised. Then to finish off his bracket Paddy performed a playful slow jig that several audience members thought sounded familiar.

'What do you call that tune, Paddy?' asked a sandy-haired bloke at the table. 'From what I can make out it seems to be a version of an old Irish harp tune by Turlough O'Carolan called "Planxty Fanny Power", though the second section is completely different than the one in the Irish tune-books.'

Paddy thought about things for a while then added, 'Well the old Dad taught me that one, and he must have got it from his own ol' dad. He did think it was one the family brought over from Ireland, sometime way back in the convict times. And we always knew it as "Mrs McGregor's Daughter". Whatever you call it, I always knowed that it was an old one. And it's been here in Tas for a very long time.'

Some of the folkies noted with interest that the old Tasmanian versions of the tunes, as Paddy had played them, contained their own regional peculiarities, a twist here, a turn there. Further there were some tune forms that many had never heard before.

⟿

Paddy had found the young folk at the pub friendly enough, and he had enjoyed the company, the drink, and the sharing of tunes. However, he relented and decided to leave as his sister's insistence that he avoid the pub and the ale came to mind. He quietly weighed the situation, thinking, *It's grand that they have their own take on the music, something different than our apple shed tunes, but kinda related. I'd like to come again and play the real old tunes for 'em, but Edie and Ivy'd scold me for it. Should know better than to frequent the town's drinking holes these days. I'll only be making a mess of things.*

Before packing away his box he turned to his newly found friends with his blue eyes twinkling. 'You know yous can always come around to the old place up the Swamp Road and share a tune or two. There'll be a cup of tea and a scone for ya if yous do. Just ask anyone what lives up there for the old Dawson home and they'll show ya where we are.'

After the night's fun he bid his fond farewells and tramped the few kilometres down the highway then up the hill to his home. It was just a humble wooden cottage built from salvaged materials and reject timber during the Depression, sitting there now amid what was once a thriving small-fruits farm; a tangle of redcurrants, blackcurrants, raspberries and blueberries.

After that night Paddy rarely returned to the folk club. His astute younger sister had anticipated the return of old demons and warned him, 'You know if you come back drunk we'll lock you out, and you'll have to sleep it off in the woodshed, Paddy. Make sure you scrub up alright for church on Sunday or we'll hide your tobacco. If you are missing the music you can always invite them musicians around here for a play with us.'

As he walked the long walk home, head full of that night's tunes, he thought, 'I still have a sister that I can play the old tunes with – in our own way. Maybe, one day or another, some of these newcomers might ask us to teach them the real old music from around here, or maybe not.'

(Over the next four decades, Australian and Tasmanian folk-music collectors did start visiting the Dawsons and some of their old mates and so recorded and saved many hundreds of the tunes that had been played in Tasmania in the old times.)

Mick and Helen Flanagan held numerous private music sessions at their cottage over the years. One day musicians from Hobart, Colin and Alison Petersfield, were down playing tunes with the Flanagans and accompanying Mick on some songs. Colin mostly played box, but he also played a little banjo. Alison was a fiddler, though she dabbled with some other instruments as well. Alison was playing a robust polka that sounded a bit like a sea shanty sped up. 'This is Colin's new tune, he's calling it "The Home Brew Polka",' she informed Mick and Helen, who soon figured out how to accompany it. Helen then went out of the room and came back holding the old beaten fiddle that they had found in their house when they moved in. 'Try it on this one, Alison!'

Alison laid down her violin and picked up the beast to play the same tune she had previously played.

'Oh! This sure has a very loud voice! Good for polkas, I guess. But it's awkward to play the higher parts, and something sounds not quite right on some notes.' With these words Alison put down the beast and switched back to playing her own instrument, and seemed all the happier for it.

The Franklin Tavern, Folk Club Night

The following weekend, the folk club was scheduled for Saturday night at the Franklin Tavern. The place was full, with people spilling out down the worn stone steps and onto the classic Victorian-era veranda with its wooden deck, timber columns and metal latticework. Locally born orchardists, loggers, and labourers rubbed shoulders with the newcomers – the artists, the craftsmen, the hobby-farmers, and the folk-revival musicians. There was always a slight feeling of apprehension between the two groups, but one that did not quite amount to distrust. Most realised that it was inevitable that they were now stuck with each other for the long haul. Consequently, most knew that they might as well try and get along.

The Flanagans were there, as were the Petersfields, along with a few dozen players of, and enthusiasts for, traditional Celtic folk music. The air was full of tobacco smoke – and something else – and fresh jugs of beer found their way to all the tables. Kon, the publican, enjoyed the extra traffic that now flowed into the bar, but he was concerned to ensure that those born in the town would not feel as if they were being elbowed out of their turf by the newcomers.

When Kon had been approached by a member of the local volunteer fire brigade to donate something for a fundraising raffle that would take place in the pub that night, it dawned on him that the folk club should also throw in a donation. This would serve as a sign of goodwill, and an appreciation of the local men and women that served as volunteer firefighters.

When Kon asked, Mick replied that they would be very happy to contribute. However, he scratched his head, trying to figure out what they might be able to donate. Helen pitched in, 'Why not donate that old fiddle as a prize. It hardly gets any use. Someone might pass it on to a child, or a student that is planning to take violin lessons, or maybe whoever wins it might just want it for an ornament. I can't think of anything else, other than a few dollars that we could muster.'

'Sounds like an idea,' said Mick, more than happy with this solution. Later the other folkies, when told what was planned, nodded their approval. That night Chris Cruise played a gutsy blues set, a couple called Stephen and Jane Ray, who had recently moved into the valley from the wild west coast, did a set of songs and some instrumentals on mandolin and fiddle, and a Welsh ex-pat sang a few unaccompanied ballads in a voice that could shake the window panes and rattle the floor boards. To top the night Frank Byrne played some intricate Irish jigs on his penny whistle.

Before the musicians proceeded to transition to an all-in session, someone from the adjacent bar came in to announce the raffle. The prizes were varied: a free stay in a shack near Cockle Creek, a meat tray, a fresh crayfish, a quarter of a side of beef, a crocheted rug, and finally, the battered old violin. The violin was made the prize for the third ticket to be drawn.

The person who held the third winning ticket was a man already in his middle years. His brown eyes smiled on hearing his number called, lighting up a tanned and a stubble-covered face. Joe Flakemore had come down from his little farm high up Braeside Road hoping to share some company and drinks with an old mate or two. Joe, though, had always been fascinated by fiddle music. His grandmother had played fiddle for apple shed dances back until World War Two. When her husband was killed, the loss of a breadwinner hit her family hard, and thus she pawned the violin to a Hobart pawnbroker in 1946 and never played again. Joe was very young when he heard her play, but the memory remained precious to him. She had played 'The Pig Tub', 'Blanchard's Hornpipe', 'The Harvest Moon Schottische' and dozens of other tunes whose names he'd long forgotten. Now that he found himself the winner of a violin, an old childhood joy arose in him.

A woman at the folk club, with a round face and an English accent, gave him a brief lesson in how to tune a violin. As soon as he was home he started practising, scraping away with the bow. Once a month, he would go to the pub to watch what more experienced folk fiddlers were doing, and try and pick up any tips he could. A beginner fiddler can rarely get a good sound from the instrument, and if they do it is either raw talent or luck. As a musician Joe had neither in any great quantity. After begging him to practise more quietly, his wife eventually insisted that he practise in the shed. He would hang the instrument on the wall there, and try to fiddle a bit between jobs. He had begun to make some progress up to a point, but somewhere around 1982 he lost half a finger, when a towing cable snapped as he was trying to pull a dead cow from a waterhole. He tried to work out a new way to play the fiddle, but it all proved too hard. In the end the beast just hung upon the shed wall gathering grime.

When Joe died, in late 2022, his granddaughter Kerry began the arduous task of cataloguing and selling his estate, including such sundry items as the old violin, that had somehow left the Testore workshop in Milan 323 years earlier, and against all odds survived.

Chapter 23

The Huon Valley, 2023

To soak up the hours, Aaron paced the cavernous workshop at the Wooden Boat Centre, distracting himself by looking at the current projects of various boatbuilders and periodically offering help sweeping the fragrant sawdust from the floors and restacking the precious timbers.

On the wall there were 'before and after' pictures of grand old ketches and schooners, first in their heyday, then half a century later, looking broken and decrepit. Finally, there were photos of the various stages of repair, culminating into full restoration and relaunch. *Ah! These craftsmen share it! The gentle care for broken things. It guides their hands and yields wonders.*

As the steaming machine worked away on the strange old piece of apple wood, Aaron took lunch by the river, millpond-still and licked by remnants of fog rising slowly as the day warmed. Sitting on the jetty among coots and wood ducks he contemplated, for a while, the unhurried patience of nature.

After watching over the steaming and bending process and making micro-adjustments to the clamps for most of the late afternoon, Aaron called time and checked the result. *Nearly there, nearly, but not quite.*

He was more or less happy with the progress from warped wood to geometrically balanced lines. He calculated, however, that another few hours, on the following day, would produce a perfect and lasting result. Calling it quits for the now, he left the sleepy riverside village of Franklin and drove into Huonville, where he picked up half a dozen craft beers, some boutique cheeses, and a crusty loaf of sourdough bread. Beneath the glass of the counter he noticed, sitting on a tray of ice, about half a dozen large red crayfish along with a sign saying 'Fresh Today'. *Now that would be a treat!* Though he wasn't sure if Haley shared his taste for rock lobster, but decided to take the chance and bought one on spec.

When Aaron arrived at Haley's cottage, the door was open, so he let himself in. He was about to call her name, when he heard the sound of two violins coming from another room. Haley had not yet finished teaching her last private student for the day. Aaron listened closely to her conversation with the student, her comments, suggestions, and corrections, and then to the renewed duet playing. He was moved by her subtle and tender way of coaxing the best out of the pupil. *This is someone who cares*, he thought, *not just someone going through the motions with her paying clients.*

Before long, the lesson was over, and Haley bid goodbye to her student, turning her attention then to Aaron. 'Hi Aaron. Welcome to my humble cottage in the Glen.'

'Thanks for inviting me. Beautiful spot! Lovely to see you again, as always.'

Haley came over and gave Aaron a polite kiss on the cheek. It was a stiff and awkward gesture, and she wondered if Aaron, arriving hands full of goodies and a face all smiles and enthusiasm, had noticed as much.

In her mind she had to deal with the memory of sharing such kisses with Richard, whenever they would greet, after university, or work, year after year. She tried to drive the uncomfortable thought from her head, but that only served to make her conflicted feelings regarding Richard even stronger. Then she reminded herself, *That was pretty much all I had with Richard in the end; the bland comforts of familiarity. I don't expect Aaron to fill that space, nor to be everything that Richard wasn't. It might never happen. For now he is a friend, a colleague. What comes next? Maybe? Who knows?*

Aaron smiled his big open smile at Haley, oblivious to her self-questioning. 'I've got us some treats for tonight, Hale. Here you go.' He opened a large brown paper bag to reveal a bag of bread and cheese, the wrapped cray, and then handed her a carboard carton containing a selection of craft beers.

She grinned with delight, then responded, 'What a treat. You are a sweety. Could you put them on the kitchen bench please?'

She watched him negotiate the space in her cottage with an effortless grace. When he had placed the groceries on the far bench he returned and looked directly into her eyes.

'I listened to you teaching, Haley, caught a good bit of that last lesson. You have such a gift for it, it's a rare thing!'

'That's a lovely thing for you to say!' Though she was flattered and sincerely delighted by his comment, she moved her head to the side to break Aaron's gaze, not wanting him to notice her blushing. She quickly directed the conversation back towards him and the business they shared. 'How did the wood-steaming and bending go today? It's a nice place there in the Wooden Boat Centre, isn't it?'

'It sure is. Helpful people too. Weren't too many tourists hanging around today, thank goodness.'

'So you got things done?'

'Yep! The neck is almost right. Just a few more hours tomorrow, then I'll take it back home and start putting the whole thing together. Once I have the neck and soundpost in place, I'll start on the French polishing. That will take me through till next Wednesday, then it is just the fingerboard, tailpiece, bridge and strings. I've arranged for two violinists to come around on Thursday. The adjudicators in Cremona have requested that they each play three pieces for the demonstration.'

Curious, Haley raised a single eyebrow. 'May I ask what pieces?'

'Some unaccompanied Bach, an extract from a Vivaldi concerto, and a Romantic or contemporary composition of their choosing.'

'Have you lined up a video camera with good audio for Thursday?'

'My mate Harry said he would bring his video gear, which has pretty good fidelity, and sort out the recording.'

'Who are the violinists? Do they have to be paid?'

'Well, I was lucky. When the word got around that I

was restoring a Testore, I had several offers from players that just wanted to come around and try it out. I was spoilt for choice. Dieter Dransfield from the Conservatorium is coming in the early afternoon, and Jing Mei from the TSO is coming a bit later. They have to each present their credentials, electronically. The adjudicators will check to ensure that they are bona fide. They then play, before giving an oral testimony as to the condition of the instrument and the quality of the restoration. They can't talk to each other before making their testimonies, so I've arranged that they come two hours apart.'

'Wow, that's so exciting. Next Thursday seems so soon, considering the old beast is still a collection of separate pieces! Have you left any fudge room in case something goes wrong with the assembly?'

'No. Afraid not. I just have to trust that the hard part has already been done. All the glues are ready. I've matched the colour of the original finish. What I think I've done that ensures a good result though, is spending ages tuning the belly and back-plate. I didn't just tune the principal, but also tuned all the overtones.'

Haley's eyes widened as she tried to get her head around this process. 'How did you do that?'

'Stethoscope, and a chromatic tuner attached to a dot-microphone, then rubbing back each section until every pitch detectable was complementary to every other.'

'That level of concord sounds nearly impossible. Funny, especially, when you consider that the beast was originally the sum of its clashing wolf-tones.'

Before it got too cold and dark, Haley took Aaron for a stroll to her favourite chilling-out spot by the river. They came to a massive flat stone, that retained the last heat of the sun, and sat there without talking. Haley surprised Aaron by taking his hand and squeezing it gently, and so they remained that way, just sitting while listening to the musical play of rapids over rocks. Before the gloaming, they returned to the cottage and ate lobster and cheeses with fresh bread. They talked the night away.

'Have you made up a bed for me, or put a mattress on the floor?' asked Aaron innocently.

Haley just looked at him and smiling softly said, 'I thought you might like to share my bed.' They moved closer together on the couch and began kissing intensely.

Emerging from the fog of sleep Haley stretched out her arm. Feeling nothing but the disturbed blankets and pillow she realised that Aaron was already up and out of the bed. In the distance there were sounds of tinkering coming from the direction of the kitchen. Haley wiped her eyes and was sitting up in bed, trying to wake up, when the phone rang.

'Hello?'

'Hello, Haley, it's Richard. A friend gave me your number. I hadn't heard back from you. I have this job interview in Hobart next week. Can we meet up, can I stay with you? How far out of town do you live?'

It was too early in the morning for Haley to process such a barrage of questions. Being only partly awake she replied, 'Oh hello Richard. I didn't expect you to call.'

'Why haven't you replied to my emails, Haley? Do you have someone else in your life now?'

Before Haley could muster a coherent answer to Richard's question, Aaron bounced into the room asking loudly, 'Would you prefer black or white coffee this fine morning, beautiful? Never takes me long to work out where the coffee and plunger are.'

'White please,' Haley replied to Aaron, before returning to Richard on the phone. 'Richard, I guess you heard that? His name is Aaron. I am sorry to sound rude, but I have a great life here. You had your chance. I moved on a long time ago. Please do not ring me again!'

Ten Days Later

In the leaf-shaded lane by the river, the timber walls of the little cottage hummed with the sound of violin music. Haley, inspired by the beast reborn, could not stop playing the Testore. She played some Handel, then a Hungarian gypsy czardas, then part of the Bruch concerto. Switching genres, she executed some crazy chromatic runs, an improvised piece comprised of a collection of Stefan Grappelli's jazz licks, some bebop lines and finally a few sets of Irish folk tunes. Playing through each piece, she heard nuances, and subtle voices within this instrument, that she had rarely heard, even in the precious Stradivarius violin that she had been allowed to play, just briefly, during a workshop given by the Australian Chamber Orchestra. Pieces of music that had seemed good enough, but a little one-dimensional, were now richer, more beautiful, and more full of meaning. It was as if, in each case, a secret truth intrinsic to the composition had been released. Haley could not but keep playing and experimenting, all the time maintaining an inner narrative about what she was experiencing.

The more she played, the harder it was for her to believe that this was the same instrument that Kerry Flakemore had given her only a few months ago. The same beaten old beast that had hung on a shed wall for decade after decade. *Aaron has truly worked a miracle, no other word for it*, she thought. If this restoration didn't win him the scholarship, she couldn't imagine what would have. She'd heard that when Dieter Dransfield and Jing Mei played it, they could not stop raving about it. Jing even offered Aaron several hundred thousand dollars for it. Maybe he, or they, should have accepted the offer. It would have set him up for years. The fact that he did not, however, confirmed that he was a person of his word.

Haley had bought a new reinforced case for the Testore. Before placing it in that case though, she wrapped the ancient instrument in a silk scarf, like a child in swaddling. When that was done, she locked each of the case's safety latches, and placed it in a coloured paper bag befitting a birthday present. She then took the instrument out to her car, and placing it on the front seat beside her, she fastened the seatbelt over it, just to be sure that it didn't move.

Late autumn had begun, and the drive south, past orchards, farms, and gardens, was alight with all the golds and the reds of the season, in that month before the leaves begin to fall.

The drive seemed longer than usual. Haley could not be sure if even the beast, now reborn into this angel, would be enough to ignite the spark which 'the girl with the blue violin' had lost, nearly three years ago. She pondered the balance of things. If Jesse didn't want the violin, it wouldn't all have been for nothing, Haley supposed. They could still sell it, probably, for a small fortune. But this whole enterprise had begun as something for Jesse, and Haley did so hope that it would end as meaning something important to her.

It was the day before Jesse's fifteenth birthday. Diane had rung Haley earlier in the morning. While Haley drank her first cup of coffee for the day, they had talked about Jesse, and about the violin, the weather and life in general. Diane seemed buoyed.

'Jesse has turned a corner, Haley. I don't know exactly what the big change has been. It's as if the cloud that has hung over her, has begun to break up, and her old light is beginning to shine through. You know she even listens to violin music again now.'

As Haley drove the winding road, through Waterloo, then Glendevie, then around the coast from Police Point to Dover, she retraced Diane's words in her mind. *I think she might well be ready for this gift, and ready too, to regain her desire to play. It was the one thing she did that made her feel special. If even a little of that returns, that will be enough.* Like Jesse's mother, Haley was almost certain that they now had a remedy, potent enough to remove the shadow that had so blighted a life.

At the Doolan household, Haley brought the Testore, in its colourful paper bag, indoors and placed it on the dining room table.

'Here it is! Is Jesse here? How's she doing?'

'She's sleeping in.' Diane explained, 'Jesse's sometimes a bit late getting up in the mornings these days. Seems her body is dealing with changes. I hope you're not in a hurry.'

'Not at all, Di. Today I have hours. No problem at all with waiting.'

Diane served tea, along with scones covered in jam and

whipped cream. In the glassed-in sunroom area, amid an indoor garden of rubber plants and monstera deliciosa, they sat and chatted. The conversation inevitably turned towards the violin in the bag upon the other table.

'I have to tell you,' Haley said, 'that this is now an extremely good violin. The restoration really has surpassed our expectations. Hard to believe that I got the instrument for free.'

Diane suddenly remembered that they had not yet talked about the cost of the restoration. She gulped at the thought of paying for a restoration that had taken months. Whether she could even pay was, as yet, unknown, as was whether or not Jesse would accept her birthday present with good grace.

'Do you think that I can afford the violin, given the months of work that have been done on it? I got quite carried away with your enthusiasm, and forgot to talk about price.'

'Well, here's the good news,' replied Haley. 'If Jesse wants it, then it's hers. If not, she can give it back to me and Aaron, the luthier, and we'll sell it on and keep the money.'

'What do you mean? You're not offering it to us for free, are you? How? Why?'

Haley began her explanation. 'I couldn't tell you this until we found out how the restoration was going to turn out. Aaron offered to restore the instrument for free, on the proviso that he photographed and videoed the process, and recorded a couple of virtuosi playing the restored instrument.'

Haley could see that Diane looked confused and so continued. 'It's all part of his application for a scholarship in Italy.'

Diane's blue eyes looked bluer than normal as they opened wide in surprise. Haley saw a shiver travel the length of her body.

Diane was clearly stunned by this turn of fate and struck

too with the generosity of the gesture. 'Shit! Haley, I'm totally blown away by all of this. Did he get the scholarship? I do hope so.'

'Don't know yet. He sent his portfolio of images, and videos, and notes, through to the selectors, last week. Then, they listened and watched, on Zoom, while two of the most accomplished violinists in the state played the revived instrument. Then they gave testimonies as to the quality of the instrument and the restoration. Aaron hopes that this will have been enough to secure his admission to the Master's program in antique violin restoration at the Academia Cremonensis in Cremona. They'll have made their decision by now. We're just waiting on an email to tell us either way.'

Diane was stunned. At first, she was unable to speak.

When she finally found her voice, she responded. 'This is so wonderful. Thank you again for your patience and generosity. Pass my deepest gratitude on to Aaron when you see him. I was wondering, are you and him a couple, or am I wrong to ask?'

Haley paused a little, looking thoughtful, before replying. 'It's still early days but yes, I think we might be in love. We can thank the violin, the Testore, for bringing us together.'

Diane's brow wrinkled. 'Why did you call it a Testore, Haley?'

Haley tried to give Diane a bit of the backstory of Jesse's new violin. 'This violin, it turns out, is very old. We think it was made by Paolo Testore, around 1700. It comes from his father's 'Sign of the Eagle' workshop. In this case, the eagle insignia was partly scratched out. That tells us that it was a reject.'

'Reject?' asked Diane.

'Yes! Usually, such rejects were smashed, or scrapped. This

one, for some reason, survived, and through Aaron's magic, it's been transformed into the equal of the best violins to come out of that Milan workshop. Aaron even considered repainting the eagle insignia, but opted instead to touch it up. Now you can see both the eagle, and the scratch marks that removed the original insignia. This honours the workshop of the Testores, but remains true to the history of this particular violin.'

'Maybe this instrument is too good for my Jess. We don't even know whether she will play it yet.' Diane had now fully understood how precious this instrument was.

Haley was quick to reassure her. 'We can only wait and see. If she really doesn't want it, we'll be happy to take it back. If she can be enticed back to music by the instrument however, then it's hers for keeps.'

Jesse

Jesse dreamed that she was playing violin with Anthea and Wattle, in the music room at school. She started noticing that she was playing her old blue violin, but with each touch of the bow, it began shrinking and melting. She kept on trying to play, but it was getting harder and harder. She started crying, and her tears fell onto the blue violin, which then melted away into water. She felt herself knee deep in tears, and blue water. When she looked around, her friends had gone. She was no longer in the music room but in the ocean. Then she heard voices, faint voices talking about her, in the distance.

Jesse awoke abruptly, remembering her plan for the morning. Looking at the time on her phone she panicked. *Shit, Shit, I'm late. I can't miss out this time! Go girl.* So, she threw herself out of bed. Put on her bathers, threw on shorts and a tee-shirt over the top, slipped on a pair of Crocs, and ran.

Even from the sunroom area, Diane heard Jesse's door open and Jesse start stamping into the corridor in a fluster. She rose to meet Jesse, unaware that her daughter was being summoned by a stronger power than her own. 'Mum, I can't stop now!' Jesse rushed through the house, noticing their guest just as she approached the front door.

'Oh, Miss McGribben, you're here again? Hello.'

'Hi Jess. I've brought you something to try out.'

'What, violin again? Sorry, but please, I must go now! Bugger!'

With that, Jesse ran out the door, and down the road, before Diane or Haley could make conversation with her, or even bid her a proper good morning. Diane once again found herself apologising to Haley about her daughter's lack of good manners. 'This is not turning out as we planned. I don't know why Jess would just barge past us like that. I saw her take one look at the violin in the bag on the table, and just shake her head. I am so sorry! I think maybe all of this is just a waste of your time. Jesse's been so much more engaged with life lately; I was hopeful, but after this episode I fear she's slipping backward.'

Haley was deeply disappointed, but still she tried to be philosophical about it. She had always known that Jesse might simply not be interested. 'Maybe she's not quite ready yet, or maybe something else is looming larger in her life just at the moment. They say that you cannot push a river. Let's not try to move things along before their time.'

Diane nodded but looked somewhat forlorn as Haley continued.

'I'll leave the violin with you for a few weeks. Present it

to her again tomorrow, for her birthday, and see if she feels any differently. If she really doesn't want to play, though, I would be the last to force the issue.'

Diane realised that Haley's approach made sense. Nevertheless, she still felt bad that Haley had done so much, for no observable reward. 'Can I, at least, shout you lunch at the Sailing Club, just to thank you for your patience, and for coming all this way?'

'You absolutely can!' replied Haley. 'A hearty pub meal might be just what I need. Thanks Di. Let's go in my car. I parked you in when I came.'

When Jess arrived at the long white beach she found Tyson sitting patiently on the sand.

'Thought you'd stood me up, or forgotten, Jess! I was almost going to go out alone.'

'Sorry, Ty! Slept in. Soon as I woke up, I ran down here. Seem to need more sleep lately. Haven't had breakfast, or a drink, or anything.'

'Will you be okay to paddle then? I usually do about an hour before coming in. Half an hour around the bay, or around one of the islands, then half an hour back.'

'I'm pretty sure that I can manage, dude. I can go a long time without eating.'

'Well, we have to wear these.' Tyson threw Jesse a life jacket and showed her how to strap it up. 'Y'know we couldn't have chosen a better morning for it. It's warm for this time of year. Not even the slightest breeze.'

When they pushed off from the beach, Jesse sat up front while Tyson sat closer to the back. He gave her a canoe paddle and instructed her on how to alternate sides each few strokes in order to maintain the craft on a straighter trajectory. Tyson himself used a two-ended kayak paddle. With this, he could dig in deep for power-strokes, and so maintain a fast and steady momentum. The water in the bay was like a perfect mirror to the cloudless morning sky. Looking ahead, everything seemed to Jess to be silver-blue and mother-of-pearl.

This was the magical world, just outside her door, that she remembered from halcyon days, in the boat fishing with her father. It was a world she had almost forgotten about. Something near, but somehow detached from the world of people, families, school, the gaggle of social life and the rest. She felt the water part willingly as the canoe moved ahead. Behind her, she could hear Tyson's regular breathing, and she could sense his strength as the canoe accelerated. As she paddled, she found a way to align with his strokes, one on each side for his two. She also sensed her own strength. She realised that she had never felt physically powerful before. It was something new, something the changes in her body had granted her, without her noticing, and she relished the sensation.

Looking down, the water was deep, but crystal clear. She could see the white sand and the kelp gardens below. Every now and then a skate, or a ray, or a flathead, would cruise past, just beneath the canoe, while schools of tiny silver whitebait formed patterns of murmuration beneath the mirror surface. In the distance they saw terns dropping from the sky into the water to feed. Near one of the islands some dolphin fins emerged, disappeared, then emerged again. Jess felt the majesty of it all filling her to the brim and her skin was tingling.

As they changed direction for the return journey, Tyson said to her, 'You must be getting thirsty, Jess.'

'Yeah, my mouth is as dry as! But I can wait ay. I could do this every day.'

'Well, this is a perfect day for it. If we had a southerly or west-nor'westerly it would have been much harder paddling. I watch the weather charts and that way I figure out when it's worth canoeing. You don't want to be out here in wind-chop or storm swells. Next time the conditions are likely to be perfect, what say I ring you, and we can do this again? You've done great today!'

'I'm so glad you think so. Kinda felt like we found our rhythm together. Felt real good to me. It's been too long since I've been out on the bay. Forgot how much I missed it till now.'

They were approaching the shore. Tyson hesitated a second to weigh his words before saying, 'It's been too long since we hung out together, Jess!'

They both jumped out into the cool water and, together, pulled the canoe up the beach and secured it to the large she-oak opposite Tyson's house.

'What a team we make, ay Ty!'

'We always did Jess, and always will!' he replied. He then walked up and put his arms around her and they hugged for a while. 'I'll grab the life-jackets Jess, you better go and eat something. Thanks for coming out with me.'

'Thank you so much for inviting me.' Before she turned, she leaned forward to give him a quick formal kiss goodbye. Neither of them had planned it, but the kiss soon became rather more than that. Both were equally embarrassed at the spontaneous passion of the moment.

'Ummm goodbye,' said Jesse. 'Thanks again.'

'Let's do it all again soon,' said Tyson, meaning both the canoeing and the kiss.

Jesse had already started walking. She knew exactly what Tyson meant. Turning her head as she walked, she called back to him. 'You bet on it. Can't wait! See you, Ty.'

Diane and Haley

Diane and Haley had finished their pub meals, and were sitting having a drink, and talking about everything other than Jesse. The view across the bay was as breathtaking as it was familiar.

'I'll never tire of this scenery,' said Haley. 'So different than Ad—' She stopped in her tracks.

Diane noticed that Haley was distracted by something 'Everything okay?'

'Sorry Di, just felt the buzzer on my phone vibrate. I'm waiting on any word from Aaron about his application. He thought that it would be today. Well, it would be around two thirty in the morning in Italy, so if he received an email it would have been over ten hours ago now. But I'll check my phone anyway if that's not being too rude.'

Diane now felt that she had her own investment in Aaron's good fortune. 'Check your messages, Haley. I'm keen to know how he went too.'

The message was simple, curt and to the point.

> I have won the Scholarship. I have a week to confirm my eligibility, to get a study-visa and to book tickets. I have delayed telling you. Should I take it? We have only just found each other. It would mean I am away in Italy for a whole year. What do you think?

Haley's eyes filled with tears.
'Everything all right, dear?' asked Diane.

Haley nodded and then smiled. Rather than message Aaron, she rang him directly.

He answered with a simple 'Hello'.

'Hello you wonderful, brilliant man. Of course, you must go! It will be the chance of a lifetime. I tell you what though. Don't expect me to wait here alone for twelve months. At the end of year break I'll schedule a trip to Europe to be with you. I can stay with you and Roberto in Cremona for seven weeks including Christmas. How does that sound?'

'That would be awesome. Really? Would you come over? I should be able to show you the sights by then. You would really do that for me? We can Skype or Zoom too.'

'One thing though, Aaron,' Haley added. 'You'll need to take time off, for a day or two, so we can go on pilgrimage to Milan. We must find the site of the "Testore Eagle Sign" workshop. I discovered that the Contrada Larga has been renamed, and that it's all modern apartments and residential in that part of the city now, but I still want to walk those streets. Just to feel the ghosts there beneath the surface.'

'I love you, Haley!' He had said it and he immediately wondered if he should have.

'I love you too, maestro!' replied Haley. 'Let's talk soon. Must go. I am down at Dover with the Doolans.' Haley said goodbye and hung up. She didn't want to destroy the magic of the moment by mentioning Jesse's failure to even look at the Testore.

Jesse

Jesse walked back along the beach, feeling as if her body had no weight at all, and as if she was floating just above the ground. She noticed the tiny shells on the sand, the scuttling of soldier crabs, a vigilant pacific gull perched in a coastal blue gum. She didn't merely feel happiness, but also the sensation of being fully awake, as if all of her senses had become more acute. She brought these feelings with her as she entered her house.

Jesse noted that Miss McGribben's car was gone. *That's a pity*, she thought. *I wanted to apologise for leaving so abruptly and without explanation. I'll try and catch up with her at school, and explain.* It then dawned on her that her mother was also not around. Perhaps she was visiting Dora down the road? She noticed again the large parcel on the table in its brightly coloured bag. She presumed that this was her birthday present. *It can't hurt if I look. It's only a day early. Guessing that as Miss McGribben dropped it in, it's a violin.* With that realisation the old disquiet reared its head. She wished her mother hadn't put so much pressure on her to play. *I'm not sure if I even want to, and less sure that I still could play if I tried. A canoe of my own would have been better, I guess. But hey, she means well and she loves me, so who am I to complain?*

She removed the case from its bag and placed it on the table. Opening the catches, one by one, she began to have a sensation of excitement despite herself and despite everything that had transpired over the last three years. The violin shone. Layer upon layer of careful shellacking, and many days of rubbing in, and rubbing back, and applying yet more shellac, then more rubbing, then a layer of fine instrument oil, also rubbed in and rubbed back, had bestowed on it an amazing sheen. Yet beneath it all, Jesse could see faint scars and blemishes that being retained, made it even more beautiful. This instrument seemed both new and ancient. She knew nothing about it, but she felt that despite her misgivings, she had to play it. The house was empty. There was no one to hear her, or judge her. She could play now just for the sake of playing.

At first, she started off by trying to remember the basics. She tried a D major scale, then did the same in G, and A, and C. Then she tried minor scales, natural and harmonic. Enjoying the weight of the new bow, she attempted to remember a little étude, then 'The Crested Hen', then whatever she could recall of 'The Old Salt Wind'.

Bit by bit, she pieced together the fragments of memory until she had found, among them, half a dozen tunes that she remembered from those years ago. Jesse noticed that as she played it, the violin kept sounding better and better; better than any violin she had ever played. The richness, volume, and complexity of the sound both amazed and disturbed something in her. She stopped playing and put the instrument up to her ear. *Am I going crazy? I'm sure this instrument is trying to say something.*

She bowed the open G string, then once again put the violin tight against her ear. She thought for a moment that she could hear an Italian village dance echoing in the overtones of the note. Then she imagined a Baroque sonata, a delicate harp playing, then an Irish pub session, a Scottish march, a gang of rowdy bushrangers laughing and singing, she heard a shearing shed dance, then the sound of crashing waves, she could hear the cry of mutton birds coming home after their annual migration, the weeping of a lonely man, the joy of a country girl playing with a band for the first time, and many lesser echoes fading as the G string stopped vibrating, and just the recollection of the note vibrated through the wood.

'Who are you? What are you?' she asked the violin. Then she picked it up and ran through the tunes and scales once more. But something happened. She couldn't keep control of the music. She started playing phrases that she had never learnt, never even heard. The violin had clutched her soul and had started playing her. She noticed that she was shifting positions and yet always the notes sounded right, always in tune, as if an inner genie was guiding her fingers. She started thinking of her old violin, of how she had loved it, then loathed it. She played the anger and self-doubt that she had felt. She played the death of her father. The emptiness, the years of despair. She played out her fear of crowds, the contempt of others, her intolerance for fools. Then the music grew into a storm, which broke, and left an abiding stillness in its place. The music became the sun on the water, a dark brown wedge-tailed eagle and a chalk-white sea eagle dancing in the sky, laughter shared with friends, the dolphins jumping in the bay, the fish weaving their mysterious patterns beneath the surface, the pearl-water droplets flying from the paddle as she stroked, the firmness of Tyson's grip, the softness of his lips.

How am I doing this? Where is this coming from? Jesse was in ecstasy, feeling pain, and bliss, and outright surprise in equal measure. Time had been bent around her as she played. She thought only of the music that poured from her and from the violin. She had no idea that other ears had also witnessed her improvised fantasia.

When Haley and Diane opened the car doors, they heard in that moment that Jesse had found the Testore, and that she had remembered how to play. They were not prepared for what they heard though. Some strange alchemy was at work. Understanding that this was a rare flight of the musical imagination, they remained outside and silent, desperate not to interrupt the flow of things and break the spell. When Jesse finally finished, they both clapped and cheered. Diane was unable to hold back the tears. The house felt different. A demon had been exorcised from their lives.

When they entered the lounge room, Jesse just stared at them at first; pale, depleted and frozen in the moment. It took her a while to register that they had heard her, heard it, heard everything. Then the spell broke and she ran directly to her mother, who simply hugged her.

Jesse reached out an arm and pulled Haley into their embrace. 'Thank you! Thank you! I love it so much! I never knew such an instrument could exist. It seems to know me. Oh! Thank you again.'

On her way home, Haley thought she might take yet one more detour down Dales Road.

Halfway along its length she noticed that some growth on the roadside verge had recently been cut. She thought she could discern the hint of a stony track, now that the tall ryegrass had been mowed. Stopping the car, she found a length of timber, half buried, paint peeled. Pulling it from the tangle of grass and dirt and brambles she tried to decipher the faded writing on it. She could just make out the words: *McGribben's Dairy. 3 Miles.*

Looking up what she now knew must be the overgrown remnant of Claytons Drive, she saw above the hills in the distance, a solitary eagle soaring.

Testore

A poem by Jesse Doolan

He is my love, and he knows my soul,
He is an eagle who has flown,
With broken wings,
Over oceans, and continents.

He is exactly 323 years old.
Created in Milan, discarded at birth,
He has died, at least, once,
But tender care has saved him, perfected him,
And raised him to apotheosis.

How many stories does he know?
He can never tell.
How many hands have held him?
Played upon him?
I shall never know.

Sometimes he cries to me, and I soothe his woes.
Sometimes he sings to me, and I sing with him.
Most times, though, it is I that cry,
and he that heals.

He is my violin, my fiddle, my love.
I do not own him, I never could.
One day, when I am long gone,
Perhaps my children, or their children
Will learn to know him,
And cherish him as I have,
Or perhaps a stranger will be saved by him,
As I have been.
What new music will they make together?

My old teacher called him the beast,
But he sings like an angel.
I call him simply, my friend.

Author's Note

This novel is dedicated to all of those who have kept folk music both in its traditional and revivalist forms alive in Tasmania. It is dedicated, in particular, to the late Dawson siblings Edie and Paddy, to the late Eileen McCoy, the late Colin Petersfield and the recently deceased Mick Flanagan. Each made contributions to music on the island that can hardly be measured and each was in some way a mentor and teacher to myself and my wife, Marjorie.

The Gentle Care for Broken Things is a book in which many different stories converge. It interweaves real persons and events with folkloric characters and stories. The latter may or may not have any real-world basis, but they have important elements in the cultural mythos of the living music portrayed in the book.

The three principal characters, Haley, Jesse, Aaron, and their families are not based upon any actual persons, nor are Charlie Dempsey, Rose Murphy and Michelle Pearson. The reject Testore violin depicted here is also a literary device rather than an actual instrument. Haley, Jesse and Aaron are products of my imagination. Their characterisation is inspired by a diverse range of people whom I have met while teaching, playing and collecting music in regional Tasmania. They are, nevertheless, characters not too different than many whom one might meet in contemporary Tasmania. However, any close similarities to actual people are purely accidental in the case of this group of characters.

On the other hand, Haley, Jesse and Aaron move in a world populated by real persons, real events and real places, contemporary and historical. The broad history portrayed in this book is mostly accurate, other than a few ventures into folkloric tales.

I have tried to keep the timeline accurate with regard to real-world events. However, I have taken a little liberty with some dates. Paolo Testore had not yet entered his apprenticeship in 1700, when Francesco Geminiani was first living in Milan. Consequently, I added a few years to his age to better fit the story. His reputation for less-than-perfect instruments was grounded in historical fact. Issues with his father over this, and other things, led to his ultimate break with the family workshop and eventually to the establishment of his own rival workshop.

Geminiani's timeline is as close to historically accurate as possible. His friendship with the blind Irish harpist Turlough O'Carolan has been passed down through multiple accounts and is a part of Irish musical folklore. However, it is impossible to determine which parts of the story are true. Turlough himself was a prolific composer of music for the Irish harp and his many tunes are still played today. Turlough O'Carolan's story has long been enmeshed with mythology. There are many magical aspects of his tale, such as his dalliances with fairy folk, that need to be seen in that light. William O'Brien, Lord Inchiquin, was a patron of O'Carolan, and Turlough dedicated the famous tune to him that still bears his name. One of Lord Inchiquin's descendants, William Smith O'Brien, was in fact sent to Van Diemen's Land as a political prisoner nearly a century after the events covered in the Turlough O'Carolan chapter.

The McBride family of Belfast are drawn from folklore, and in particular the folk song variously called 'Arthur McBride' or 'Arthur McBride and the Recruiting Sergeant'. The events depicted in that song took place at exactly the time when Alexander Laing was in Ireland working as a recruiting officer for the British Army. Their meeting as imagined in this book, was a perfect fit between history and fiction.

Laing himself was a real character. The events leading to his transportation as depicted here are all accurate. Laing's meeting with the infamous Tasmanian bushranger Michael Howe is taken directly from Laing's own account of that day. Laing's transformation from indentured convict to constable and celebrated colonial fiddler is all well documented, as is his relationship with the Champs. With the late historian Peter MacFie, my wife Marjorie and I wrote the book *On The Fiddle*, about the life and music of Alexander Laing.

The Laing and Foggo sections of the book are dedicated to Peter, who also uncovered the details of the life of Neil Gow Foggo.

Like Laing, Neil Gow Foggo was a real character, and his life largely accords with the account in this book.

The story of the Donohue clan, from Liam to Gundy and Dan et al., is mostly historically accurate, though the names of Liam and his sons were contrived as I could not determine their actual first names from available records. Gundy was very real, as was Dan, and both were extremely influential in folk music circles of Northern Tasmania from the 1910s through to the middle of the twentieth century. I conversed with Gundy's son Leo, himself a fine traditional musician, back in the early 2000s. I also have an old tape of the playing of Gundy made in the 1960s, when he was already a great age but could still play like a demon.

Affie Saltmarsh is a fictional character. His first name is based on the title of a Cape Barren Island fiddling tune called 'Uncle Affie's Tap Dance'.

The surname Saltmarsh is taken from the name of a character, Salty Saltmarsh, invented by my wife Marjorie, who features him in her novel, *Golden Valley*.

I contrived that Affie as depicted in my book is the father of Salty Saltmarsh in hers. The two books are set in different eras but there are some crossovers. Another character featured in *Golden Valley*, Malcolm Johnstone, also has a minor role in *The Gentle Care for Broken Things*, appearing in Chapter 20, when he helps Tops McGuire and her cousin Tommy get their truck across a flooded Huon Bridge.

Tops McGuire was a real person and a well-known country dance piano player. The story of her meeting with Paddy Dawson, Lyall Mansfield and Norm Burgess (all musicians from the Huon Valley's Apple Shed Dance days) along with the missing recording made that rain-swept night, was conveyed to me by someone who was there, who rang me after I enquired about old family recordings of local music. Most of the details about Tops's life are contrived. Her cousin Tommy is fictional, as is Marek.

Joe Flakemore is meant to be a fictional character, but coincidentally there was a Joe Flakemore living in Franklin during the eras described in the book. Any similarity with the members of the Flakemore families of the Franklin region is entirely coincidental. In fact, Kerry Flakemore's daughter Liz, who is mentioned just once in passing, is herself a character from fellow Tasmanian writer John Tully's detective novels and is mentioned with his permission, and a bit of licence taken with the dates.

Eileen McCoy was very much a real person. She was already well into her eighties when she came to stay with us in 2004. From her we learnt a host of old Tasmanian folk and country dance tunes directly from the source. The same applies to Paddy Dawson and his sister Edith, residents of Franklin who lived and played music well into their nineties. They became our dear friends, teachers and mentors and gave Marjorie and me a direct link to the local tradition of Apple Shed Dance music.

Brian the Flute, Phillipa the fiddler, Sandra and Jake from the Franklin Post Office, Rachel from the Van Diemen's Band, Brendan from Belfast, Dorothy the counsellor, Kon from the Franklin Tavern, Aaron's friend and fellow instrument maker Harry, and several others are based, more or less, on real people and importantly, these people have all given their permission to be referenced in the ways I have done in this book.

Helen and Mick Flanagan, Colin and Alison Petersfield, Ian and Liz Crelin, Chris Cruise, Stephen and Jane Ray and a few others mentioned are all actual persons either alive or deceased and each has been treated with respect. Some events were slightly different than the way they have been portrayed here. For example, Paddy Dawson's first encounter with Mick Flanagan was not at the pub but at a session at Mick's place. He walked up the lane, being drawn by the sound of the music emanating from Mick and Helen's cottage.

I hope that readers enjoy this web of tales. I consider it a work of fiction designed to serve, not distort, the cultural history of this island, be it called lutruwita, Van Diemen's Land, or Tasmania. Please enjoy.

Included as an appendix to the novel are several of the tunes mentioned in this book. Apart from the 'Tarantella', the extract from the 'Geminiani Violin Solo in C', and 'O'Carolan's Concerto', these are all pieces either collected in Tasmania or composed by Tasmanian musicians. Each is still played by lovers of traditional Tasmanian music. Obviously, I could not include every piece mentioned in the book; rather I have chosen those I felt were most pertinent to the story.

I hope that those who can read music might play through these tunes and get some feeling for each era and episode.

Acknowledgements

I would like to acknowledge some of the people that have helped make this book possible.

My wife, Marjorie, is a wonderful writer and musician. She has shared my journey through the collecting, performing, and teaching of traditional Tasmanian music for nearly a quarter of a century and now shares the new journey into literature and writing.

I also owe a huge debt to my editor, Susan Young, who has been thorough and tireless in her work, and patient with me as I blundered throughout the process. Susan's commitment to local literature through Ashwood Publishing continues to enrich the cultural life of the Huon and of Tasmania more generally.

A very big thankyou should go to Kristie Knight (@ krillknight on Instagram) who donated the photo of Dover used in the cover art, and to my old friend Chris Kelly, who drew the chapter icons. The Canadian fiddler Danny Armstrong gave me the idea for writing the poem 'Testore' at the end of the book.

I acknowledge the help of Helen and Mick Flanagan in correcting details regarding the early days of the Franklin Folk Club. Sadly, Mick passed away before the publication of the book. It is my profound hope that it does justice to his legacy.

I would also like to thank those who helped me on my journey to rediscover the almost lost treasures of Tasmanian country dance music. In particular the folklore collectors, Rob Willis, Fred Pribac, Julie Edwards and Stuart Graham have all inspired my own work and helped nudge me in the directions I needed to go.

This book would not have been possible if not for the traditional Tasmanian musicians that I have been proud to call friends. Edith and Paddy Dawson, Eileen McCoy and several others have all passed on but were always forthcoming with deep friendship and generous with their music, as was Leo Donohue who sent me recordings of his family music.

Finally, a big thank you to the hundreds of music students that Marjorie and I have had the honour of teaching, and to the many musicians that have participated in our ensembles over the years. You have all helped me understand the value of music in everyday life and its associations with community, place, and history.

The author and publisher wish to acknowledge the traditional Palawa custodians of lutruwita. This includes, especially but not solely, the Indigenous people of the Huon Valley and the broader South of Tasmania: the Muwinina, Nuenonne, Melukerdee and Lyluequonny peoples.

Appendix

The following section contains a small number of the tunes mentioned, hinted at, or pertinent to the various tales within this book. They are set out more or less in chronological order, with some exceptions. The Tarantella is the oldest tune here, having been published in 1700, the year the Testore 'beast' was made.

I have had to remove a section of the Geminiani violin solo for the sake of brevity. Hopefully it still stands faithful to the playing and musical imagination of the composer.

Folk tunes are usually written monophonically, that is as a single line with chord names above to suggest accompaniment or harmony. Ornamentation, dynamics, tempo, syncopation and playing styles are usually learnt by ear from established players or invented afresh to suit the player's own musical vision. If any reader chooses to play these tunes, or finds a musician to run through them, it is my hope that the music will enrich the reading of this novel, in which melody and music play such an important part.

Tarantella Anonimo 1700

Extract from Violin solo in C
by Francesco Geminiani

O'Carolans Concerto

O'Carolan

Arthur McBride's Jig

Mrs Champ's Fancy

Alexander Laing

The Onboard Waltz

D. Hellstrom

Gundy Donohue's Set Tune

Gundy Donohue

Orm's Mazurka

The Black Cat Piddled
In The White Cat's Eye

Trad Cape Barren Tasmania

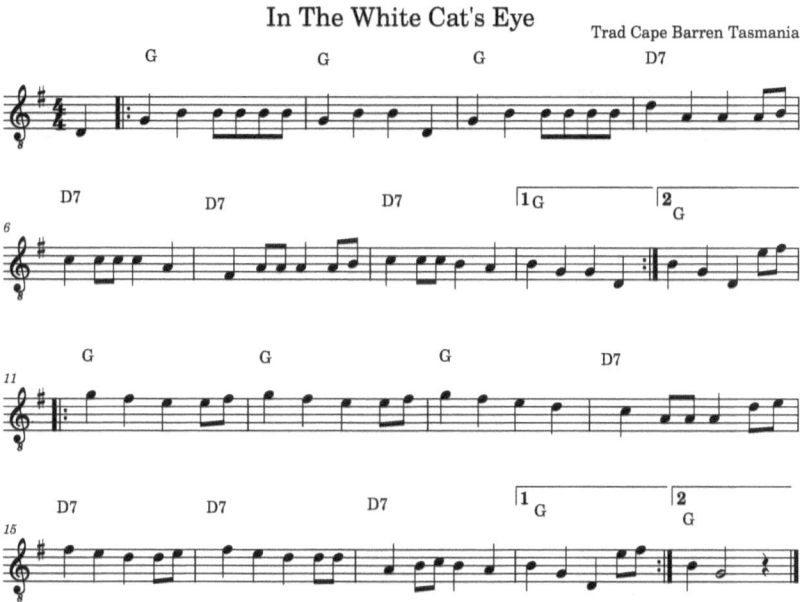

Eileen McCoy's Varsovienna 1

Trad Collected E. McCoy

Uncle Affie's Tap

Trad. Cape Barren Tasmania

Down Longford Way

Kitty Parker

Mountain River Schottische

collected from Paddy Dawson

Old Huon Schottische

collected from Paddy Dawson

310

Home Brew Polka

Colin Petersfield

The Old Salt Wind

S.Gadd

The Druid's Prayer

www.ingramcontent.com/pod-product-compliance
Lightning Source LLC
Chambersburg PA
CBHW030526120726
47904CB00005B/1650